DETERMINED INTERFERENCE

LINDA WAGNER

Copyright

Copyright © 2024 Linda Wagner. All rights reserved.

The characters and events portrayed in this book are fictitious. Any similarity to actual persons, living or dead, is coincidental and not intended by the author.

Table of Contents

Oh, the delightful chaos! Our furry friends, those agents of mischief! Will love blossom at the end?

Dedication

This story is dedicated to my husband. He's my best friend, and he patiently listens to me while I describe the antics of the characters in a story.

Description

'*D*etermined Interference' is a heartwarming story based on Jane Austen's classic *Pride and Prejudice*. In this non-canon tale, familiar characters take on new roles and face unexpected challenges that lead to profound personal growth.

In the autumn of 1811, Netherfield Park acquired new tenants whose arrival brought opportunities and complications to the neighborhood. Family expectations, friendly meddling, and the antics of beloved pets create obstacles that ultimately strengthen Darcy and Elizabeth's relationship.

Will the arrival of the Bingleys and Mr. Darcy disrupt the lives of Jane and Elizabeth Bennet? Can a letter from Colonel Richard Fitzwilliam alter Darcy's prideful demeanor? What devious plans does Caroline Bingley have up her sleeve? As tensions rise, will Mr. Bennet, Mr. Gardiner, and Lord Matlock intervene to steer events toward a favorable outcome? And can the mischievous antics of four furry friends—Jasper, Bacon, Sir Whiskers, and Miss Poppy—create enough mayhem to bring about happily ever afters for our beloved characters?

Discover what happens when three determined patriarchs, one insightful matriarch, two supportive cousins, a shy younger sister, and four endearing pets join forces—intentionally or not—to transform Darcy into a gentleman of true worth. *'Determined Interference'* celebrates the idea that love can flourish even amid chaos and that, sometimes, interference leads to the most cherished outcomes. Join us in this enchanting story where family, friends, and a quartet of playful animals help shape the futures of Jane and Elizabeth in the most delightful ways.

Chapter 1

Friday, November 15, 1811
Darcy

Striding down the hallway of Netherfield Park, Fitzwilliam Darcy's boots echoed against the polished marble floors... a scathing letter burned in his pocket like a hot coal. Darcy abruptly stopped at the library entrance, his gaze narrowing upon seeing the single occupant.

Miss Elizabeth Bennet stood with her back to the door, gazing out the window, her shoulders slightly trembling, a handkerchief clutched in her hand. As he watched, her hand rose to deftly dab a tear from her eye, a delicate, heartbreaking gesture that made Darcy's chest tighten. Unable to face her, he backed away from the door and silently retreated, passing several rooms before a shrill voice caused him to pause.

The door to the drawing room was slightly ajar, and Caroline Bingley's hateful words pierced through the gap with shocking clarity. Her eyes blazed with anger as she hissed, "No, Louisa, this situation is beyond the pale! Those Bennet chits must leave here immediately." Her lips curled in disdain, and her voice dripped with contempt. "I don't care what the apothecary said, and I don't care about Jane's health; I only care about getting Eliza out of this house."

"Are you mad?" Louisa Hurst's brow furrowed in confusion, her voice tinged with disbelief. "The Bennets are the first family in this neighborhood. I will not evict them. It would be a shocking display of poor manners, ruinous to the hopes of our brother."

"What about my hopes?" Caroline's voice rose in desperation, her hands clenched into fists. "I will not standby while Mr. Darcy is distracted by that hoyden, Eliza. Her presence hinders my plans to be mistress of Pemberley." Her eyes darted around the room, searching for a sympathetic gaze. "And Charles will forget about his angel once we return to town. We must get out of this place and back to London, where we can find him another, more appropriate angel to swoon over."

"Caroline, you are never going to be mistress of Pemberley," Mr. Hurst said, his voice firm as he leaned forward, his eyes piercing into Caroline's. "Mr. Darcy dislikes you. You are the only person who does not hear the disdain in his voice when forced to speak to you." He slammed his hand on the table, causing his teacup to clatter. "He will never marry a tradesman's daughter who decries the country and its inhabitants. You need to lower your sights and keep your hands to yourself." Mr. Hurst stood up, towering over Caroline. "Only a desperate flirt grabs a man's arm before it is offered or attempts to show her bosom while bending over. You have nothing the wealthy grandson of an earl wants."

Darcy quietly walked away from the door, Caroline Bingley's shrill voice fading as the distance increased. His jaw clenched, and his eyes narrowed in frustration at her relentless scheming. Seeking relief outdoors, he left the house, heading for the kennels where his Great Dane, Jasper, currently resided. Well, that would change. From now on, his dog would stay inside the manor as a guard against Caroline Bingley's unwelcome attentions.

After collecting Jasper, he headed north, cutting through the fields until reaching a footpath to the woods where the dog could hunt. The tension in his shoulders eased as he entered the peaceful surroundings, the sounds of nature soothing his troubled mind. Darcy searched for a fallen log or boulder to use as a seat, his brow furrowed in concentration. Eventually, he found a large boulder and promptly sat, letting out a sigh of relief as he settled down upon it, grateful for the solitude the woods provided and the companionship of his canine friend.

Darcy removed the letter from his pocket and perused the pages again, wondering whether his cousin, Colonel Richard Fitzwilliam, was exaggerating the family's reaction to the events in Meryton. With a shaking hand, he unfolded the pages and read the message for the fourth time.

November 13, 1811

Matlock House, London

Cousin,

You are a fool... a buffoon... an idiot... a coxcomb, and an arse. When will you learn to behave in a civilized manner? Have you no regard for the feelings of others? Who are you to treat the gentlefolk of Hertfordshire without respect? How dare you speak ill of all and sundry and a gentlewoman within the hearing of the lady and her neighbors? You have placed yourself in the disapprobation of my parents and several close friends. Do you even know how badly you have behaved?

I will enlighten you. Mr. Thomas Bennet is my father's close friend, just as he was of your father. They attended school together. Mr. Bennet and my father still correspond regularly. They meet a few times yearly with Mr. Edward Gardiner, Mrs. Bennet's brother, to play cards and discuss business investments. Those business investments supply a tremendous amount of revenue to their coffers. Your father was one of their circle until he died, and if you check the investments you hold, you will find that most of the highly profitable ones are with Mr. Gardiner.

Do you know who owns the estate where you are staying? Did you or Bingley bother to inquire? Mr. Gardiner owns it...a gentleman by any standard and a tradesman by choice. The Bennets are very familiar with Netherfield Park because their uncle owns it. The daughters do not need to pursue a wealthy husband, no matter how loudly their mother decries her fate. The hedgerows will never be the home of a Bennet.

The only reason Charles Bingley was allowed, yes allowed, to lease the place was because Mr. Gardiner thought he might be an eligible match for the eldest Miss Bennet. Your friend is amiable, outgoing, and kind. These qualities would help Miss Jane overcome her extreme reserve. However, Gardiner never met Caroline Bingley, and after receiving Mr. Bennet's letter describing the shrew, he explores ways to remove Miss Jane from Bingley's presence before her heart is engaged.

That brings me back to the infamous assembly. How dare you disparage the residents of the entire neighborhood? Call a beautiful woman tolerable but not handsome enough to tempt you? Walk about the assembly room with your nose in the air? Ignore matrons who try to converse with you? You are naught but a gentleman's son and definitely not acting as a gentleman. Did you bother to apologize to Miss Elizabeth? Did you take your sorry arse to Longbourn to meet Mr. Bennet? Have you done anything to rectify your poor impression on the area's residents? Have you noticed that no single lady has attempted to garner your attention?

In case you didn't know, I often met Mr. Bennet, Miss Jane, and Miss Elizabeth when they were visiting the Gardiners. They dine here at Matlock House, and we dine at Gracechurch Street; by we, I mean my parents, my siblings, and I. Mrs. Bennet is unaware of the connection. Neither Miss Jane nor Miss Elizabeth would accept a man for his wealth. Both wish for a love match. You may ask my sister if you doubt my words.

You have been taught sound principles but have never learned to implement them. You must stop listening to the harpies of society and become a man of true worth. I will arrive on Saturday to begin instructing you. Inform Bingley to prepare for my visit. Do not inform the Bingleys about the Bennets' connections. Burn this letter before Caroline Bingley finds a way to read it. I put nothing past the conniving termagant.

Yours in disgust,

RF

DARCY REREAD THE LETTER several more times, committing each word to memory, the biting accusations etched into his mind. Humiliation and regret churned within him, mingling with a burgeoning anger at the family's determination to interfere in his life. He stalked through the underbrush, gathering dead leaves and twigs, his movements sharp and purposeful.

When he knelt to build a small fire, the cold ground seeped through his breeches, but he barely noticed, his thoughts consumed by the harsh letter. The familiar motions of stacking twigs and leaves brought a modicum of calm, the growing flame a small beacon of light fighting against his dark thoughts. When the fire was strong enough, its heat warming his hands, he took a deep breath, steadying himself.

With deliberate slowness, he tore the letter into strips, each rip of the paper a small act of defiance against the condemnation it held. He fed the strips into the dancing flames, watching as the edges curled and blackened, the words disappearing into the fire. The paper crackled and disintegrated, turning into ash that swirled up with the smoke, carried away by the late autumn breeze.

As the last piece vanished into the flames, Darcy's thoughts turned inward, a storm of confusion and betrayal. Why had none of his family informed him of their connection with the Bennets? The question gnawed at him, the uncertainty twisting like a knife in his gut. His cousin's reproachful words replayed in his mind, each sentence a brutal reminder of his perceived failings. He stared into the fire, its light flickering in his eyes, casting shadows across his features.

The silence of the woods pressed in around him, broken only by the crackle of the fire and the distant rustle of leaves as Jasper chased a rabbit. The dog bounded through the underbrush, his movements a blur of energy and enthusiasm, oblivious to his master's mood. Jasper returned to Darcy's side, nuzzling his hand for a brief moment of reassurance before darting off again.

As the flames died down, Darcy remained seated, lost in contemplation. The letter was gone, but its impact lingered. He knew he had much to rectify. Jasper returned and settled beside him, resting his head on Darcy's knee, offering silent companionship. Darcy absently stroked the dog's head, drawing comfort from the loyal canine as he contemplated ways to rectify his mistakes.

Chapter 2

Friday, November 15, 1811
Elizabeth

Staring at the garden through the library window did nothing to alleviate Elizabeth Bennet's concern for her sister, Jane, who lay in a fevered and restless sleep in an upstairs guestroom under the care of a maid. Her brow was furrowed with worry, and tears welled in her eyes, blurring her vision. She dabbed at them with her handkerchief, determined not to show weakness. Giving any resident of this house the satisfaction of knowing her discomfort was unbearable.

The garden outside, usually a source of comfort, seemed dreary and uninviting. Elizabeth's mind was a whirl of anxiety and frustration. The neatly trimmed hedges stood barren of flowers, mirroring her sense of bleakness.

About to turn away from the view, Elizabeth saw Mr. Darcy walking toward the kennels. Her shoulders slumped with a heavy sigh of disappointment, and another tear escaped her eye, trailing down her cheek. She had been excited to learn the man was coming to the area. After listening to her friend, Rebecca Fitzwilliam, speak about Darcy's tall, muscular figure, handsome face, exceptional intellect, moral behavior, charitable endeavors, and care for his estate and tenants, she had expected a wonderful gentleman... a man she might like.

How could a gentleman be so arrogant and rude? Her eyes narrowed with anger as she remembered his conceited attitude. At the Meryton assembly, he refused to dance with anyone outside his party, barely acknowledged introductions to the gentry, insulted the area residents, and called her tolerable but not handsome enough to tempt him. Everyone who overheard his remarks deemed him proud.

The memory of his disdainful expression and haughty demeanor sent a fresh wave of tears cascading down her cheeks. She hastily brushed them away, frustration mingling with her sorrow. How could a man who appeared so perfect in description be so flawed in reality? The dissonance between the Darcy her friend, Rebecca, spoke about and the Darcy she met was almost too much to bear. Elizabeth's thoughts churned with the injustice of it all. She felt betrayed by her hopes and expectations, each recollection of his arrogance stinging more deeply than the last.

As Elizabeth watched from the window, Darcy emerged from the kennels with his Great Dane, Jasper, trotting obediently at his side, blending into the landscape until they disappeared. Elizabeth turned away and walked to the center of the room. Her steps were slow and heavy, and each movement reflected her troubled thoughts.

She wiped her eyes again, taking a deep breath to steady herself. Jane needed her. No matter how distressing her encounters with Mr. Darcy were, Elizabeth must keep her composure for her sister's sake.

As Elizabeth made her way down the hall toward the staircase, she paused when Caroline Bingley's shrill voice filtered through an open door.

"No, Louisa, you and your husband are wrong. Mr. Darcy will marry me," Caroline hissed, her voice dripping with venom.

"You are delusional," Louisa Hurst responded. "The man lives in the country most of the year."

"What about it?" Caroline's voice rose in desperation. "I will be mistress of Pemberley."

"Caroline, you are never going to be mistress of Pemberley," Mr. Hurst loudly interjected. "Mr. Darcy dislikes you. You are a tradesman's daughter. He can have his pick of the ton's noble daughters."

"You know nothing! He won't have a choice," Caroline shrieked. "Once the Bennets are gone, I'll make him propose."

Mr. Hurst laughed raucously before loudly proclaiming, "He will never propose. Others have tried to force his hand, but nobody has succeeded in getting a proposal. Several ladies were ruined after their failed attempts at compromising the man. The Fitzwilliams and Darcys are powerful families with ties to royalty. One word from Lady Matlock will guarantee your downfall. You are a fool, Caroline!"

Elizabeth's heart pounded as she absorbed the conversation. The desperation of Caroline's words and the harsh dismissal from Mr. Hurst were disturbing. The idea of such heartless discussions filled her with indignation, not just for herself but for Mr. Darcy, who, despite his faults, did not deserve to be ensnared by such a woman.

Determined not to hear more of their conversation, Elizabeth quietly continued to the staircase, gliding past several footmen lingering in the hallway. She must be with Jane, away from the cruelty of Caroline Bingley and the Hursts. As she ascended the stairs, she resolved to stay here for her sister's sake, no matter what petty grievances and plots swirled around her. Nursing Jane was her priority, and Elizabeth would not allow anyone to diminish the care her beloved sister received.

Reaching Jane's sickbed, Elizabeth paused, taking in the sight of her sister lying pale and fragile against the pillows. Her heart ached at the sight. Sitting beside her, she gently took Jane's hand, feeling the warmth of the fever beneath her cool touch. Jane stirred slightly, murmuring in her sleep, and Elizabeth brushed a stray lock of hair from her sister's forehead. She looked for the basin of cool water only to find it gone. Where was the maid?

As if on cue, the door opened, and Sally, the maid her father sent from Longbourn, entered, carrying a basin of cool water and soft cloths. Her steps were quiet, and her expression was one of genuine concern.

"I'm sorry, Miss Lizzy," the maid whispered. "Miss Jane's fever hasn't broken yet, and I had to fetch more cool water." Sally set the basin on the bedside table, dipped a cloth into the cool water, wrung it out, and handed it to Elizabeth. "Here, Miss Lizzy. This should help."

Elizabeth took the cloth and gently dabbed Jane's forehead, her movements tender and precise. "Thank you," she said, grateful for Sally's assistance. "You've been very kind."

"It's my duty, Miss," the maid replied, though a warmth in her tone suggested it was more than mere duty driving her actions. "Miss Jane is a sweet lady. We all hope she recovers quickly."

Elizabeth smiled faintly, appreciating the sentiment. "I hope so, too. She's the kindest of us all."

The maid took another cloth and began to dab Jane's hands and arms, working in silent harmony with Elizabeth. The room was quiet save for the soft sounds of their ministrations and Jane's occasional murmurs.

As they worked, Elizabeth's mind wandered back to the overheard conversation. She felt a surge of protectiveness toward Mr. Darcy. Should she interfere and warn him about Caroline? Could she find the courage to speak to him despite her hurt and anger?

"Miss Lizzy, is something troubling you?" Sally asked, noticing the furrow in Elizabeth's brow.

Elizabeth hesitated, unsure how much to reveal. "I overheard something troubling that could affect a Mr. Darcy."

The maid paused, her eyes widening slightly. "Do you think it's something serious?"

Elizabeth nodded. "Yes, very serious. But I'm not sure how to approach the matter. The gentleman and I... we do not see eye to eye."

The maid considered this for a moment. "If it's important, Miss Lizzy, you must find a way to tell him. Even if it's difficult."

Elizabeth sighed. "You're right. But I must prioritize Jane right now. Her health comes first." She continued dabbing Jane's forehead with the cool cloth.

"Of course, Miss Lizzy," the maid agreed. "But do not wait too long. Some things cannot be left to chance."

Elizabeth sighed, her mind a tangled web of conflicting emotions. Whether she liked it or not, Mr. Darcy had to be informed. The question was how and when.

Chapter 3

Saturday, November 16, 1811
Netherfield

The morning sun's rays illuminated the breakfast room with abundant light. The clinking of silverware and the soft murmur of conversation between Caroline Bingley and Louisa Hurst filled the air as the assembled individuals enjoyed their morning meal. Mr. Hurst was devouring his second plate of food, ignoring everyone else in the single-minded pursuit of satiating his hunger.

Elizabeth Bennet sat silently at the table, her eyes intermittently drifting over the spread of pastries, fruit, and assorted breakfast favorites. Despite the sumptuous offerings, her plate boasted a small portion of scrambled eggs, a buttered roll, and one small slice of ham. She was preoccupied with worry for Jane and the overheard conversation about Mr. Darcy. She glanced across the table at him, noting his reserved demeanor and the occasional flicker of unease in his eyes.

Sitting beside her brother Charles, whose plate boasted a large apple sconce, Caroline Bingley exuded a haughty demeanor as she engaged in light conversation with Louisa. However, her eyes frequently darted toward Mr. Darcy, who sat quietly, seemingly lost in his thoughts. Caroline's gaze was calculating, a reflection of her scheming nature.

The sound of horses snorting and the crunch of gravel on the driveway announced the arrival of the Matlock traveling coach. Charles Bingley's face lit up with anticipation as he rose from his seat, smoothing his waistcoat with nervous hands. "We have another guest," he announced, his voice brimming with enthusiasm. "Colonel Fitzwilliam has arrived."

The room's occupants turned their attention toward the door, curiosity piqued. Mr. Hurst raised an eyebrow, and Louisa exchanged a glance with Caroline, whose eyes narrowed slightly at the mention of another guest. Caroline's thoughts raced; why hadn't her brother informed her or Louisa of this visit? And how long was Colonel Fitzwilliam planning to stay in this backwater?

A few moments later, the butler entered, followed by Colonel Richard Fitzwilliam, whose military bearing was evident in his upright posture and confident stride. He removed his hat, revealing a head of dark blonde, fashionably styled hair, and scanned the room with keen, intelligent blue eyes.

"Colonel Fitzwilliam!" Charles exclaimed, stepping forward to greet him with a hearty handshake. "Welcome to Netherfield Park!"

"Thank you, Bingley," the Colonel replied, his voice warm and cordial. "It's a pleasure to be here."

The Colonel gazed at the occupants of the breakfast room, where everyone rose to greet him. Mr. Darcy stood first, a rare smile tugging at his lips as he extended a hand to his cousin. "Richard, it's good to see you."

"And you, Darcy," the Colonel replied, firmly shaking his cousin's hand. "It's been too long since we rusticated together."

Charles gestured to the table. "Please, join us for breakfast, Colonel."

"Thank you," Richard said, moving to one of the empty seats beside Elizabeth. "Good morning, Miss Bennet, Mrs. Hurst, Mr. Hurst, Miss Bingley." He nodded to the others and took his seat after the ladies sat.

"Good morning, Colonel," they chorused in response, with Caroline adding a charming smile as she tried to catch his eye. She was so surprised by his arrival that she overlooked his greeting, Elizabeth, by name and without an introduction.

Elizabeth observed her old friend with interest, noting his easy manners and the respectful way he interacted with everyone. As the Colonel settled in, the conversation gradually resumed, albeit with more participants.

"How was your journey, Colonel?" Charles asked, his tone genuinely curious.

"Uneventful and swift," Richard replied, helping himself to a slice of toast while a footman placed a cup of coffee near his plate. "The weather held fair, and the roads were in decent condition. My father was kind to lend me his coach."

Caroline leaned forward slightly, her voice dripping with practiced charm; she asked, "What brings you to Netherfield, Colonel Fitzwilliam? We are always delighted to welcome such a distinguished guest to our home."

Colonel Fitzwilliam smiled politely. "I have come to visit my cousin and to see how he fares in Hertfordshire. I have heard much about the charms of this region." He surreptitiously winked at Elizabeth.

Elizabeth noticed the slight tension in Mr. Darcy's posture as the conversation continued. It appeared the arrogant man did not entirely welcome Richard's presence.

During the following minutes, Elizabeth became increasingly drawn into the conversation, her initial curiosity about Richard's unexpected arrival giving way to genuine pleasure at seeing him again. Colonel Fitzwilliam's engaging manner and insightful comments made him a delightful addition to the table. Even Darcy seemed more at ease, his guarded demeanor softening in his cousin's company.

At one point, the Colonel turned his attention to Elizabeth, his eyes full of concern. "Miss Elizabeth, I have heard about your sister's illness. How is she faring today?"

Elizabeth's expression softened, and she smiled gratefully. "Thank you for asking, Colonel. Jane is still feverish, but I am hopeful she will recover soon."

"Miss Bennet is fortunate to have such a caring and devoted sister," he remarked kindly before taking a sip of coffee.

Elizabeth blushed slightly at the compliment. "Thank you, Colonel. Papa sent our maid to help with the nursing. He didn't want me to carry the full burden of her care."

"Your father is a good man," remarked Richard before adding, "Was the staff here inadequate in some way?"

"When I arrived, no maid was assigned to care for Jane. I am sure it was an oversight, but happily, my father spoke to the apothecary when he stopped by with the bill, realized Netherfield must be understaffed, and rectified the problem." Elizabeth glanced up at Richard with a glint of mischief in her eyes.

Caroline glared at Elizabeth. Turning to the Colonel, she asked, "How did you know about Miss Jane Bennet's illness?"

"My cousin mentioned it," came the curt reply. He turned a disapproving stare on the woman. "I hope your household can bear the expense of feeding me and my entourage."

Shocked, Charles Bingley looked up from his meal. "Heavens! Of course, I can afford to house guests. Why would you think otherwise?"

"Because you failed to provide a maid to care for an ailing young lady and sent the apothecary to collect payment from her father," retorted Richard. "Does the local man cost more than a shilling or two for a consultation?"

"What?" An astounded Bingley looked at Louisa. "Is this true, Louisa? You failed to provide a maid? Why didn't you send Mr. Jones to me for payment? Do you wish to ruin me in the eyes of our neighbors?"

Louisa stared blankly at her brother. She answered slowly, "I assigned a maid to help her undress. How was I to know she needed more than that? You sent for Mr. Jones. You should have made the payment arrangements." Louisa put down her cutlery, rose, and excused herself. She left the room with Bingley hot on her heels.

Everyone began to disperse, each with their plans for the day. Elizabeth lingered momentarily, watching Mr. Darcy and Colonel Fitzwilliam converse quietly by the window. The sight of them together stirred a new sense of curiosity within her. Perhaps the Colonel's presence would offer an opportunity to better understand the enigmatic Mr. Darcy.

Determined to seize the moment, Elizabeth approached the pair, her steps light and purposeful. "Mr. Darcy, Colonel Fitzwilliam," she began, her voice steady, "I wonder if I might have a word with you both."

The two men turned to her, their expressions curious. Darcy nodded, his eyes meeting hers with a hint of anticipation. "Of course, Miss Elizabeth. We are at your service."

"Thank you," she replied, a smile on her lips. "Shall we say in the drawing room, now?"

"That sounds perfect," Colonel Fitzwilliam agreed, his gaze warm and encouraging.

Elizabeth led the way to the drawing room, her mind racing. She must warn Mr. Darcy about Caroline's plans and inquire why Richard had come to Netherfield, but she didn't wish to sound like an interfering busybody. The trio walked away from the open doorway to the farthest end of the room. Richard glanced at the open door, raised a finger to his lips, and whispered, "The family sends their regards, Lizzy. I've come to save you from the Bingleys and Darcy. Has it been awful staying here with them?"

Before Elizabeth could answer, Darcy loudly sputtered, "What! I haven't done anything awful!"

Richard clamped a hand over Darcy's mouth and shook his finger warningly. "Whisper, Darcy. Those harpies are probably lurking out of sight in the hall, attempting to hear our conversation."

Elizabeth covered her mouth with both hands, trying to suppress her laughter. Darcy's shocked countenance was too much, and an uncontrollable gurgle of laughter escaped. Richard joined her, and they soon wiped tears of mirth from their eyes as Darcy, released from the Colonel's grip, stood expressionless, watching the pair laugh. A tiny twitch of his upper lip indicated Darcy's amusement.

Finally, Elizabeth whispered, "They are awful. When I arrived, my sister was burning up with a fever without anyone in attendance. Mrs. Nichols, the housekeeper, slept in Jane's room but had duties to perform, and in her estimation, none of the maids could care for a patient. Papa sent our maid from Longbourn to help me nurse Jane. I pray Jane recovers quickly. Neither Mrs. Hurst nor Miss Bingley have checked on Jane since I arrived yesterday morning. I never thought I'd be anxious to leave this place, but being here with these inconsiderate people is unpleasant."

"I haven't done or said anything unpleasant to you," protested Darcy in a shocked whisper.

Two pairs of eyes gazed at him in wonder. Richard shook his head in disbelief while Elizabeth raised an eyebrow.

"Fine," Darcy murmured, looking at Elizabeth. "I apologize for the uncouth, untrue words that flowed from my mouth at the assembly. But I've been polite to you ever since."

Colonel Fitzwilliam snorted in disbelief and spoke before Elizabeth could say anything. "Lizzy, what's on your mind?"

"Yesterday," she whispered, "as I was passing this room, I overheard part of a conversation between Miss Bingley and the Hursts. Miss Bingley plans to trap you, Mr. Darcy, into marriage. The Hursts told her it would not work, but she disagreed. That's all I know because I kept walking. The servants may know more since several footmen were stationed in the hall."

The men straightened their posture; anger flashed in their eyes.

"That will not happen," stated Darcy.

"Never," growled Richard.

"Jane will be awake by now. I must go to her. I'm sure you two have things to discuss." Elizabeth curtseyed and left the room, closing the door behind her.

Chapter 4

Saturday, November 16, 1811
Netherfield – Discussions

"This is a problem," Darcy said quietly, running a hand through his hair. His brow furrowed in frustration. "Caroline Bingley's scheming must end. I, too, heard her arguing with the Hursts about her intention to compromise me."

Richard rubbed his chin thoughtfully, his eyes narrowing as he considered their options. "I agree that Caroline is a problem," Richard replied, his voice equally low. "She's desperate and determined." He folded his arms across his chest. "Perhaps if Charles knew the full extent of Caroline's plans, he would be persuaded to leave Netherfield and take his family with him."

Darcy paused, considering the idea. "You're right," he said, lowering his hand and gazing at Richard with a furrowed brow. "Charles is a good man. He wouldn't condone such behavior if he knew about it." Darcy's frown deepened, confusion creasing his forehead. "But I don't understand why you claim the whole family should leave Netherfield."

Richard's expression hardened, and he leaned forward, his tone gruff. "Mr. Gardiner wants them gone from Netherfield permanently," he replied, his blue eyes reflecting his determination. "Jane Bennet deserves a worthy man, not a milksop led about by conniving sisters."

Darcy's frown deepened, his thoughts racing. "We need to discuss this further, but not here," he said, glancing around the room for the servant's entrance. "Let's go to my room. We can speak there."

Richard agreed, and the two men quickly went upstairs to Darcy's private quarters. As they entered the sitting room, Darcy's dog bounded over, greeting his master with a wagging tail and a friendly nuzzle. Darcy's face softened as he patted the dog's head.

Richard raised an eyebrow, his lips curling into a knowing smile. "I see you've got Jasper staying with you."

Darcy smiled slightly, scratching the dog behind the ears. "Yes, I've found his presence comforting since bringing him inside yesterday, especially after I overheard an unmarried woman declare her intention to compromise me. Plus, he's a good listener."

Richard chuckled, a glint of amusement in his eyes. "Indeed. A large guard dog can be invaluable when fighting off hordes of females."

Darcy closed the door securely, ensuring their conversation would remain private. He motioned for Richard to sit, and they both took seats by the window, Jasper lying down at Darcy's feet, his head resting on his paws with a contented sigh.

"About the letter," Darcy began, his tone somber, his gaze fixed on Richard. "The one you wrote detailing the family's connection to the Bennets. I had no idea."

Richard's expression softened, his brows furrowing slightly in empathy. "It must have been a surprise. But that's because you seldom attend family dinners, and we never talk about our friends on Gracechurch Street at balls."

Darcy's jaw firmed, his eyes narrowing in frustration. "I know that I have many lucrative business contracts with Gardiner Enterprises. I did not know Mrs. Bennet was Edward Gardiner's sister. You could have told me about Mr. Bennet's friendship with your father. You knew I was going to stay here."

Richard leaned forward, his tone becoming more earnest. "Agreed," he said firmly, his gaze unwavering. "But Mr. Bennet wanted to see your true character. Lizzy has listened to Mother and Rebecca praise you to the heavens for years and was looking forward to meeting the handsome, intelligent, modest gentleman of excellent character who might be an agreeable companion for an intelligent young lady who reads extensively, plays chess, and might be found walking for miles every day on her father's country estate."

Darcy's expression shifted to one of regret, his shoulders slumping slightly. "I cannot defend myself," he admitted, his voice tinged with remorse. "No matter my exhaustion and irritation at that assembly, I acted like a lout. My mother would have boxed my ears for speaking such deplorable insults about anybody. It doesn't matter that it was a private conversation. I didn't bother to lower my voice or see if anyone stood nearby. Miss Elizabeth must hate me."

Richard placed a reassuring hand on his cousin's shoulder. "We'll handle this tactless bent of yours by privately practicing how to respond in social situations, Darcy. I should have taken you to task years ago. You are lucky Lizzy has a forgiving nature, and Bennet is a good man."

Determination in his eyes, Darcy said, "We shall go to Longbourn today. You can introduce me to Mr. Bennet. Let's make the necessary arrangements and leave as soon as possible."

With that, the two men left the room. Jasper followed behind Darcy, who went to the stable and instructed his groom to prepare the carriage while Richard sought the privacy of his chambers to prepare for the short trip.

UPON ARRIVING AT LONGBOURN, Darcy and Richard were greeted by the butler, Mr. Hill, who looked surprised to see them.

"Good day, gentlemen," he said, bowing slightly. "How may I assist you?"

"We need to speak with Mr. Bennet," Darcy replied politely, handing over their calling cards. The butler took the cards and disappeared down the hall. A few minutes later, he reappeared.

"Very well, sirs. Mr. Bennet is available," the butler said, leading them through the house.

As they walked, Darcy noticed Longbourn's lived-in atmosphere. Family portraits and lush tapestries covered the walls, and the aroma of fresh flowers filled the air. Longbourn's manor had a warm and inviting charm.

Mr. Hill led them to Mr. Bennet's study, where he knocked lightly before opening the door. "Colonel Fitzwilliam and Mr. Darcy to see you, sir," he announced.

Mr. Bennet looked up from his book, mildly curious. "Colonel Fitzwilliam, Mr. Darcy, this is quite an unexpected visit," he remarked, setting the book aside. "To what do I owe the pleasure?"

Richard stepped forward, his expression earnest. "Mr. Bennet, thank you for seeing us. May we sit?"

Mr. Bennet's eyes widened slightly, and he gestured to the chairs opposite his desk. "Of course, please, sit down. What has happened?"

Darcy and Richard took their seats, and Richard introduced Darcy to Mr. Bennet. He explained the situation, detailing Caroline Bingley's schemes and Mr. Gardiner's desire to rid Netherfield Park of the current renters. Mr. Bennet listened intently, his expression growing more contemplative with each passing moment.

When Richard finished speaking, Mr. Bennet leaned back in his chair, his face thoughtful. "This is indeed troubling news. I appreciate your coming to inform me. Caroline Bingley's intentions are clear, and I hope you take precautions to prevent a compromise. But I can do nothing except offer advice on that subject. However, once my daughters are safely home, getting the residents of Netherfield to decamp to London will be easy." Bennet tapped his nose and grinned at Richard. Richard laughed, knowing the tricks Bennet might employ to drive the Bingleys from Netherfield.

Darcy cleared his throat and shifted in his chair. "Mr. Bennet, before we continue this topic, I want you to know that I apologized to Miss Elizabeth this morning for my ungentlemanly words and behavior at the assembly. I extend this apology to you and your family. Please forgive me."

Darcy's voice was sincere, and Mr. Bennet studied him before speaking. "Mr. Darcy, I accept your apology. However, forgiveness must be earned. I cannot speak for Elizabeth; I can tell you she is a kind girl. As for Caroline Bingley, tread carefully."

Richard leaned forward, his tone earnest. "Mr. Bennet, we believe the only solution is for the Bingleys to leave Netherfield. We need your advice on achieving that without causing undue scandal or harm."

Mr. Bennet tapped his fingers on the desk thoughtfully. "Convincing Charles Bingley to leave might be easier if he has no reason to stay. Perhaps Jane and Elizabeth should visit the Gardiners in London once Jane is healthy enough to travel."

Darcy smiled. "We could arrange to send them in the Matlock carriage. Then we can leave Netherfield a day later, claiming we're going to Derbyshire."

"Indeed," Mr. Bennet agreed. "I can send a letter to Mr. Gardiner."

Richard smiled. "An excellent suggestion. Sending the ladies to London could be the key to resolving this situation." Richard's expression changed. "No, that wouldn't separate Miss Bennet from Bingley. He would call on the Gardiners. That puppy is relentless while pursuing an angel. Of course, his infatuations are legendary in London for their brevity."

"I don't want my daughter to attach herself to that man. His sisters would make her life miserable. Do you have any other suggestions?" Bennet raised his brow as he looked from Richard to Darcy.

Darcy paled, Mr. Bennet was correct. Shifting in his chair, he said, "My sixteen-year-old sister, Georgiana, is at Pemberley, my estate in Derbyshire, with a middle-aged companion. She is in dire need of friends who are closer in age. Would you consider sending Miss Bennet and Miss Elizabeth to Pemberley if the Matlocks, especially Lady Matlock and her daughter Lady Rebecca, agreed to accompany them for an extended visit that would last through the winter? Colonel Fitzwilliam and I would be part of their escort. Of course, you can come, too."

Mr. Bennet's eyebrows rose in surprise. "That is quite an offer, Mr. Darcy. Traveling to Derbyshire may be a suitable solution. Your sister would benefit from their company, and Jane would be away from Charles Bingley. Lizzy loves to travel and would consider a trip to Derbyshire a grand adventure."

Thomas Bennet stared at Darcy and began tapping his fingers on the desk. "Why would you go to these lengths to help us separate my Jane from Mr. Bingley?"

Redness crept up Darcy's neck. Did Bennet suspect Darcy's partiality to Elizabeth? "I want to make up for my errors since entering Hertfordshire. Plus, Miss Elizabeth and Miss Bennet would help Georgiana recover from the betrayal of a false friend."

Darcy continued earnestly, "I assure you, Mr. Bennet, they would be well taken care of at Pemberley. Cousin Richard informed me that Lady Matlock and Cousin Rebecca are very fond of your two eldest daughters, and they would have every comfort."

Mr. Bennet stood, extending his hand to Darcy. "Mr. Darcy, I appreciate your candor and willingness to address this issue. I accept your invitation for my two eldest daughters and expect to receive confirmation of Lady Matlock's agreement within the week." Bennet glanced meaningfully at Richard.

"If you allow me to use your writing supplies, I'll send an express to my parents immediately outlining the plan." At Bennet's nod, Richard glanced around the room, went to a mahogany writing desk, and began to pen a letter to his mother.

Darcy shook Mr. Bennet's hand, feeling a sense of relief. "Thank you, Mr. Bennet. Your support means a great deal. If Miss Bennet can come downstairs for dinner tonight, we will bundle her up in blankets and escort the ladies home after services tomorrow. Then we will return to London on Monday morning."

"I'll inform Mother to expect us Monday afternoon. Do you believe Miss Jane will be well enough by Wednesday to leave for Derbyshire, Bennet?" Richard held his pen poised above the paper.

Mr. Bennet, anxious to get back to his book, replied, "Yes, yes, that should be sufficient time." Then, a low chuckle rumbled from his chest. "Tell the Bingleys you are going to Kent to visit Lady Catherine. Otherwise, Miss Bingley will follow you to London and be knocking on your door at Darcy House." All three men laughed uproariously.

"That's an excellent idea," Richard gasped when he reclaimed his voice. We will stay hidden within Matlock House until Wednesday. Since we don't want the locals to know your daughters are going to Derbyshire, can you bring them to meet us at Stevenage? Do you wish to send a maid, or shall we provide one?"

Mr. Bennet replied, "I'll send Sally with the girls and accompany them to the posting station in Stevenage. Would nine in the morning be an acceptable time to meet, Colonel?"

Richard nodded. "Yes. We can transfer everyone's luggage, and you can finalize arrangements with my parents or come to Pemberley."

Bennet sighed, "Sadly, I cannot travel to Pemberley now. I expect guests to arrive next Friday and must be here to greet them."

"What will you do about the Bingleys?" asked Darcy. "They will still be at Netherfield after we depart, and Mr. Gardiner wants them gone."

Eyes twinkling with mirth, Bennet said, "Do not worry, young man. They will be long gone from Netherfield before the end of the month. I have a few ideas on how to arrange it." At Darcy's quizzical look, Mr. Bennet shook his head. "No. Telling you would spoil my fun and cause you to worry. I am sure your friend will correspond with you after his departure."

As they left Mr. Bennet's study, Richard turned to Darcy. "We must go to Meryton and arrange for an express rider to deliver this letter."

"Agreed. The sooner we have your parents' approval, the better. We need to get away from Netherfield." Darcy gazed intently at his cousin. "Richard, is there anything you wish to share regarding the Miss Bennets?"

Richard turned to Darcy with a severe expression. "No. Let's speak about how to avoid a compromise. Having Jasper in your room is a safeguard, but he can't always be at your side. We should share my room at night. Your valet and my batman can sleep in your room. Those two can discover any servants' gossip and keep us informed."

"Agreed. The sooner we take precautions, the better."

The two cousins became silent as the carriage rolled along the road to Meryton, each man lost in his thoughts. Darcy's mind raced with the complexities of their situation and the urgency of their plan while Richard pondered the best way to approach Bingley about his sister's scheming.

Upon reaching Meryton, they quickly arranged for an express rider to deliver Richard's letter. With the message dispatched, they turned to the next pressing matter: confronting Bingley.

Back in the carriage, Richard broke the silence. "We need to handle Bingley delicately. You must tell him about the conversation you overheard; it will be a shock."

Darcy said, "Indeed. He's a good man who deserves to know the truth."

As they approached Netherfield, the two men steeled themselves for the upcoming conversation.

Chapter 5

Saturday, November 16, 1811
Bingley

"You cannot be serious!" Incredulous, Charles Bingley gazed at the two men sitting across from him. "Caroline would never stoop so low. She has a dowry of twenty thousand pounds and accomplishments garnered at the finest finishing school. Her pleasing figure and beautiful face might capture the heart of a suitable man from the ton. Why would she scheme to compromise you, Darcy?"

Silencing Darcy with a gesture, Richard leaned forward, his expression grave. "Bingley, we understand your reluctance to believe this about your sister. But Darcy overheard her plotting to trap him into marriage. She was speaking to the Hursts. You know Darcy would not bring such a matter to you lightly."

Bingley shook his head, his face turning red with anger. "This is absurd! Caroline is many things, but she would never use deceitful tactics. You must be mistaken."

Darcy's eyes narrowed in anger. "I assure you, Charles, there is no mistake. Louisa and Edwin tried to dissuade her. Caroline expressed herself loudly and refused to believe I had no interest in her. I heard her, clear as day. The servants in the hallway heard her. Ask Hurst."

Bingley's frustration boiled over. He stood up, pacing the room. "I refuse to believe it! Caroline is my sister. She has flaws but would never risk our family's reputation like this. It's preposterous!"

Bingley turned his gaze to Richard, his eyes pleading. "Richard, please. Tell me there's been some misunderstanding. Caroline is ambitious, but she's incapable of such a scheme."

Richard remained seated, his voice calm but firm. "You know my cousin wouldn't fabricate something like this, Bingley. We're trying to protect you and your family."

Darcy sighed, standing to face his friend. "Charles, I wish it were a misunderstanding. But I'm afraid it is not. Caroline is desperate to secure a high-status match and sees me as her best opportunity. You must send her away. Don't you have an aunt up north?"

Bingley's anger flared again. "No! I cannot accept that. She wouldn't do this to us. She wouldn't jeopardize everything we've worked for."

Darcy stood several inches taller than Bingley, his expression resolute. "Are you calling me a liar? I know this is hard to hear. But ignoring it won't make it go away. You must act and curtail her plans before it's too late."

Bingley clenched his fists, his face a mask of turmoil. "This is madness. I can't just pack her off to our aunt in Scarborough because of an accusation."

Richard placed a reassuring hand on Bingley's shoulder. "We're not asking you to abandon everything. Just take a step back; give us time to figure things out without the immediate threat of scandal."

Darcy stared coldly at his friend, his jaw tightening. He loudly repeated his question. "Are you calling me a liar, Bingley?"

Bingley's eyes widened, and he raised his hands defensively. "No, of course not, Darcy. I'm just finding it hard to believe. Caroline has always been ambitious, but this seems... extreme."

Bingley shook his head, determination hardening his features. "I'm sorry, but I can't abandon Caroline. We are settled here, and I won't disrupt our lives based on something that has not happened."

Darcy's face tightened with frustration. "It is clear that you do not believe me. If Miss Bingley stays, we cannot. You risk everything... your reputation, your future. This isn't just about your sister. You must protect your family."

Bingley's eyes flashed with anger. He disregarded Darcy's words, knowing his friendship with Darcy and Colonel Fitzwilliam might be lost. "I appreciate your concern, Darcy, but my decision is final. She is staying at Netherfield."

Richard glanced worriedly at Darcy before turning back to Bingley. "If that's your decision, we'll respect it. But you must be vigilant. Miss Bingley's schemes could ruin your family."

Bingley spoke through clenched teeth, "Caroline is my sister, and family comes before friendship. If you cannot stay, I will understand." He slammed his palm down upon the desktop, emphasizing his words.

Darcy sighed, "Very well. Richard brought an urgent request from our aunt, Lady Catherine de Bourgh. We'll leave to attend to this family matter when travel arrangements are complete. There's no need to inform your sisters."

Bingley's expression softened slightly. "I'll miss your company, but I understand. Perhaps some distance will do us all good."

"Yes. I believe distance will affect us all in varied ways. In the future, I will not recognize Miss Bingley if she approaches me on the street. She will not be welcome in my homes or on my properties. My connections will no longer invite her to their homes. She has demonstrated an unacceptable lack of character. We will retreat to our chambers pack." Darcy's final words, spoken with arrogant disdain, ensured they would be acquaintances who met only by chance.

As Darcy and Richard left the study, they encountered Edwin Hurst in the hallway. His face bore an expression of determination as he stepped forward, halting before the two cousins.

"Gentlemen, is Charles in a pleasant frame of mind?" Edwin asked, his voice steady but insistent.

Darcy nodded curtly. "You must judge for yourself, Hurst. He appears a bit put out, but who am I to render an accurate opinion of a man wearing blinders." Richard snorted but said nothing.

With that, Darcy and Richard made their way to Richard's room, leaving Edwin Hurst to confront his brother-in-law. Hurst entered the study and closed the door, turning to face Bingley, who still paced the room in agitation.

"Charles, we need to talk," Hurst began, his tone serious.

Bingley stopped pacing and looked at Hurst with frustration and disbelief. "Edwin, please tell me you are not here to spout nonsense about Caroline. Darcy and his cousin believe she is plotting a compromise. It must be a terrible misunderstanding."

Hurst shook his head. "I'm afraid it's not, Charles. I was there. I heard Caroline's plans myself. She is scheming to compromise Darcy. I tried to dissuade her to no avail."

Bingley's face turned pale as he sank into a chair. "I can't believe this. Caroline would never do something so reckless."

Hurst sighed, moving to sit across from Bingley. "I know it's difficult to accept, but you must understand that Caroline is desperate and sees Darcy as her last chance to secure a prestigious match. Louisa and I tried to talk her out of it, but she wouldn't listen."

Bingley's eyes filled with pain and confusion. "But why, Edwin? Why would she risk everything we've built?"

"Because she's blinded by ambition," Edwin replied. "She believes that landing Darcy will elevate her and secure her future. She doesn't realize the potential consequences of her actions."

Bingley buried his face in his hands. "What am I supposed to do, Edwin? I can't just send her away without proof. It would devastate her."

"Proof? My words are proof!" Edwin leaned forward, his voice firm. "Charles, you need to protect our family. If Caroline's plan succeeds, it will bring scandal upon all of us. You don't have to send her away permanently, but perhaps a temporary stay with your aunt in Scarborough would give her time to reflect and calm down."

Bingley looked up, his eyes searching Hurst's face for answers. "And what about Darcy and Richard? They are angry because I wouldn't believe their story. They've decided to visit Lady Catherine in Kent."

"They're not talebearers," Hurst advised. "Their absence will help ease the tension here. We can handle Caroline in their absence."

Bingley nodded slowly. "Very well, Edwin. I'll speak with Caroline about maintaining propriety with our guests. I hope this will be enough to prevent any further complications."

Hurst placed a reassuring hand on Bingley's shoulder. "It's the best course of action, Charles." Bingley shrugged off his brother's hand.

As Hurst watched Bingley head for the door, he said, "Charles, wait."

Bingley turned back, his expression one of weary frustration. "What is it, Edwin?"

Hurst took a deep breath and stepped closer. "You don't seem to grasp the magnitude of the repercussions if Caroline attempts to compromise Darcy after you are warned of her intentions. This isn't something that will blow over."

Bingley's brow furrowed with irritation. "Edwin, Caroline will give up her schemes once Darcy leaves for Kent. She's ambitious but not foolish enough to continue pursuing someone who isn't here."

Hurst shook his head, his voice growing more urgent. "You're underestimating the situation, Charles. The servants are already gossiping about Caroline. They've heard her words and seen her behavior. Word is spreading, and it won't be long before this household becomes the center of a scandal."

Bingley's face flushed with anger and disbelief. "Caroline is a good woman, Edwin. She has flaws, but she's incapable of malicious deeds. She wouldn't risk her reputation or ours. Once Darcy is gone, everything will settle down."

"Charles, open your eyes," Edwin insisted, his tone full of exasperation and concern. "The servants' gossip alone can ruin us. Even if Caroline doesn't follow through, the rumors will persist. This isn't just about her reputation; it's about the reputation of our entire family."

Bingley shook his head vehemently. "I won't believe it. Caroline has always been headstrong but never used such underhanded tactics. This is all a misunderstanding."

Hurst's eyes bore into Bingley's, his frustration growing. "You're being naive, Charles. Caroline's ambition blinds her to the consequences of her actions. We're not just talking about idle gossip but about potential ruin. If Darcy is the victim of a compromise or an attempted compromise, he will not marry your sister. If even a whisper of this gets out, it will destroy us."

Bingley's jaw tightened, his stubbornness unwavering. "I won't abandon my sister based on hearsay and paranoia. Caroline will give up her dream of marriage once Darcy is gone. She'll stop." Bingley looked away, trying to remember Darcy's parting words. Had the man threatened to cut Caroline and withdraw all support in society? Bingley shrugged. After all, Darcy's opinion was irrelevant. Wasn't it?

Hurst sighed deeply, realizing the futility of arguing with Bingley. The idiot could not take anything seriously and refused to hear or see anything unpleasant. "I hope you're right, Charles. But remember, this determined self-deception won't protect you or Caroline from the consequences of any nefarious actions she takes. The stakes are higher than you realize, and I pray you don't regret your decision to ignore my words."

With that, Hurst turned and left the study, leaving Bingley alone, his mind full of denial and trepidation.

Chapter 6

Sunday, November 17, 1811
Longbourn

Jane and Elizabeth Bennet sat in their father's study, their expressions curious and slightly anxious. The room was filled with the faint smell of old books and the sound of the crackling fire. Mr. Bennet looked up from his papers and cleared his throat, capturing their full attention. "My dear girls, I have some news regarding your upcoming trip."

Elizabeth raised an eyebrow, glancing at Jane before focusing on their father. "What trip, Papa?"

Mr. Bennet leaned back in his chair, a small, knowing smile playing on his lips. "You will be traveling to Pemberley, Mr. Darcy's estate in Derbyshire. Lady Matlock and her daughter, Lady Rebecca, will accompany you and possibly Lord Matlock. Colonel Fitzwilliam and Mr. Darcy will also be part of your escort."

Jane's eyes widened in surprise, her head tilting to the right. "Pemberley? But why, Papa?"

Mr. Bennet folded his hands on the desk, his expression growing serious. "It seems Mr. Darcy's sister, Miss Georgiana Darcy, needs friends closer to her age. Moreover, this arrangement will help separate you, Jane, from Mr. Bingley to allow everyone to reflect on the consequences of aligning oneself with an inappropriate family."

Elizabeth frowned slightly, her fingers tightening around the armrest of her chair. "Separate Jane from Mr. Bingley? Is something amiss?"

Mr. Bennet sighed, his gaze softening as he looked at his daughters. "Yes. There have been some complications involving Mr. Bingley's sister, Caroline. Your Uncle Gardiner and I believe it would be best for all parties if you were away from the Bingleys."

Jane's concern deepened, her delicate features creasing with worry. "Caroline? What has she done?"

Mr. Bennet hesitated, choosing his words carefully. "Miss Bingley mistreats the servants and rules her brother's actions through deceit. The man cannot see her shrewish behavior and follows her directions like a puppy. She overspends her allowance and makes unreasonable demands. Gardiner regrets leasing the estate to Mr. Bingley. The termagant has been scheming underhandedly to secure a match with Mr. Darcy. Mr. Darcy overheard her plans and is taking precautions to avoid scandal."

Elizabeth's eyes narrowed in thought, her mind racing. "So, we are to help Miss Darcy and simultaneously remove ourselves from the Bingleys?"

Mr. Bennet nodded. "Precisely. This will provide you both with a change of scenery and some time away from the local gossip. You will be in good company, and it is an opportunity to see a different part of the country."

Jane looked at her father, concerned. "But what about Mr. Bingley? If we leave, will he think we are abandoning him?"

Mr. Bennet sighed again, his tone gentle but firm. "I do not care what Mr. Bingley thinks. You hardly know the man. His reputation in London includes his inconstancy regarding women. He flits from beauty to beauty, calling each lady an angel. I will never bless a match with a man of his ilk."

Jane was silent. She looked down at her hands as a tear rolled slowly down her cheek. She impatiently brushed it away. "I thought him the most amiable man of my acquaintance and all that a gentleman should be... kind, honest, cheerful, and handsome. Was I mistaken?"

Mr. Bennet rubbed his forehead in frustration. His eldest daughter constantly looked for the goodness in people and overlooked the bad. He answered, "All of this you learned after two dances at a public assembly and fifteen minutes of conversation during a dinner party at Lucas Lodge?"

Jane looked abashed. "He was very concerned while I was ill, always asking Lizzy about my health."

Mr. Bennet scrutinized his daughter. "Jane, it is time you stopped seeing the world through a colored lens. Anyone hosting a sick guest would inquire about their health. Romanticizing this behavior is a disservice to yourself. Charles Bingley is a handsome flirt. How kind or honest is a man who compliments a lady, raising her hopes, only to abandon the lady when he moves on to the next angel? An inconstant man before marriage will be inconstant during marriage. Do you want to marry a man who will have affairs? How much of his income will he continue to spend supporting his sisters? Would you be content allowing Miss Bingley to run your household?"

Horrified, Jane vehemently shook her head. She slumped in the chair and buried her face in her hands. Elizabeth was ashamed of herself. Why had she teased Jane about the man?

Glancing sympathetically at her sister, Elizabeth's eyes glowed with a determination to keep her unfounded speculations to herself in the future. She reached out to place a comforting hand on Jane's arm. "Very well, Papa. When are we to leave?"

Mr. Bennet smiled, relieved there would be no protracted argument. "Do not tell anyone about this trip. You will depart on Wednesday. Pack for a long visit and include your winter clothes. Do it yourselves. I do not wish the staff or the rest of the family to know about your plans. We will meet your fellow travelers at Stevenage, and I will ensure you are safely on your way. Sally will accompany you as your maid. After you are gone, I will inform your mother and sisters that you are visiting friends. Your destination is to remain a secret. Do you understand? Direct All correspondence to your Aunt Gardiner. "

Jane and Elizabeth exchanged glances, each lost in her thoughts about the unexpected journey ahead and its secrecy. Jane's heart ached with the idea of leaving Mr. Bingley, while Elizabeth's mind buzzed with speculation about Pemberley and the intriguing Mr. Darcy.

Jane broke the silence, her voice trembling slightly. "Lizzy, what do you think Pemberley will be like?"

Elizabeth smiled, trying to lighten the mood. "I imagine it will be grand and imposing, much like Mr. Darcy. But I also hope it will be a place of comfort and beauty, where we can find peace away from all this nonsense."

Jane nodded, her tears beginning to dry. "Do you think we will like Miss Darcy? She sounds quite reserved."

Elizabeth squeezed her sister's hand reassuringly. "I'm sure we will, Jane. And we will have each other, no matter what. Plus, Rebecca and Lady Matlock will be there. This journey may be exactly what we need to clear our heads and find some clarity."

Jane took a deep breath, drawing strength from her sister's words. "I suppose you are right, Lizzy. It will be an adventure, at the very least."

Mr. Bennet watched his daughters with concern. He knew the journey would be challenging but believed it was necessary for their growth and happiness. "Remember, girls, you are doing this for your well-being. Stay focused and keep your wits about you. Pemberley is far from Hertfordshire, but you will always have a home here."

Jane and Elizabeth considered their father's words as they left the study and headed toward the drawing room. When they entered, Mrs. Bennet's voice rang out, "Well, girls, what did your father want?"

Jane and Elizabeth exchanged glances, each trying to mask their emotions. Elizabeth spoke first, her voice light and controlled. "Papa wanted to discuss our stay at Netherfield."

Mrs. Bennet's eyes lit up with curiosity and hope. "Oh, I do hope Mr. Bingley was mentioned. He seems so fond of you, Jane. What did your father say?"

Jane forced a smile, trying to keep her voice steady. "He did mention Mr. Bingley, Mama. He learned from an acquaintance in London that Mr. Bingley is a notorious flirt. He also spoke about maintaining proper decorum and ensuring I do not rush into anything."

Mrs. Bennet huffed, clearly dissatisfied with such a prudent response. "Nonsense! Mr. Bingley is clearly in love with you, Jane. There is no need for all this caution."

Elizabeth jumped in, steering the conversation away from dangerous waters. "Mama, have you seen the new lace Mrs. Philips sent over? It is lovely and would look splendid on a new gown for Jane."

Distracted, Mrs. Bennet's attention shifted to the promise of finery. "Oh, indeed! We must see about having a new gown made immediately. We cannot have you looking anything less than perfect, Jane."

Kitty and Lydia, who had been half-listening from their corner of the room, perked up at the mention of new dresses. "Oh, Mama, can we have new gowns as well?" Lydia asked eagerly.

Mrs. Bennet waved them off. "We shall see, we shall see. Jane must take priority now. She has caught the eye of a very wealthy gentleman, after all."

As the conversation turned to talk of lace and gowns, Mary, observing from her spot near the window, spoke up, her tone dismissive. "I have heard rumors about Caroline Bingley's treatment of the servants at Netherfield. She mistreats them terribly, berating them for the slightest mistakes and making unreasonable demands."

Elizabeth's eyes widened slightly. "Where did you hear this, Mary?"

Mary shrugged, setting her book aside. "Mrs. Long mentioned it to Aunt Philips, who told me. The servants are afraid of her, and some have even considered leaving."

Jane's brow furrowed with concern. "That is dreadful. I never imagined Miss Bingley to be so harsh."

Mary's expression remained severe. "It only shows her true character. And as for Mr. Bingley, any regard he has shown is suspect. A man who allows such behavior in his household is no true gentleman."

Mrs. Bennet's eyes flashed with irritation. "Oh, Mary, do not be so harsh. Mr. Bingley is a good man. He may not be aware of his sister's actions."

Mary shook her head, her tone firm. "Ignorance is no excuse, Mama. If he were a good man, Mr. Bingley would ensure his household was run with kindness and respect. Instead, he skips from one beauty to another. His behavior was in the gossip column almost daily before he came here. It is the behavior of a rascal, not a gentleman."

Jane spoke softly, "In the London papers? Why didn't you say something earlier?"

Mary shrugged. "You never wish to find fault with anyone. Showing you the paper wouldn't matter. You would claim it was all a misunderstanding and continue to deceive yourself."

"Hush, Mary. Stop your prattle. The man has five thousand a year. I'm sure he would change his ways for Jane," hissed Mrs. Bennet.

Sensing her sister's distress and the mounting tension, Elizabeth reached out to hold Jane's hand. "Jane, you must not let these things trouble you. We cannot judge Mr. Bingley based on his sister's actions or the gossip columns. You must examine his actions and words."

Mrs. Bennet, unwilling to relinquish her hopes, softened her tone slightly. "There, there, Jane. Elizabeth is right. We must be cautious but not lose hope. Mr. Bingley has shown you great attention, and perhaps, in time, things will become clearer."

Jane nodded slowly, though the sadness in her eyes remained. The room fell into a contemplative silence. Each Bennet sister was lost in her thoughts about the swirling rumors.

Suddenly, Lydia jumped up with a bright smile. "I'm so excited! The militia is coming to town soon!"

Kitty, catching Lydia's excitement, clapped her hands. "Oh, that will be wonderful! We should have a dinner party to welcome them. A ball might be too much, especially with all the preparations, but a dinner would be perfect."

Mrs. Bennet, distracted from her concerns about Jane and Mr. Bingley, looked at her younger daughters with amusement and indulgence. "A dinner sounds like a delightful idea. It would be an excellent way to make their acquaintance," she said.

Mary interjected with a note of caution. "Mama, I must remind you that officers, while charming, often have minimal pay and cannot afford marriage. Their attention is fleeting, and their prospects are limited. Some are rakes, looking only to the pleasures of the flesh."

Lydia's smile faltered slightly, but she quickly regained her enthusiasm. "Oh, Mary, don't be such a spoilsport. Hosting a dinner party for the officers will be fun. It's the excitement and novelty that count. I'm sure they are honorable men, not rakes."

Elizabeth, seeking to balance the conversation, gently added, "Lydia, while it's delightful to look forward to new acquaintances, let's remember the importance of good sense and practicality. There is no way to know a soldier's background. A handsome, smiling face can hide a black heart. It's important to remember there is no future with a poor man. We must marry men who can afford to provide us with a decent home. None of us can cook, clean, or sew an evening gown."

As Lydia continued to flutter around the room, the rest of the family sat in contemplative silence. Still affected by the earlier conversation, Jane gazed out the window, lost in thought about her inability to recognize Mr. Bingley's faults and how she missed seeing Caroline's duplicity. Elizabeth remained by her side, offering silent support.

Chapter 7

Monday, November 18, 1811
Netherfield

When Mr. Darcy and Colonel Fitzwilliam joined the Bingleys and Hursts at the breakfast table, the dining room at Netherfield was alive with the sounds of silverware scraping against plates. Sunlight streamed through the tall windows, casting a warm glow over the polished mahogany and the generous spread of morning fare.

With a cheerful grin, Charles Bingley watched the cousins fill their plates and begin eating. All thought of their previous disagreement slipped his mind.

After finishing a plate of eggs and toast, Bingley inquired, "Have you made any specific plans for your day, Darcy?"

Darcy finished chewing a slice of bacon, sipped his coffee, and calmly responded, "We plan to leave for Kent to visit our aunt, Lady Catherine de Bourgh, and our cousin, Anne."

Colonel Fitzwilliam glanced around the table, fork in hand, smiled, and added, "Indeed. Lady Catherine has extended a gracious invitation, and we intend to depart shortly after breakfast."

Louisa Hurst looked up from her plate, her curiosity piqued. "I didn't realize you were leaving today. It seems rather sudden."

Darcy grimaced. "Yes, Mrs. Hurst. The urgency of Lady Catherine's invitation has made the trip to Kent rather immediate."

Caroline Bingley, her surprise evident, interjected with a hint of feigned casualness. "How very sudden. I hoped we would have more time to enjoy your company."

Darcy maintained his composed demeanor. "We are, of course, grateful for your hospitality. However, we must go at once. Our aunt expects us to arrive today."

Colonel Fitzwilliam chuckled. His piercing gaze caught Caroline's eye. "I trust you and your family will manage well in our absence."

Edwin Hurst, who had been quietly eating, was relieved. He said, "I must admit, this is an interesting turn of events. I wish you a safe and pleasant journey."

Charles Bingley, puzzled, looked at Edwin and then turned to Caroline. "It will be nice to spend more time with the family. And with the militia arriving soon, plenty of officers will afford the area more distractions and entertainments."

Caroline's smile tightened. "I do hope you are not suggesting that the arrival of the militia will overshadow the refined conversation we've been accustomed to. The company of poor officers is no substitute for our departing guests."

Edwin, noticing her displeasure, shrugged slightly. "The militia's presence might bring some lively diversion, though I understand it may not be to everyone's taste."

Charles quickly changed the topic to avoid further tension. "Darcy, when exactly are you planning to leave for Kent?"

Darcy lowered his cup to its saucer and reiterated. "We'll be departing immediately after breakfast. The servants are currently loading my carriage. Jasper will enjoy roaming the park at Rosings."

Caroline gripped a fork tightly, and her smile faltered. "Very well. I shall have to reconcile myself to the loss of your dog with the arrival of penniless soldiers."

Colonel Fitzwilliam, unable to resist, chimed in with a teasing grin. "Ah, Miss Bingley, are you so fond of Jasper that his absence will be deeply felt? He has a peculiar talent for avoiding social niceties."

Caroline's eyebrows shot up. "I assure you, Colonel, I have no particular attachment to the beast. His departure is a blessing."

Edwin Hurst, with a wry smile, added, "Indeed. The militia will more than compensate for any lack of canine companionship. Though, I must say, their arrival might also stir up excitement in a lady's heart."

Caroline gave a curt nod and tossed her napkin onto the table before rising abruptly. She was in no mood to be teased about worthless officers or dogs. Her terse comment, "I shall leave you to your preparations," preceded her exit.

Richard's eyes twinkled with amusement as a fuming Caroline left the room. "It seems Miss Bingley has grown rather sensitive about our departure and the arrival of the militia."

Darcy and Colonel Fitzwilliam exchanged amused glances. The breakfast conversation was sparse, and they bid farewell when they rose from the table. The two cousins had successfully concealed their true destination—London—behind the pretense of a journey to Kent.

A short time later, the cousins boarded the Darcy carriage; Jasper sprawled across the rear-facing seat, clearly enjoying their departure. The tension from the morning's conversation dissipated as the carriage rolled away, and Mr. Darcy and Colonel Fitzwilliam began discussing their upcoming stay at Matlock House.

Colonel Fitzwilliam leaned back against the deeply cushioned squabs, a playful glint in his eye. "You know, Darcy, I must say, our plan to stay at Matlock House is rather clever. I doubt anyone at Netherfield will suspect we're headed to London instead of Kent."

Darcy nodded with a satisfied smile. "Indeed. It's a much safer destination to avoid any unwanted scrutiny. Besides, Lady Catherine would never countenance the presence of a Great Dane in her home."

Colonel Fitzwilliam laughed. "Aunt Catherine will never know we're enjoying London's finer offerings rather than enduring her lectures on proper decorum."

Darcy grinned. "Precisely. Staying hidden inside Matlock House for today and tomorrow, watching your mother and sister prepare for our journey to Pemberley, won't compare to the entertainment we might find at a club. However, it will be vastly entertaining compared to Aunt Catherine's lectures and Anne's sullen stare."

Jasper shifted slightly, his tail thumping against the carriage door as if in agreement. Colonel Fitzwilliam's eyes twinkled. "It seems Jasper is as eager for a change of scenery as we are. Though I must admit, I hope he behaves himself. A footman will exercise him in Hyde Park, but there won't be any games of fetch. The gossips will think Father has bought another dog for the Viscount."

Darcy laughed softly, his eyes crinkling in amusement. "Jasper is quite the companion. I'm sure he'll find new amusements in the park and perhaps even a few new friends among the city's dogs. Does your father still have that Standard Poodle?"

Richard laughed and shook his head. "Oh, yes. Bacon is his favorite companion. I still can't believe he named the dog Bacon after it devoured an entire plate of bacon from the sideboard in one swift, mischievous move."

"Does Lord Matlock have Bacon sit beside him while he is driven in an open carriage through the park during the fashionable hours?"

Colonel Fitzwilliam raised an eyebrow. "Not as much these days. He has relegated the task to Viscount Hedley. My brother loves the attention the dog commands from the ladies. However, it would be a scandal if Jasper were out of the limelight. I must instruct the footmen to walk Bacon and Jasper together."

Darcy's grin widened. "Of course. We wouldn't want either dog to feel neglected. We should arrange a private playdate with Bacon in your garden before sending them out into Hyde Park... to ensure they remain friends."

The two men continued their light-hearted conversation, easing the journey. Sensing their good spirits, Jasper nestled further into the cushion on the rear-facing bench and closed his eyes.

Chapter 8

Monday, November 18, 1811
Longbourn

In the Longbourn library, Mr. Bennet paced restlessly, his hands clasped behind his back. The room, usually a refuge from the outside world, felt stifling today, filled with the heavy silence that followed a heated conversation.

A plainly distressed Mrs. Bennet, perched on a delicately embroidered chair, looked up at her husband. "I cannot believe you are dismissing Mr. Bingley so lightly! He was to be the very pinnacle of a suitable match for Jane. Now, you call him a rascal. And the officers..."

Mr. Bennet cut her off with a sharp gesture. "My dear, suitability is not merely a matter of income or a red coat. Charles Bingley is a fool, swayed by every charming face and every pretty word. His fickleness is evident, and his sister's actions only reinforce my concerns. I will not see Jane's future tied to such an unreliable man."

Mrs. Bennet's eyes brimmed with tears as she stood, her hands twisting the edge of her shawl. "But you must reconsider. Mr. Bingley is attentive to Jane and shows a rare interest in her society. Are we to disregard this simply because of some gossip about his sister? And the officers... how can you so easily dismiss them?"

Mr. Bennet sighed, his expression softening but remaining resolute. "The soldiers, my dear, are a frivolous distraction. Inviting them into our home is an absurdity. Officers with minimal pay will do nothing but stir up idle chatter and detract from the quiet comfort we are accustomed to. The idea of them being invited into our family sphere is impractical and undesirable."

Mrs. Bennet shook her head in dismay, her voice trembling. "You speak of them as though they were mere commoners. They are officers, after all. Surely, they must possess some decency and respect for gentlewomen."

Mr. Bennet's stern tone was tempered with gentleness. "Respect is not easily traded among such men. Their attention is often fleeting, and while their manners might dazzle in public, they rarely reflect the true depth of their character. I have no desire to see our home besieged by their insipid chatter and pretensions. More importantly, I will not risk seeing our daughters compromised by a rake."

Mrs. Bennet's distress mounted, her voice rising in a pleading crescendo. "But what of Jane and her future? She is heartbroken. If Mr. Bingley is truly unsuitable, you should have revealed it sooner. And as for the officers, you cannot simply dismiss them as unacceptable!"

Mr. Bennet moved closer to her, placing a calming hand on her shoulder with a look of affectionate sympathy. "I assure you, my dear, that every decision I make is with the utmost concern for our family's well-being. Jane's happiness is, of course, paramount, and while Mr. Bingley's charms are indeed evident, they are superficial. The man is ruled by his younger sister, and she despises us. As for the soldiers, their presence here would only bring chaos. Please remember that I was a captain in the regulars and am familiar with such men. They are not interested in marriage... they cannot afford it. Their pursuits generally revolve around seduction, gambling, and drinking."

Mrs. Bennet's hands wrung a lace handkerchief, and her voice softened to a sorrowful murmur. "Then what of our daughters, Mr. Bennet? We must think of their futures with due consideration."

Mr. Bennet's gaze softened, filled with affection. "Rest assured, my dear, that my intentions are solely for their benefit. Jane and Elizabeth will find their paths, and I will ensure they are not led astray by fleeting whims or transient distractions. Moreover, Lydia and Kitty must learn restraint and social decorum. We have allowed them too much freedom because the neighborhood is small. The arrival of the militia means the area is no longer safe for unattended females. Effective immediately, Lydia and Kitty will no longer be seen in society, and Mary's social interactions will be limited. None of our daughters will be allowed to wander without a footman. Additionally, a governess will soon arrive to educate our younger girls and assist you in training them for household responsibilities."

Frustrated, Mrs. Bennet sank back into her chair. She sighed deeply. "Why? Why are you doing this?"

"Because I must," Mr. Bennet replied firmly, gesturing toward the door to signal the end of the discussion. With a disheartened expression, Mrs. Bennet flounced out of the library, slamming the door and retreating to her chambers, where she collapsed onto the bed and wept.

The afternoon sun filtered through the curtains of Jane Bennet's bedroom window. Jane and Elizabeth sat by the fire, wrapped in shawls, as they spoke in low, excited tones about the journey ahead.

Elizabeth picked up a small, intricately woven pillow and fluffed it thoughtfully. "Jane, can you believe we're going to see Pemberley? It's almost too good to be true. Rebecca speaks so warmly of Darcy's home. I imagine it must be as splendid as she describes."

Jane's face lit up with a gentle smile. "Lady Matlock has always been so kind to us. I look forward to catching up with her and Lady Rebecca. I'm sure we'll enjoy our visit."

Elizabeth nodded enthusiastically. "Yes, it will be delightful to spend time with friends. The Fitzwilliams are such a nice family, especially Richard. The journey itself will be a pleasant chance to view new places."

Jane leaned back in her chair, her eyes sparkling with anticipation. "I wonder about the journey. I hope Mr. Darcy is not too staid and Colonel Fitzwilliam is his affable self. Mr. Darcy can be rather reserved."

Elizabeth chuckled softly. "True, but they are both such fine gentlemen. I imagine they'll be good travel companions, though I suspect they might try to maintain their composure. Colonel Fitzwilliam has always been quite amiable, and Mr. Darcy has moments of warmth despite his reserve. He roams the countryside with a large dog. I've seen him playing fetch with the creature on Netherfield's front lawn."

Jane's expression turned contemplative. "I hope they don't feel obliged to be overly formal because Lady Matlock is present. I would rather enjoy the journey and the sights without any stiffness."

Elizabeth's gaze wandered to the window as she considered their upcoming adventure. "We're in for a treat, regardless. The countryside in autumn is quite lovely. And Rebecca claims that Pemberley's grounds are breathtaking any time of year."

Jane's eyes softened with appreciation. "Yes, it will be wonderful to see the estate and experience a new part of England. And we mustn't forget Miss Georgiana Darcy. We've heard so much about her shyness and gentle nature. I look forward to meeting her."

Elizabeth nodded, a thoughtful look on her face. "Indeed. I've gathered that Georgiana is a delicate flower shielded from the world's harshness. Some consider her a musical prodigy. I hope she will feel comfortable with us."

Jane's face brightened at the thought. "It will be lovely to befriend her."

Elizabeth reached out and took Jane's hand. "We'll make the best of it, Jane. We'll have our friends with us, which makes all the difference. Besides, the change of scenery will be refreshing."

Jane squeezed Elizabeth's hand gratefully. "You're right, Lizzy. I'm sure it will be a memorable experience, no matter what. And perhaps, with the Fitzwilliams around, we'll have some light-hearted moments to look forward to despite Mr. Darcy's reserve."

Elizabeth smiled warmly at her sister. "Indeed. Let's focus on the excitement and the new experiences. We'll have plenty of time to enjoy ourselves and to be with friends who care for us."

As the sunlight waned and the room grew dimmer, the sisters continued to discuss their upcoming journey with increasing enthusiasm. Their imaginations were filled with the promise of new experiences, cherished company, and the anticipated meeting with the shy Georgiana Darcy.

Supper that evening was almost over when Mr. Bennet cleared his throat and addressed his family with unusual seriousness.

"Well, my dear daughters," Mr. Bennet began, his tone firm yet tinged with a trace of resignation, "it has become clear that we must make some changes to ensure your futures are secure and respectable."

Lydia, her mouth full of food, inquired, "Papa, what are you talking about?"

Mr. Bennet set down his fork and looked around the table, meeting the wide-eyed stares of his three younger daughters. "As you know, the social expectations for young women are quite stringent, and we must refine our behavior to ensure you are not led astray by transient whims or inappropriate influences. Also, speaking with your mouth full of food is gauche, Lydia."

Mary, her eyes wide with curiosity, leaned forward. "What kind of changes, Papa?"

Mr. Bennet took a deep breath, then continued, "First and foremost, Lydia and Kitty, you will no longer be out. All females in this family will be escorted by a footman whenever they leave the house. This will prevent inappropriate encounters and ensure you maintain a respectable appearance."

Lydia's face twisted into a pout. She whined, "But Papa, I enjoy going out with my friends and meeting new people!" She tossed her napkin on the table and kicked her chair's leg.

Mr. Bennet's expression remained unyielding. "Lydia, it is not about enjoyment but about propriety. Your behavior and social interactions must reflect the respectability expected of a gentlewoman. Furthermore, Mary will now be enjoying a more limited society, and we have secured a governess who will arrive shortly to further your education and instruct you in household responsibilities and proper conduct. Also, a music master will ensure your ability to play the pianoforte or harp."

Mary spoke up with indignation. "A governess? But Papa, I've always prided myself on my knowledge and education. Surely, I don't need another instructor?"

Mr. Bennet's gaze softened slightly, but his tone remained firm. "Mary, it is not solely about possessing knowledge but also how it is applied daily. We need to ensure that all of you are adequately prepared to handle the demands of society with grace and dignity."

Kitty, clearly distressed, glanced at her sisters before asking, "But Papa, what about our social activities? Will we be restricted from attending events and gatherings?"

Mr. Bennet shook his head gently. "You can still attend dinners at home with more supervision and under stricter guidelines. We must project the image of a well-regulated and respectable family."

Kitty's shoulders slumped as she stared down at her plate, clearly disheartened by the news. "This is so unfair. We're not allowed any freedom."

Mr. Bennet's expression softened with a touch of sympathy. "I understand this may seem harsh, but it is for your good and to ensure that you each find suitable matches and maintain our family's reputation. I only wish to protect you from the pitfalls of too much freedom and too little guidance."

The room fell into a heavy silence as the sisters absorbed their father's words. A contemplative stillness replaced the usual light-hearted chatter as each girl grappled with the implications of their father's decisions.

"Mama, surely you won't permit this change!" exclaimed a recalcitrant Lydia. All eyes turned to a red-eyed Mrs. Bennet.

To the surprise of everyone, Mrs. Bennet replied, "You will do as your father says. He is the master of Longbourn and the best of men. I cannot go against my husband's wishes. If you ever marry, you will understand that a wife cannot defy her husband, so choose wisely."

With the discussion over, the family quietly finished their meal. A short time later, everyone retreated to their respective rooms instead of gathering in the drawing room.

Chapter 9

Monday, November 18, 1811
Netherfield - Evening

The room was bathed in the fireplace's warm glow, its flames burning low. Caroline Bingley stood by the mantel in her elegant evening dress, her fingers nervously toying with a delicate glass perfume bottle. The air was thick with unspoken irritation. This situation was intolerable. How could Charles allow Darcy to leave? The gentleman was supposed to stay another three weeks. This unexpected arrival of his cousin and subsequent departure disrupted her meticulously crafted seduction plans. Her frustration bubbled over, and she began muttering curses as she tapped the bottle on the mantel.

In a sudden surge of rage, Caroline hurled the bottle into the fireplace. The glass shattered on impact against the stone, its shards scattering like tiny stars across the hearth. The liquid within poured out, and time seemed to stand still as the contents splashed into the flames.

Then, with a whoosh, the flames leapt higher, their hungry tongues licking at the alcohol-laden perfume. Caroline watched, transfixed, as the blaze crackled and popped, its vibrant hues painting the room with an unsettling orange glow. The brilliant burst of fire illuminated the room, casting flickering shadows that danced frenetically on the walls. The scent of jasmine mingled with the acrid stench of burning alcohol, and the flames' wild dance seemed to mock her. Caroline stepped back from the intense heat, her eyes wide with fear and awe as the flames surged higher and the fire roared louder, temporarily engulfing the ornate interior of the fireplace and shooting up the chimney, consuming the remnants of the perfume.

Her hands trembled slightly as she retreated from the conflagration, a cold realization dawning on her. The destruction of her cherished perfume symbolized the unraveling of her carefully laid plans. She hoped to secure Mr. Darcy's affections and gain control over his fortune, but everything slipped through her fingers. Her thoughts raced as she struggled to formulate a new plan, her mind already spinning with schemes to salvage what remained of her grand designs.

In a desperate bid to regain some semblance of composure, Caroline grabbed the fire poker and pushed at the logs with an unsteady hand, trying to subdue the fire's fury. This only made the flames leap higher. Another woosh, louder and more frightening, and the fire expanded, reaching outward toward Caroline.

Hurried footsteps echoed in the hallway, growing louder and more urgent as the servants raced toward the room. The door was banged upon with desperation, punctuating the staff's increasing alarm.

"Miss Bingley! Miss Bingley, are you in there?" a voice called out, strained with panic.

Caroline, her face pale and eyes wide with fear, stared at the conflagration, her thoughts momentarily frozen. Her hand trembled as she fumbled to open the door. The servants burst into the room, their faces etched with concern and anxiety.

"What on earth has happened?" Mrs. Nichols, the head housekeeper, gasped, her eyes widening as she viewed the scene. The housekeeper ordered the servants, "Quickly, bring sand to smother the flames!"

The fire crackled fiercely, sending occasional bursts of sparks up the chimney. The perfume's flames licked the air, and the acrid stench of smoke overpowered the scent of jasmine. One of the footmen, eyes wide with alarm, grabbed a heavy woolen blanket from the bed and threw it onto the flames, attempting to smother the fire while others dashed to fetch buckets of sand from the stockpile in the closet at the end of the hall.

"Miss Bingley, you must leave at once!" Mrs. Nichols ordered firmly despite the tremor of fear racing up her spine. "The fire could spread! We need to get it under control before it does more damage."

Caroline's composure shattered. She took a step back, her mind racing. "I... I didn't mean for this to happen. I was only..."

"Miss Bingley!" Mrs. Nichols cut her off sharply. "There's no time for explanations! Get out of this room, now!"

Caroline stumbled out of the room, her face flushed and her breath coming in short, panicked gasps. The servants worked frantically, tossing sand onto the flames, weighing down the blanket, and trying to contain the hissing fire's wrath. The crackling of the waning fire and the murmur of distressed voices permeated the smoke-filled room.

"Is everyone all right?" one of the footmen called out, his voice tinged with urgency.

"Everyone's safe, but we need to get this fire out quickly," Mrs. Nichols replied, her tone brisk and authoritative. She glanced at the crackling, sputtering fire with a worried expression, watching it intensely as it struggled against the suffocating materials.

As the fire gradually began to sputter into extinction under the diligent efforts of the servants, Caroline stood outside the room, her mind a whirlwind of regret and frustration. She looked back at the dying fire, her plans and pride in ruins, and knew everything had irrevocably changed.

Charles, Louisa, and Edwin arrived in a flurry of rapid footsteps. Charles's face was a mask of worry as he saw the smoldering logs and the scattered shards of the broken perfume bottle. Louisa's eyes were wide with concern, and Edwin was angry.

"Caroline! What on earth happened here?" Charles loudly demanded, waving a hand at the open door. He glanced at the servants busy clearing out the remnants of the logs and ashes from the fireplace, their movements quick and purposeful.

One of the footmen looked up, his face smeared with soot when Caroline failed to speak. "Mr. Bingley, there was a small fire in the hearth to heat the room. Miss Bingley threw a bottle of something into the fireplace, and it ignited."

Louisa's eyes narrowed, her voice filled with disbelief. "A bottle? Caroline, you must explain yourself immediately!"

Still visibly shaken, Caroline wrung her hands as she stood outside the room, her face pale. "I didn't mean for it to get out of hand. It was just a moment of frustration. I was holding my perfume bottle. I lost my temper and threw it."

Edwin stepped forward, his voice stern and clipped. "This is utterly unacceptable. You could have caused serious damage to the house and endangered everyone's safety. Do you know how reckless you've been?"

Caroline's eyes welled with tears. She struggled to maintain her composure. "I am deeply sorry. I didn't think…"

"We'll sort out the damage later," Charles interrupted, his tone softening slightly but still tinged with frustration. "For now, we must ensure everything is dealt with properly."

Under Mrs. Nichols' direction, the servants worked diligently to clear out the fireplace. The ashes were removed while the maids hurried to empty Caroline's clothes from the wardrobe, airing out her gowns and ensuring the smoke damaged as little as possible. They quickly removed any affected items, and the footmen cleaned up the soot in the room before opening a window to clear out the smoke.

"Miss Bingley," Mrs. Nichols called out, her voice authoritative despite the chaos. "We'll move your belongings to another room while we air this one out to eliminate any lingering smoke."

Caroline nodded, her face flushed with embarrassment. "Of course. Where shall I go?"

"A room will be prepared as soon as possible," Mrs. Nichols replied, her tone practical but not unkind. "In the meantime, you may use the yellow guest room."

Charles turned to his sister, his expression exasperated. "Caroline, this reckless behavior must stop. You need to be more careful."

With a tense expression, Louisa added, "We'll make sure everything is sorted. But you must be more mindful in the future."

Caroline was escorted to the designated room, and the Hursts descended the stairs. Charles stayed behind to oversee the final cleanup. The atmosphere was heavy with tension. The fire's damage was contained, but the incident cast a long shadow over the day.

An hour later, Charles Bingley entered the guest room where Caroline Bingley sat on the edge of the bed, her posture rigid and her hands fidgeting with the skirt of her dress. Though unscathed by the fire, she trembled.

Charles closed the door behind him and stood with his arms crossed. "Caroline, we need to talk."

Caroline looked up, her eyes narrowing with irritation and defiance. "Charles, this is hardly the time. I am still in shock."

Charles moved a chair and sat opposite her, his face a mask of stern determination. "It is precisely the time. Your actions today have been anything but accidental. You know that perfume contains a large amount of alcohol. You know its effect if thrown into a fire. Any remaining items in your room that are dangerous have been confiscated."

He glared at her. "I need to address a larger issue. Did you think that a plan to compromise Darcy would succeed?"

Caroline's eyes widened in disbelief, her mouth opening in a sharp intake of breath. She stood abruptly, pacing the small room with agitation. "How dare you accuse me of such underhanded schemes! I merely sought to secure a future for myself, not to compromise anyone."

Bingley's gaze remained steady, his frustration unmistakable. "Your so-called plans were overheard by Darcy, the servants, and shouted at the Hursts. It's not just about what you want for yourself... it's about the harm your words inflicted on others, including me."

Caroline stopped pacing and faced Charles, her face flushed with anger and wounded pride. "So, you think you know everything about my motives? Do you think you understand what I've been through? You know nothing of the sacrifices I've made."

Bingley's voice grew firmer, though his eyes were sympathetic. "I know enough to see that your methods are damaging. Trying to manipulate situations and people to your advantage without regard for the consequences must stop. Today's fire directly resulted from your continued unfettered disregard for consequences."

Caroline's eyes flashed with defiance as she crossed her arms, her chin jutting up. "You act as though I have been deliberately malicious. I was only trying to better my situation in a world that offers few opportunities for women like me. I want Pemberley. I must marry Darcy to get it."

Charles leaned forward, his hands resting on his knees, his tone softer. "Darcy will never marry you. You will never have Pemberley. This obsession of yours is not about a desire to improve your situation. It's pure greed. Your actions have been calculated and deceitful. Throwing a substance that hastens combustion into a fire manifests the chaos you've been sowing. Thank heavens the creosote in the chimney didn't ignite! You almost set the entire house ablaze with that reckless act. Do you realize how close we came to disaster? If you don't change your selfish ways, you risk destroying not just your future but everyone and everything you claim to hold dear."

Caroline's gaze wavered as she sank back onto the bed, her hands clasped tightly in her lap. Her voice, though still defiant, held a tremor of vulnerability. "You think I wanted all this to happen? I didn't mean to create an imbroglio."

Bingley's face softened slightly. He stood up, his gaze steady. His sister would never change. "Caroline, I am asking you to reconsider your approach. To act with honor and integrity."

Caroline looked down, her shoulders slumping as crocodile tears filled her eyes. She wiped at them with her hand, her voice cracking. "I will try. I never meant for things to go this far."

Charles nodded in relief. "That's all I ask. Understand that your actions have consequences, and now is the time to reflect and make things right."

After Charles left Caroline, he slunk slowly down the hallway, his slow footsteps reflecting the state of his heart... unspoken regrets and unresolved tensions. Charles Bingley was a defeated man. He felt a deep sorrow for his sister. Her defiance appeared diminished, but her actions were indefensible. The emotional scars he suffered from discovering her true nature would take time to heal.

The servants would undoubtedly spread tales of his sister's words and actions, stories that would soon reach London. Caroline's recklessness and disregard for the values held dear by their family doomed her to become a social pariah, and her family would share in the disgrace. Charles knew he might pray for his sister's soul every night for the rest of his life, hoping she might change, but knowing it was impossible.

Chapter 10

Tuesday, November 19, 1811
London – Matlock House

Light streamed through Matlock House's tall windows on the clear autumn day, casting a soft glow over the opulent drawing room. Rich tapestries depicting pastoral scenes hung from ceiling to floor and covered the walls. Stylish sofas, chairs, and polished mahogany tables accentuated the room's elegance, contrasting with the air's tension.

The Earl of Matlock, a stern and imposing figure, stood by the fireplace, hands clasped behind his back, his demeanor radiating disapproval. His cold and piercing blue eyes were fixed on his nephew, Fitzwilliam Darcy, who stood rigidly before him, a flush of discomfort on his face. Darcy shifted nervously, struggling to maintain his composure under his uncle's unrelenting scrutiny.

Lord Matlock's voice, sharp and commanding, broke the silence.

"Nephew," the Earl began, his tone heavy with reproach, "I am deeply disappointed in you. The news of your recent actions towards Miss Elizabeth Bennet has reached my ears, and I must express my severe displeasure. How dare you refuse to dance with her? Worse, how dare you say she was *tolerable but not handsome enough to tempt you?*"

Darcy's gaze fell to the floor, unable to meet the intensity of his uncle's stare. "Uncle, I..."

The Earl waved his hand, his frustration evident. "Do not attempt to justify your behavior. You have treated Miss Elizabeth with a lack of respect and consideration. Such conduct toward any woman is beneath you and reflects poorly upon our family."

Darcy's cheeks reddened, and he stammered, "I did not intend..."

"Intention is irrelevant," the Earl interrupted forcefully. "It is your actions that speak volumes. Miss Bennet is a young lady of admirable character, and your behavior was disgraceful. You dismissed her feelings and treated her with unacceptable coldness."

At this, Richard Fitzwilliam, lounging on a sofa with a barely concealed smirk, sniggered softly. The sound was a low, mocking note in the tense room. Though he tried to stifle his amusement, the flicker of laughter in his eyes did not escape Lord Matlock's notice.

Lord Matlock's gaze shifted sharply to his son. "Richard," he said, his voice cutting through the room like a blade, "if you find this situation amusing, I suggest you reconsider. The matter at hand concerns the honor and dignity of our family. Miss Elizabeth, whose beauty and character were insulted by your cousin's behavior at the Meryton assembly, suffered a marred evening. Plus, the incident was an affront to my friend Bennet's family that I will not tolerate."

Richard straightened up, his smirk fading as he met his father's stern gaze. "Apologies, Father. I meant no disrespect to Miss Elizabeth. I have the highest regard for the Bennet sisters. I expressed my opinion regarding Darcy's behavior in a letter before joining him in Hertfordshire."

Lord Matlock's expression softened slightly, though his tone remained severe. "It is not just about respect; it is about recognizing the worth of others. Miss Elizabeth is a lady of extraordinary beauty, virtue, and intelligence. These qualities deserve our admiration, not disdain. Her hurt feelings reflect our failings if we do not correct this wrong."

Darcy nodded solemnly. "I understand, Uncle. After receiving Richard's letter, which castigated me completely, I apologized to Miss Elizabeth and her father. I will strive to show Miss Elizabeth the respect she deserves and my regard."

Lord Matlock's gaze lingered on Darcy. "You should take this upcoming house party as an opportunity to demonstrate genuine contrition. The journey to Pemberley with your aunt and cousins should be used to rectify your actions and prove yourself capable of behaving as a gentleman rather than an insufferable prig. Let it be a chance to show Miss Elizabeth you recognize her worth."

A more somber expression replaced Richard's earlier amusement. "Father, you mentioned Mr. Gardiner would be arriving soon?"

Lord Matlock nodded gravely, his face taut with concern. "Indeed. Mr. Gardiner is expected later today. He is coming to meet with Darcy and expects an apology for the affront to his niece. This is a crucial opportunity for you to mend bridges, Darcy."

Darcy's brow furrowed, his shoulders sagging slightly as he inwardly cringed with remorse. "I will convey my sincere apologies to Mr. Gardiner."

Lord Matlock's posture relaxed slightly, though his tone remained stern. "It is imperative that you make amends. This is not merely about formality but restoring honor and demonstrating genuine respect. Miss Elizabeth's hurt must be acknowledged and addressed, and Mr. Gardiner's feelings must be respected."

Darcy replied, "I understand, Uncle. I will do my utmost to make things right."

Sensing the need to shift the conversation from Darcy's apology to a more pleasant topic, Lord Matlock addressed his daughter and wife as they entered the room.

"Ah, my dears, just in time," he greeted the ladies warmly, a subtle shift in his demeanor signaling a change in focus. "We were just discussing the forthcoming journey to Pemberley. Richard wants to show the Bennet sisters some of the interesting sights."

Lady Rebecca Fitzwilliam, eyes sparkling with interest, sat beside her brother. "Richard, have you been planning special stops as we travel from Stevenage to Derbyshire? It would be lovely to break the journey with some sightseeing."

Lady Matlock smiled and added, "Indeed. I've heard there are several charming towns and estates along the way. It would be wonderful to see something of the countryside before we reach Pemberley."

His lordship nodded thoughtfully, his demeanor lightening. "I was just about to mention that you could consider stopping at St. Albans. It boasts a beautiful cathedral and some delightful old architecture."

Lady Rebecca leaned forward, her enthusiasm evident. "And what about the market town of Baldock? I've heard it has lovely inns and a variety of shops. It might be a pleasant diversion."

As she twirled a curl around a finger, Lady Matlock smiled. "That sounds splendid. It would be nice to stretch our legs and enjoy fresh air while we rest the horses."

Lord Matlock's eyes twinkled with approval. "Excellent suggestions. You might also explore some historic sites around the Cotswolds. The countryside is charming and should provide a lovely contrast to London."

Darcy, listening attentively, added, "Those are wonderful suggestions. I'm certain that the journey will be enjoyable. I look forward to showing the Bennets the sights and having the opportunity to spend time with everyone. Georgiana will be thrilled to have so many agreeable companions at Pemberley."

Lady Matlock's gaze turned to Darcy, a hint of satisfaction in her eyes. "Yes, indeed. The journey should be most agreeable. I sent an express assuring Georgiana that she will love Jane and Elizabeth."

Lady Rebecca clapped her hands together in delight. "We're planning several charming activities once we reach Pemberley that will complement whatever Georgiana is planning. Georgiana will be pleased to share her favorite pieces on the pianoforte, and I can play the harp. I am certain everyone will enjoy our performances."

Lady Matlock smiled warmly. "And, if Elizabeth feels inclined, she might grace us with a song or two. Her voice rivals the best professional vocalists in London. Music will be such a delight when shared among friends."

Richard, lounging on a nearby sofa, leaned in with a grin. "And let us not forget the various indoor games and outdoor activities."

Lady Rebecca ignored her brother and chimed in eagerly. "Oh, and we must visit the Roman ruins at Verulamium. It will be a delightful educational experience. I know Elizabeth and Jane have always had a passion for history."

Richard, attempting to rejoin the conversation, cleared his throat. "Indeed, it sounds like you have quite an itinerary planned. Perhaps we should also consider visiting..."

Lady Matlock gently interrupted. "Oh, Darcy, have you remembered to provide extra carriages to accommodate the Bennets' luggage and servants?"

Darcy chuckled, his attention shifting back to the ladies. "Yes, yes, it's all taken care of. Though I must confess, I'm more interested in hearing what you think of these little detours."

Lady Matlock's eyes sparkled with excitement. "It sounds absolutely wonderful. I am particularly looking forward to the Roman ruins. I've heard so much about them."

Lady Rebecca nodded in agreement. "There will be plenty of time to enjoy Pemberley's grounds before heavy snow covers them in January. It will be such a treat to share your estate's beauty with everyone."

Mr. Darcy attempted to interject. "Perhaps we should also..."

But Lady Rebecca, still bubbling with enthusiasm, continued without missing a beat. "And let us not forget to plan a few cozy evenings by the fire at Pemberley, where we can all share stories and enjoy each other's company."

Lord Matlock sighed softly, conceding that the ladies firmly controlled the conversation. He was content to let them plan the trip's diversions while he and Richard exchanged amused glances. Mr. Darcy, feeling somewhat sidelined, excused himself from the discussion and left the room.

Darcy went to the enclosed garden, where Jasper rested in the sun beside Bacon, Lord Matlock's Standard Poodle. The sight of the two dogs brought a smile to Darcy's lips. He crouched beside Jasper, gently stroking the dog's fur.

"Well, Jasper," Darcy murmured, "it seems our three-day journey is going to be quite the expedition." Jasper looked up with attentive eyes, his tail wagging slightly in response. Bacon lifted his head and let out a soft bark.

Darcy continued, "The ladies have planned an extensive itinerary filled with extra stops and sightseeing. I'm not entirely sure how it will all turn out, but at least we'll have some moments of peace. While they shop, we can take walks." He gave Jasper a reassuring pat.

Jasper nuzzled against Darcy's hand, offering his form of comfort. A very social dog, Bacon rolled over, positioning himself closer to Darcy, and nudged his knee, seeking attention. Darcy chuckled and gave Bacon a gentle scratch behind the ears. "And I suppose you'll be joining us for those walks, won't you, Bacon?"

Bacon wagged his tail enthusiastically and gave a short, happy bark. Darcy smiled and added, "We should be prepared for anything. From ancient ruins to shopping in marketplaces, our trip to Pemberley promises to be eventful. I'm counting on you both to keep me company when the ladies desert me."

Jasper stretched and shook himself when Darcy stood while Bacon rolled onto his back, inviting a belly rub. Darcy leaned down and obliged, scratching Bacon's belly with a grin. "Yes, you two will make the journey far more enjoyable. I hope Miss Elizabeth likes dogs," Darcy mused, giving each dog one last affectionate pat.

With a deep breath, Darcy headed back inside, pleased by the unabashed affection of two furry creatures who demonstrated their devotion by wagging a tail or nuzzling his hand.

Chapter 11

Tuesday, November 19, 1811
London – The Gardiners

The afternoon light cast a warm glow over the streets of London as Mr. and Mrs. Edward Gardiner arrived at Matlock House. Their carriage, drawn by a pair of matching chestnut horses, came to a smooth halt before the imposing entrance of the Matlock townhouse. The butler greeted them with courtesy.

"Welcome to Matlock House," the butler announced, ushering them into the elegantly appointed foyer.

Mr. Edward Gardiner, a man of distinguished bearing and thoughtful demeanor, acknowledged the butler's greeting. Mrs. Madeline Gardiner gave the butler a warm smile as she stepped inside, her eyes taking in the grandeur of their surroundings.

"We are delighted to be here," Mrs. Gardiner said, removing her gloves and handing her coat to a waiting footman. "Thank you for the kind welcome."

Lord Matlock, Lady Matlock, and their children rose to greet the Gardiners as they were shown into the drawing room. The large drawing room, decorated with rich fabrics and antique furnishings, provided a fitting backdrop for entertaining distinguished guests.

"Mr. and Mrs. Gardiner, it is always a pleasure to have you here," Lord Matlock said, extending a hand with genuine warmth to his friends. "Please, make yourselves comfortable." He gestured toward the brocade sofa.

Mrs. Gardiner accepted the greeting graciously. "Thank you, Lord Matlock. We appreciate your hospitality."

Lady Matlock warmly added, "We hope your journey through London was pleasant. The cook is prepared to serve dinner once Mr. Darcy joins us."

Richard, who had been lounging on a sofa, glanced up with mild interest. His gaze lingered on his mother with a trace of curiosity before he refocused on the ongoing conversation.

Lord Matlock began speaking of Darcy as the Gardiners settled into their seats. "Mr. Gardiner, I understand your concerns regarding my nephew's recent behavior in Hertfordshire."

Mr. Gardiner, his expression sober, said, "Indeed, Lord Matlock. I wish to discuss his treatment of Elizabeth and the residents of Meryton."

Unable to conceal a smirk, Richard interjected, "I trust my cousin will offer another apology once the footman retrieves him from the library. His propensity for verbal missteps is well-known. Everyone keeps flogging him for his error at the Meryton assembly."

Darcy paced the width of the library, casting occasional glances at the clock. An air of nervous anticipation marred his usually composed demeanor. He was tired of apologizing for the blunder at that blasted assembly. While he appreciated his family's interference to a certain extent, this constant rehashing of the topic was absurd. Forcing him to await the arrival of the Gardiners in a separate chamber exacerbated his discontent and, in his opinion, magnified the importance of the event.

A footman gently knocked on the open door and announced, "Mr. Darcy, Mr. and Mrs. Gardiner are here."

Darcy took a deep breath, straightened his cravat, and adjusted his waistcoat. He strode out of the library and down the corridor. Each step seemed heavier than the last, and his mind rehearsed the words of the apology he was about to deliver.

When he entered the drawing room, Darcy saw Mrs. Gardiner seated comfortably, engaged in light conversation with Lady Matlock and her daughter. Mr. Gardiner, Lord Matlock, and Richard stood nearby, their eyes surreptitiously watching the doorway.

"Darcy," Lord Matlock began, his tone authoritative, "allow me to introduce you to Mr. Edward Gardiner and his lovely wife, Mrs. Madeline Gardiner."

Darcy stepped forward and bowed, his heart pounding as he faced the Gardiners. Mr. Gardiner bowed in return. "Mr. Darcy, it is a pleasure to make your acquaintance."

Darcy replied, "Mr. Gardiner, Mrs. Gardiner, the pleasure is mine."

Mrs. Gardiner, her demeanor gracious and understanding, offered a warm smile. "Mr. Darcy, we are glad to be here. We've heard much about you from your family."

Darcy stood quietly, feeling like a bug under a magnifying glass. He glanced briefly at Lady Matlock and Richard.

"Mr. Darcy," Mr. Gardiner began, his voice steady and measured, "I trust you understand the purpose of our visit?"

"Yes, Mr. Gardiner. You came to dine with my family. I cannot imagine you wished to meet someone as insignificant and obtuse as myself for any other reason."

Lord Matlock's brow furrowed at the droll response. "Darcy, this is not the occasion for jesting."

Richard chuckled softly, and Lady Rebecca hid a smile behind her fan. Mrs. Gardiner and Lady Matlock exchanged glances, their whispers adding to the room's tension.

Darcy leaned slightly toward Mr. Gardiner, his voice dropping in volume. "Sir, I am fully aware that my behavior in Meryton was deplorable. I deeply regret my actions and any distress they may have caused Miss Elizabeth. I sincerely apologized to Miss Elizabeth and her father last Saturday."

"Is that all you have to say for yourself, young man?" demanded his uncle in a no-nonsense tone. Darcy glared at Lord Matlock, his gray eyes taking on a steely glint that caused most of his subordinates to inwardly quake. The Darcy mask fell into place as he turned to face Mr. Gardiner. He was tired of this constant interference in his life.

"I sincerely apologize to you and Mrs. Gardiner for any discomfort you have experienced on Miss Elizabeth's behalf. Everyone in this room must be more distressed over an incident that incited the young lady's laughter than necessary. Miss Elizabeth overheard a private conversation between me and Charles Bingley. My voice was not raised nor lowered. The music was loud. The young lady sat on a chair at least six feet to our rear on the other side of the pillar I leaned against. I was unaware of her presence until she walked away to join her friends across the room where she shared my words, causing the entire town to hold me in contempt."

Darcy took a breath to calm his nerves. "I shall endeavor to amend my behavior because after twenty-seven years of believing myself well-mannered, discovering my mistake has been a disheartening experience. Sadly, this mistake cannot be forgotten after numerous apologies to interfering friends, family, and strangers. Will my life or, God forbid, the lady's future be forever blighted by this incident? Shall I look for a sword and fall upon it to satisfy the world with my death? Will a victory over the French overshadow the heinous mistake of an insignificant, rude man who refused to dance with a stranger and said the lady was tolerable? Please enlighten me. What form should my next apology take?"

Mr. Gardiner's lips curled into a faint smile, a touch of amusement in his eyes. "Mr. Darcy, your self-deprecating humor is noted, though it does little to alleviate the effect of your earlier actions. Nonetheless, your contrition and chastisement is appreciated. Let us hope your future conduct gives a better impression."

Darcy was visibly relieved by Mr. Gardiner's words. "Thank you, Mr. Gardiner. I am committed to improving."

At that moment, the butler entered the room and cleared his throat gently. "Dinner is served," he announced.

Lord Matlock gestured toward the door. "Shall we proceed to the dining room?"

"Indeed," Lady Matlock said, standing gracefully. "Dinner will be a pleasant diversion after listening to Darcy." She gave her nephew a playful wink as she glided past him.

When the group entered the dining room, Lady Matlock offered Darcy a reassuring smile. "Let us enjoy the meal and the company. We have much to look forward to in the coming days."

Darcy allowed his mask to slip. "Yes, Aunt Jessica. I am looking forward to spending time with friends and family. Will Bacon come with us?"

Lady Matlock laughed, her eyes twinkling with amusement. "Matlock takes that poodle everywhere. Last night, in undeniable selflessness, he declared that Bacon must accompany Richard on the trip. I believe the dog has become a fixture in our lives."

With a fond look at his wife, Lord Matlock added, "Indeed. Bacon is rather attached to me, though if he could speak the king's English, he might argue he's the Lord of Gladstone Park whenever we go there. I know he'll enjoy spending time with Richard, much like the rest of you."

Mr. Gardiner chuckled, "It seems Bacon will be quite the star on this journey. And what of your dog, Mr. Darcy? Will he be joining the party as well?"

Darcy smiled, "Jasper will certainly be coming along. I daresay he'll be pleased to have Bacon's company, though I suspect Bacon will be rather aloof. Jasper, on the other hand, will be enthusiastic."

The convivial conversation continued until dinner ended. Lady Matlock rose from the table and led the ladies away, leaving the men to enjoy their brandy in the study. The gentlemen settled into comfortable chairs with glasses of brandy. The soft crackle of the fire and the rich aroma of the brandy gave the men a short respite from any conversation.

The comfortable silence was broken by Mr. Gardiner, sipping his brandy and glancing around the room with a hint of humor, began, "My judgment is more cautious than impulsive, but I must confess I was wrong about Charles Bingley. The Netherfield servants have been reporting the most astonishing tales about his sister, Caroline. Mr. Phillips sent an express concerning her latest exploit."

Richard, intrigued, raised an eyebrow. "Oh? What have you heard?"

Mr. Gardiner lifted his eyes heavenward and sighed slightly, a twinkle of mischief in his expression. "Apparently, Caroline has been quite a spectacle at Netherfield. My servants speak of her antics with disbelief and amusement. From her attempts to garner Mr. Darcy's affection to her less-than-favorable opinions of the local gentry, she's made quite an impression. Yesterday, she threw a bottle of perfume at the hearth, resulting in a blaze that shot up the chimney with a ferocious roar."

Lord Matlock chuckled. "I have heard similar accounts. Miss Bingley does not shy away from making her presence known. Her control of Charles Bingley is well-documented, and her methods leave much to be desired."

Darcy, his gaze thoughtful, added, "Caroline's behavior has always been somewhat... assertive. I suspect she sees herself as a key player in the social scene, though her tactics often do more harm than good. It's no wonder she's managed to stir up quite a bit of unfavorable gossip about herself."

Mr. Gardiner nodded, his expression reflecting exasperation. "Indeed. Her actions have been noticed. I've heard that her recent escapades have been the talk of several social circles, with varying degrees of criticism and incredulity."

Richard muttered, "It appears Caroline Bingley has a knack for attracting attention, whether she intends to or not. Her penchant for drama is well-suited to the social stage she eagerly wants to occupy."

Lord Matlock leaned back in his chair and sneered. "Well, her behavior certainly adds an element of intrigue to the social scene. I must admit, I'm more interested in how her actions will affect your upcoming journey."

Darcy took a sip of his brandy. "That termagant has no inkling that we are off to Pemberley. She thinks we are visiting Aunt Catherine. After my last conversation with Bingley about Caroline's behavior, I trust that, with time, there will be no social interactions with that family." He gazed at Richard for confirmation of his help to turn the subject.

Never one to prevaricate, Richard boldly stated, "True. Bingley implied we were liars when we told him his sister was scheming to compromise Darcy. The imbecile claimed the chit was beautiful, kind, and too honorable to deceive anybody." The men shook their heads at this proof of Bingley's stupidity.

"Will you boys cut the clodpate," asked Lord Matlock.

"No. We'll greet Bingley if our paths cross, but never send him an invitation again. We will give Caroline the cut-direct if she dares to approach us again," answered Richard.

"Mr. Bennet has a plan to remove them from Netherfield," stated Darcy to distract the older men.

Mr. Gardiner smiled, appreciating Darcy's comment. "I do not doubt Bennet will manage things with his usual perverse humor and grace us with the tale."

The conversation in the study gradually shifted to lighter topics as the evening wore on. The men discussed the upcoming trip and shared anecdotes from their recent experiences. The atmosphere grew more relaxed, with laughter punctuating their exchanges.

The clock approached the hour for tea, and the men rejoined the ladies in the drawing room. Lady Matlock served the tea with her characteristic grace while conversing pleasantly with Mrs. Gardiner and Rebecca about the latest fashion trends. Lord Matlock and Mr. Gardiner discussed their mutual interest in horticulture, exchanging tips on gardening and plant cultivation. Richard and Darcy spoke amiably about the itinerary for the upcoming journey.

Eventually, the Gardiners prepared to leave. They exchanged warm farewells with their hosts, expressing their gratitude for the hospitality and the opportunity to discuss recent events. The couple departed with promises to meet with Lord Matlock soon.

With their guests gone, the remaining occupants of Matlock House retired for the night, knowing that they must wake early to depart for Stevenage before dawn.

Chapter 12

Wednesday, November 20, 1811
Stevenage

Before dawn, a cavalcade of coaches and outriders departed from Matlock House. The early morning air was crisp, with a hint of light on the horizon. The carriages rolled through the quiet streets of London, their wheels turning steadily as they made their way out of the city.

The procession arrived at the Swan Inn near Stevenage's main thoroughfare shortly before nine o'clock in the morning. The inn was a welcome sight, the smoking chimneys hinting at the interior's warmth amidst the chill of the early hour. Mr. Darcy, accompanied by his cousin Richard, stepped out of their coach and breathed in the fresh morning air, feeling the relief of completing the successful first leg of their journey. Two dogs disembarked with them, their tails wagging as they prepared for a brisk morning walk.

Darcy led the way, his long strides purposeful as he navigated the path behind the inn. Jasper trotted beside him, eager for exercise, while Bacon followed slowly, sniffing at each bush.

With his hands stuffed into his coat pockets, Richard glanced over at Darcy with a grin. "The early start is not quite my favorite when off duty, but it has advantages. Fresh air and a quiet moment before the chaos begins wakes a man up."

Darcy smiled slightly, his gaze fixed on the horizon. "Indeed. It's a rare opportunity for a moment of peace before the day's events. Spending time with the dogs before the Bennets arrive is relaxing."

The two men walked in companionable silence for a few more minutes, enjoying the morning's serenity. The dogs sniffed around with keen interest, their excitement growing as they explored the area.

When the distant sound of an approaching coach became louder, Darcy and Richard turned, watching as the Bennet coach drew nearer. The sight of the familiar vehicle and its occupants renewed their anticipation for the journey ahead... Elizabeth and Jane were inside that coach.

When the Bennet coach finally discharged its occupants at the inn, the two groups greeted each other warmly. Elizabeth and Jane, both beaming, were immediately enveloped in affectionate hugs from Lady Matlock and Rebecca.

"Oh, how lovely to see you both!" Lizzy exclaimed, her eyes shining as she embraced Rebecca.

Jane followed suit, giving Lady Matlock a warm hug. "It's wonderful to see you again, Lady Matlock. I'm so looking forward to our time together."

Richard, Darcy, and the dogs joined the scene as well. Darcy and Richard bowed to the Bennets. Richard, with a grin, said, "Good morning! I hope your journey was comfortable." Darcy smiled warmly at Elizabeth, never taking his eyes from her face. Richard poked him in the ribs.

Mr. Bennet greeted Lord Matlock with a hearty handshake. "Well, this is a surprise, my friend! I thought you would be tied up with business in Parliament."

"Yes, yes. Parliament demands my time, but I wanted to see you, Bennet, and the girls. I will have to return to Matlock House after breakfast."

Darcy signaled an outrider to leash the dogs as the Bennets' trunks were transferred from Bennet's coach to Darcy's luggage coach. With characteristic mischief, Jasper evaded the man, circling the party. During the commotion, Jasper bumped into Elizabeth. She stumbled, her arms flailing wildly before Darcy stepped forward to steady her with a firm but gentle hand.

"Are you hurt, Miss Elizabeth?" Darcy inquired, his voice tinged with concern. His gaze was earnest as he looked her over.

Elizabeth blushed from embarrassment and shrugged, her smile reassuring. "No harm done, Mr. Darcy. Though I must say, your dog's enthusiasm is as impressive as his size."

Exasperation and amusement warred within Darcy. He reprimanded Jasper. "Careful there, Jasper!" He grabbed the dog by the scruff of the neck, and the outrider attached Jasper's collar and leash. "You'll have to behave around the ladies, or we'll be forced to keep you in the carriage."

Elizabeth laughed softly, "I think Jasper has taken a liking to me. Perhaps he wanted my attention." She leaned over and scratched behind Jasper's ear.

Darcy chuckled, a genuine smile warming his features. "I suppose it is a possibility. He certainly has a knack for causing chaos."

The servants completed the luggage transfer, and the group entered the inn to eat a hearty breakfast. The travelers gathered around the dining table, the aroma of freshly baked bread and sizzling bacon filling the air. Conversation flowed easily between the Fitzwilliams and the Bennets, with Darcy listening quietly.

While most of the party listened to Colonel Fitzwilliam spin an outrageous tale of heroism in saving Bacon from a savage goose, Darcy found a moment to speak with Elizabeth. He leaned closer to her with a slight hesitation, saying, "Miss Elizabeth," he began, his tone sincere, "I hope the journey thus far has been to your satisfaction. I must admit, I am looking forward to our time at Pemberley."

Elizabeth turned to face him, her eyes alight with mischief. "The ten miles from Longbourn to Stevenage was pleasant in its way. Papa gave us a list of dos and don'ts, then fell asleep. Sally pressed her nose to the window and exclaimed at every new sight. Jane watched Sally with a gentle smile, and I read Papa's list before burying it at the bottom of my reticule. Then I closed my eyes and pretended the trip to Stevenage was over."

"Did pretending it was over expedite your arrival?"

"No, but we were here when I opened my eyes." Elizabeth smiled at Darcy. "I look forward to visiting your home and meeting your sister."

"Georgiana is eager to meet you and your sister." Darcy paused, looking down for a second to gather his thoughts. He desperately wanted this woman to like him. He murmured, "I trust that our time together will be pleasant. I know my behavior in Meryton was less than ideal, and I hope to make amends and show you my better self."

Elizabeth's gaze softened, and she offered him a warm smile. "I appreciate your sentiment, Mr. Darcy. I would like to know your better self."

Darcy looked relieved, his shoulders relaxing slightly. "I am grateful for your understanding. And I assure you, I will make every effort to be an agreeable companion." They turned their attention back to Richard's story.

After breakfast, Lord Matlock led the men to a private parlor. Sitting with a satisfied sigh, he began, "Bennet, I trust you are enjoying your little excursion from Longbourn?"

Bennet laughed. "It is refreshing to be away from the house briefly." He smiled wryly and added, "When I return, my wife's inquisition will start."

"I imagine Fanny will want to know where Jane and Elizabeth have gone." The earl shook his head in sympathy. "You must be brave."

Mr. Bennet, settling into the chair with a cup of coffee, replied with a wry smile, "Ah, yes, this is the quiet before the storm. I plan to inform her that Lizzy's godmother has taken our eldest daughters on a trip."

Matlock, knowing that Lizzy's godmother was dead, stiffened slightly. "Is it wise to lie to Fanny? She might remember that Elspeth died in 1801."

"True, but I won't tell her their actual destination. Don't look so glum. I'll think of something plausible before she notices they are gone." Bennet's twinkling eyes caused Lord Matlock to smile.

"Fanny will forgive you. She always does." Matlock sighed and tapped his old friend on the shoulder. "How are you planning to remove the Bingleys from Netherfield?"

Bennet, brow furrowed in worry, slowly answered, "There is one scheme that will get the job done quickly, but Bingley appears determined to stay. Though I must admit, removing the Bingleys from Netherfield may be easier now that Miss Bingley almost burned the place down."

"What in blazes are you talking about? When Mr. Gardiner mentioned the incident last night, the fire appeared innocuous," interrupted Darcy.

A grave Mr. Bennet pointed a finger at Darcy's chest. "No, not a harmless incident. It has caused quite a stir. The chit threw a bottle of perfume into the fireplace. The bottle shattered, splashing its contents into the flames, creating a conflagration that took over thirty minutes to extinguish. The stench from the incinerated perfume and the smoke permeate the family wing. Luckily, the manor still stands. Otherwise, Bingley would pay a fortune to rebuild the place and replace the contents."

Rendered speechless by Mr. Bennet's words, Richard and Darcy stared at the man.

Darcy's concern for his erstwhile friend was evident when he asked, "Was anybody hurt?"

"No, Mr. Darcy. The staff controlled the fire before it spread. The room stinks, and most of Miss Bingley's clothes will have a lingering odor of smoke until they are washed and aired. The only true tragedy is Mr. Bingley's inability to protect his family and staff from Miss Bingley," explained Mr. Bennet.

"However, on the plan to encourage that family to leave, our neighbors are being encouraged to call on Netherfield every morning to offer sympathy over the incident, bombard the family with tales of the Netherfield ghost, sympathize with Miss Bingley's encounter with ghostly control, and complain about the awful odor that permeates the air. A group of scholarly ghost hunters will also converge on the place, asking for a tour. Several staff members will be hiding to rattle chains and moan pathetically to enhance the experience starting tonight."

Lord Matlock chuckled. "The Bingleys will be irritated about the ghost stories and sound effects. I hope they leave before you try one of your less humorous tricks."

Richard could not contain his mirth, but Darcy, less inclined toward injurious jests, was not amused.

As the conversation shifted to lighter topics, the men's camaraderie deepened. They enjoyed a relaxed discussion about the plans and expectations for the journey ahead. When the horses were ready for the trip's next leg, Thomas Bennet and Lord Henry Matlock waved at the departing cavalcade.

The two cronies returned to the private parlor and discussed Jane and Elizabeth Bennet's future before Bennet returned to Longbourn and Lord Matlock returned to London.

Chapter 13

Wednesday, November 20, 1811
Netherfield

Louisa Hurst entered the drawing room after taking a few deep breaths to compose herself. She took a moment to survey the room, her gaze shifting from one face to another, noting the curious glances and the subdued murmurs of the Lucas and Goulding families. The fire at Netherfield had certainly stirred the neighborhood, and she wondered if everyone in the area was now compelled to visit out of sheer curiosity.

Mr. Hurst, who was lounging on a chaise with a cup of tea instead of his usual brandy, looked up. "Ah, Louisa. Just in time. We've been entertaining a steady stream of callers eager to know the details of Caroline's incident."

Louisa sighed and sat beside him, her eyes reflecting fatigue and irritation. "I can only imagine. The fire has become quite the spectacle, hasn't it?"

Sir William Lucas, who was seated opposite them, chuckled. "Indeed, Mrs. Hurst. It seems that news of the fire has spread. If only to satisfy their curiosity, every neighbor seems to be coming here."

Lady Lucas, seated beside her husband, nodded sympathetically. "The interest has been quite remarkable. The appeal of such misadventures is a diversion from the mundane happenings of daily life."

As Louisa settled into the conversation, she glanced around the room, noting Caroline standing near the open door. The steady stream of visitors continued to arrive. Some expressed concern, while others seemed more interested in the latest gossip as they greeted Caroline before moving further into the room, where they stood in small groups.

Charlotte Lucas leaned in toward Louisa, her expression thoughtful. "I must say, Mrs. Hurst, the fire caused quite a stir. But I wonder... what possessed Caroline to throw a perfume bottle into the fireplace?"

Louisa shook her head, her lips pressing into a thin line. "It is beyond me, Miss Lucas. The whole affair is utterly baffling. I was shocked by her recklessness."

Charlotte's brow furrowed in concern. "Do you think she might be suffering from some form of instability? Her actions appear erratic and dangerous."

Louisa sighed heavily. "I am concerned for my sister. The staff here certainly speak of her mood swings with a measure of unease."

At that moment, Sir William leaned forward, his eyes twinkling. "Ah, but perhaps we are overlooking a most intriguing possibility. There have been tales of an evil spirit that roams these very halls. Some say that it causes people to behave in the most irrational ways."

Louisa and Charlotte exchanged puzzled glances, and Lady Lucas raised an eyebrow in curiosity. "An evil spirit, Sir William? That sounds like the tale the old women tell to frighten naughty children."

"Yes, indeed," Sir William continued, his voice taking on a dramatic tone. "It is said that this spirit, which has been dubbed the Netherfield Ghost, is responsible for various disturbances in the house. Late at night, one can hear strange noises: footsteps echoing in empty corridors, doors creaking open by themselves, and the whispers of unseen voices. Some believe the ghost affects the minds of those who dwell here, driving them to perform acts of folly."

Charlotte's eyes widened slightly. "How fascinating! And do you believe there is any truth to these stories?"

Lady Lucas, her expression thoughtful, joined in. "Charlotte, I recall hearing a chilling tale about the Netherfield Ghost. There was a story of a previous resident who almost drowned in the lake here."

Louisa leaned in, intrigued. "Do tell, Lady Lucas."

Lady Lucas continued, her tone growing solemn. "It was said that a young lady, quite some years ago, had been walking by the lake late one evening. She was found later, nearly drowned, claiming she had been pulled into the water by unseen hands. Some attributed the incident to the spirit that roams these grounds."

Charlotte added, her voice low and conspiratorial, "I recall the story. The local gossip was that the ghost had been active again, disturbing the young lady's thoughts and causing her to wander into the lake. Of course, there were no witnesses, and no one could explain it definitively."

Sir William nodded, his expression reflecting both amusement and a touch of seriousness. "Exactly. And while it's easy to dismiss such stories as mere superstition, they provide an interesting backdrop for the current disturbances. Perhaps Miss Bingley's behavior is just another manifestation of this spectral influence."

Mr. Hurst chuckled loudly, a hefty dose of skepticism in his tone. "This spirit is conveniently blamed for every misstep and mishap."

Sir William bobbed his head up and down. "Perhaps. But it does make for an interesting story, don't you think? If nothing else, it provides an entertaining explanation for the inexplicable."

Lady Lucas sipped her tea, amused. "Well, whether or not the spirit exists, it is clear that Netherfield has become quite the topic of conversation. You must make the best of it until things settle down."

As the conversation continued, Mr. Goulding, a neighbor who had joined the gathering, came forward. He had been quietly listening to the tales of the Netherfield Ghost, and now he was eager to contribute.

"You know," Mr. Goulding began, his loud voice tinged with dramatic flair, "I have a particularly curious story about that very ghost. It involves one of the stablehands from several years ago."

Everyone turned their attention towards him, intrigued.

Mr. Goulding continued, "It was a dark and stormy night when the ghost made its presence known with a series of eerie noises resembling rattling chains. The poor stablehand, alone in the loft, was so frightened that he lost all sense of reason. He bolted out of the stable, brandishing a pitchfork as if he were preparing for battle."

Louisa's eyes widened with curiosity, and Charlotte leaned in closer. "What happened next?"

"Ah, well," Mr. Goulding said with a grin, "he chased the horses around the paddock, shouting and waving his pitchfork wildly. The horses, understandably panicked, scattered in every direction, making the scene even more chaotic. It was quite the sight... horses galloping, the stablehand shouting, and the pitchfork flailing about."

Lady Lucas chuckled, her eyes dancing with amusement. "That sounds like quite the spectacle. Did the stablehand ever recover from this madness?"

Mr. Goulding nodded, his expression serious. "Indeed, he did. The poor fellow was eventually subdued by several footmen and subsequently seen by the local apothecary. As for the horses, they were unharmed, though they were quite shaken. The stablehand, however, was said to be deeply affected by the experience. The tale of his frantic chase became a local legend, and it was said that the ghost was to blame for his sudden fit of madness."

Charlotte shook her head in disbelief, though a smile tugged at her lips. "These stories are certainly entertaining, though I wonder how much truth there is to them."

Mr. Goulding shrugged. "One can never be too certain. But the stories do persist, and they add an intriguing layer to the history of Netherfield. Whether or not the ghost is real, the ghost is a convenient explanation for the inexplicable."

A true skeptic, Louisa sighed, shaking her head. "Well, apparently, this imaginary ghost is proving to be quite the topic of conversation. Perhaps we should all be wary of wandering the halls alone at night."

As the laughter and conversation continued, Caroline Bingley, lingering nearby, could no longer contain her irritation. Her face was flushed with anger and embarrassment, her sharp eyes glaring as she stormed over to the offending group.

"Really," Caroline said, her voice laced with disdain, "must we continue with these absurd ghost stories? It is bad enough that the entire neighborhood has taken to speculating about that tiny fire. Now we must entertain ourselves with tales of phantom influences controlling our actions."

Her tone was accusatory as she fixed her gaze on Mr. Goulding and the others. "Are you suggesting that my behavior, or indeed anyone's behavior, can be attributed to this so-called ghost? Any faults or follies of mine are not the result of some supernatural force."

Lady Lucas, who had been engaged in the conversation, raised an eyebrow. "Miss Bingley, we were merely sharing local legends. No one intended to imply that you or anyone else is under the influence of a ghost."

Caroline's eyes flashed with irritation. "Well, it sounded like you were hinting at such nonsense. It is rather embarrassing to have one's actions scrutinized and blamed on imaginary entities."

Mr. Goulding, taken aback by her reaction, tried to smooth things over. "I assure you, Miss Bingley, the tales are meant to entertain, not to cast aspersions on anyone's character. The stories of the ghost are part of the local folklore, and any resemblance to current events is purely coincidental."

Caroline crossed her arms and tapped her foot impatiently. "Coincidental or not, it seems that such stories only reinforce the notion that something supernatural is afoot. I must insist that you cease these discussions immediately. They are not only tiresome but also rather unsettling."

Louisa Hurst interjected with a calming tone. "Caroline, I understand your frustration. Please do not allow these tales to overshadow the true purpose of our visitors. We should focus on enjoying each other's company."

Caroline gave a huff of resignation, nodded curtly, and walked away, saying, "Very well, if it will end these ridiculous speculations."

"Sir William," Mr. Hurst said, his voice low and confidential, "I must say, Caroline's behavior is becoming increasingly tiresome. She has a way of turning every little thing into a grand drama. Yet, she makes a valid point. No imaginary phantom controls her actions. She creates mayhem wherever she goes with her cavalier attitude toward the rest of humanity."

Sir William chuckled, shaking his head. "I can imagine. She does seem to have a penchant for making mountains out of molehills. These ghost stories are harmless enough, but she took them as a personal affront."

"Indeed," Mr. Hurst replied with a sigh. "I've seen her become rather agitated over the smallest things. One would think the ghost was an actual threat to her peace of mind."

Sir William raised an eyebrow. "I remember when she insisted that the tiniest draft in my parlor was the cause of her headache and precipitously left our card party. My wife was insulted. Is she always that dramatic?"

Mr. Hurst nodded in agreement. "Yes. I sometimes wonder if she sees slights and insults where there are none, simply because it fits her narrative of victimhood."

"Quite right," Sir William agreed. "Keeping one's composure when surrounded by such theatrics must be challenging. But we must all remember to navigate situations females create with patience."

"True enough," Mr. Hurst said with a wry smile. "At least we can find some amusement in her antics."

Sir William chuckled again, raising his cup in a gesture of fellowship. "Finding humor in the absurdities of social life is a skill."

Mr. Hurst raised his cup in return. "To absurdities and to enduring them with good humor."

The two men clinked their cups together, their shared amusement providing a lighthearted gesture as the conversation continued to flow until the final guest departed.

Chapter 14

Thursday, November 21, 1811
Netherfield

The morning dawned gray and dreary, with thick clouds hanging low and a promise of rain in the air. The atmosphere was heavy, mirroring the tension that lingered within Netherfield.

At breakfast, the mood was somber and strained. Caroline, Louisa, and Edwin discussed the visitors from the previous day and the unsettling stories about the fire circulating through the neighborhood. Charles Bingley, who had been out with the steward the previous day inspecting a broken fence, was bewildered by the conversation about ghosts.

Caroline's voice was sharp as she commented on the tales. "I cannot believe the audacity of some people. It is as if they wish to make our lives a public spectacle. The tales of ghosts and madness are preposterous."

Louisa, her face a mask of exhaustion, added, "Indeed. It seems every visitor we received had a new ghost story to tell. The whole neighborhood is abuzz with these absurd rumors."

Sipping his coffee, Edwin remarked dryly, "And to think this is the result of Caroline's tantrum. The spirit of mischief seems to have taken residence here, as though our misfortunes are entertainment for others."

Charles Bingley, who had been listening with growing confusion, finally spoke. "I must admit, I'm perplexed. I've just learned of these ghost stories from my valet. Is it true that strange noises were heard last night? It's all quite unsettling."

Caroline's eyes flashed with irritation. "Yes, Charles, apparently strange sounds were heard. As if that wasn't enough, Sir William Lucas has been spreading tales of an evil spirit that roams the halls and causes residents to behave irrationally."

Charles looked aghast. "Ghosts causing mischief? I had no idea it had reached such a level. I thought it was all merely idle gossip."

Louisa sighed heavily. "That's exactly what I thought. But now it seems everyone is caught up in these ridiculous stories of the Netherfield Ghost. The latest claim is that a previous resident almost drowned in the lake."

Charles shook his head in disbelief. "I was so occupied with inspecting the broken fence yesterday that I had no idea this nonsense was circulating the neighborhood."

The conversation took a turn as Charles recounted the tales he had heard from his valet. "According to a servant, Mr. Goulding shared an alarming story about a ghost causing a stablehand to go mad. The poor fellow chased the horses around the paddock with a pitchfork. It's all quite bizarre."

At this moment, Caroline joined the conversation. Her face was flushed with anger. "So now everyone believes I'm under the influence of a ghost? Is this the explanation we're settling on for my actions?"

Charles looked at her in surprise. "No, Caroline. We're merely trying to make sense of the stories circulating. There's no need to take offense."

Mr. Hurst, visibly frustrated, interjected, "It's not just the stories that trouble me but Caroline's behavior. It's becoming increasingly difficult to manage the situation. Her constant agitation only seems to fuel these rumors."

Louisa proudly added, "The tales of this spirit have taken on new life. The ghost is believed to be the root of all our troubles."

Caroline's face flushed as she angrily retorted, "I'm right here! Do not speak about me as though I were not! I will not be accused of being controlled by ghostly forces. I am quite capable of managing my actions without supernatural interference."

Charles, trying to mediate, suggested, "Perhaps we should consider a different approach. Instead of focusing on these unsettling stories, we might visit some of our neighbors. It could help shift the focus away from Netherfield and offer a reprieve from these incessant rumors."

Louisa nodded in agreement, grateful for a possible solution. "That sounds like a sensible idea. Engaging with our neighbors might distract them and us from the ghostly gossip."

The group agreed, but rain began to fall as they ate breakfast, a fitting accompaniment to the day's somber mood and an excuse to discard their plan.

The steady patter of rain against the window was interrupted by a sudden, sharp knock on the front door. Charles, with a frown, glanced at the clock. "At this hour? Who could it be?"

Mr. Hurst, lifting an eyebrow, murmured, "It better not be more ghost story enthusiasts."

Louisa, taking a deep breath, glanced toward the door. "We'll find out soon."

The butler, Mr. Nichols, opened the front door to reveal two distinguished men in scholarly attire, carrying leather-bound notebooks and a selection of curious instruments. They introduced themselves as Mr. Reginald Ashford and Dr. Jonathan Blythe, noted ghosthunters of the region.

"Good day," Mr. Ashford began, his tone formal as he addressed the butler. "We are Mr. Ashford and Dr. Blythe. We've come at the invitation of several local residents who have been rather concerned about the recent spectral disturbances here at Netherfield."

Adjusting his spectacles, Dr. Blythe added, "We hope to clarify the matter and perhaps provide solutions."

Nichols gestured for the men to wait and left them in the foyer while he inquired whether Mr. Bingley was home to a pair of ghosthunters.

Caroline's eyes widened with disbelief. "Ghosthunters? I've never heard of such a thing. We hardly need another group spreading tales of hauntings."

Exasperated, Mr. Hurst interjected, "We've heard more than enough about ghosts already. What could they possibly add to the existing stories?"

Caroline, crossing her arms, gave a skeptical look. "I must insist that our home is not a subject for sensational investigations. We are dealing with enough issues without adding professional curiosity."

Trying to mediate, Charles said, "Perhaps they can tell us about their methods. It might help us understand how to address these concerns more effectively." Turning to the butler, he added, "Show them into the parlor. We'll join them shortly."

Nichols returned to the callers and explained that the family was eating breakfast as Mr. Ashford and Dr. Blythe were escorted to the parlor. The pair meticulously placed their instruments, examined the room's atmosphere, and took preliminary readings, which they entered into their notebooks before settling into comfortable armchairs near the fireplace to await the family.

When the family entered the parlor, introductions were exchanged.

Bingley took the lead, his voice tinged with skepticism. "Gentlemen, why are you here?"

Mr. Ashford, unfazed, explained, "We wish to investigate the claims that Netherfield is haunted, including reports of recent strange noises and apparitions. We have been studying the phenomenon of spectral disturbances for many years. Our approach is scientific and methodical."

Dr. Blythe nodded in agreement. "Indeed. We aim to either confirm or dispel these accounts with evidence. We've brought along our instruments to conduct a thorough examination." He pointed to the various instruments.

Charles raised an eyebrow, clearly dubious. "Have you found any ghosts using these methods?"

Dr. Blythe met Charles's gaze steadily. "While we cannot guarantee results, we have succeeded in various other locations in dispelling unfounded rumors. Our instruments are designed to measure environmental changes that could indicate supernatural presence."

Louisa, still uneasy, asked, "What exactly will you be doing?"

Mr. Ashford replied, "We'll use several tools to monitor electromagnetic fields, temperature variations, and other unusual activity. We'll also conduct interviews and gather testimonies to support our findings."

Charles, still perplexed, glanced at his sister. "And what if you don't find anything?"

Dr. Blythe answered, "If we find no evidence of supernatural interference, we will report that. Our goal is to seek the truth and dispel fear."

Still visibly annoyed, Caroline added, "I hope your investigation doesn't cause further distress. We've already had more than enough excitement."

Mr. Ashford assured her, "We aim to be as unobtrusive as possible. Our work is conducted with the utmost respect for the property and its occupants."

Still visibly perplexed but determined to handle the situation rationally, Charles Bingley approached Mr. Ashford and Dr. Blythe.

"Gentlemen," Charles began, trying to sound as authoritative as he could, given his uncertainty. "I must admit that the idea of a formal investigation into these ghostly reports is quite unexpected. However, if it will bring clarity or ease the minds of my staff and neighbors, I will permit your investigation."

Mr. Ashford and Dr. Blythe exchanged pleased glances, and Mr. Ashford responded, "Thank you, Mr. Bingley. We appreciate your cooperation. We assure you that our methods are designed to be thorough yet respectful."

Charles continued, "I will instruct the staff to cooperate fully with your investigation. They should assist you in any way you require. Do not hesitate to ask if there are specific details you need from them."

Dr. Blythe nodded in acknowledgment. "Your support is most appreciated, Mr. Bingley. We will endeavor to minimize disruption."

Turning to Nichols, Charles added, "Please ensure that the staff is informed of the ghosthunters' presence and instruct them to offer their full assistance."

The butler nodded and stepped away to relay the instructions. Standing nearby with resigned frustration, Caroline muttered, "This is the last thing we needed."

Charles, catching her words, gave her a reassuring look. "Caroline, I understand this situation is far from ideal. I will ensure our home is not subject to unnecessary distress."

Caroline sighed but agreed, albeit reluctantly. "I suppose we must make the best of it."

As the ghosthunters began their preparations, Charles returned to them. "I trust this will help in resolving the ghostly rumors once and for all. If you need anything further, do let me know."

Mr. Ashford and Dr. Blythe set about their initial tasks. They started by interviewing the staff to gather information on the reported disturbances. They split their time between the kitchen, the servants' quarters, and other areas where the staff might have witnessed or heard unusual occurrences.

In the kitchen, Mr. Ashford interviewed the apprehensive cook.

"Mrs. Smith," Mr. Ashford began, "we've heard reports of strange noises and shadowy figures. Can you tell us if you've experienced anything unusual?"

Mrs. Smith wiped her hands on her apron, her face paling slightly. "Well, I can't say I've seen any ghosts, but there have been times when I've heard scratching noises from the walls. It's more annoying than frightening, but it does make me wonder."

Dr. Blythe took note and asked, "And when did these occurrences happen?"

Mrs. Smith thought for a moment. "Usually late at night, when everyone is asleep. It sounds like it's coming from inside the walls or the attic."

Meanwhile, Mr. Ashford spoke with the maids in the servants' quarters. Mary, a young chambermaid, recounted her experiences with visible distress.

"I've seen shadowy figures near the stairwell," Mary reported. "They move quickly and disappear when I try to look closer. Sometimes I hear squeaks. It's quite unsettling."

Dr. Blythe asked, "Have these occurrences been consistent?"

Mary shook her head. "They're not consistent. Sometimes it's every night, and sometimes I might go a day without seeing or hearing anything."

Mr. Ashford interviewed the stablehands. Tom, the head stableman, seemed particularly anxious.

"Last week, I heard something scratching at the stable door," Tom said, his voice trembling slightly. "It was so loud that it woke me up. I rushed to check the stalls. Nothing was in the stable except agitated horses. One of them even kicked at the door."

Dr. Blythe noted this and asked, "Have you heard or seen anything else?"

Tom shook his head. "No, just that. It was enough to unsettle me, though."

After their initial interviews, Mr. Ashford and Dr. Blythe regrouped in the parlor. The ghosthunters discussed the interviews when the family joined them for an update.

"We've heard a range of reports," Mr. Ashford began. "Scratching sounds, moans, shadowy figures... each account is different, but there seems to be a pattern of disturbances primarily at night."

Dr. Blythe added, "We will need to examine the areas where these disturbances have been reported. The fact that the noises are heard predominantly at night suggests there may be a structural or environmental explanation, but we will also consider the possibility of supernatural activity."

Caroline, her frustration evident, interjected, "I must ask... do you truly believe that there might be a ghost behind all these reports?"

Mr. Ashford met her gaze calmly. "We must investigate all possibilities. We approach each case with an open mind, aiming to either confirm or disprove the presence of a spectral entity."

In seeking to defuse the tension, Charles said, "I trust your investigation will provide some clarity. If there is an explanation, whether natural or otherwise, I hope it will help put everyone's minds at ease."

The ghosthunters began their more detailed investigation, moving from room to room with their equipment. The family and staff watched with apprehension, hoping the day's efforts would resolve the unsettling rumors.

As night settled over Netherfield, the steady rhythm of rain against the windows became a backdrop to an increasingly unsettling atmosphere within the house. The investigation appeared thorough, and the residents hoped for a peaceful night after the day's scrutiny. However, as the hours wore on and the house fell silent, the ghostly activities intensified quickly.

Around midnight, the first unsettling sound broke the stillness: a high-pitched scream echoed through the empty corridors of the guest wing. The sound seemed to come from nowhere and everywhere, causing everyone who heard it to stir in their beds, though the source remained elusive. Louisa Hurst, already on edge from the day's events, clutched her pillow tightly, her eyes wide with anxiety.

Moments later, loud, deliberate footsteps resounded through the hallways. The sound was heavy and purposeful, echoing from one end of the house to the other. Caroline Bingley, unable to ignore the noise, tossed and turned in her bed before finally throwing off the covers and venturing into the hallway. There, she found nothing out of the ordinary... only an oppressive silence and the lingering echo of the footsteps.

A series of crashes and bangs erupted from the attic as if some unseen force were hurling objects around. The sound of furniture being overturned and heavy thumps reverberated through the floors, rousing the staff. Huddled together in their quarters, their faces pale, the female servants shook with fear.

Charles, failing to sleep through the ruckus, rose and went to the attic, hoping to find a rational explanation. As he ascended the stairs, the noise grew louder, a cacophony of unsettling sounds. Reaching the attic door, he hesitated, his hand shaking as he turned the knob. The door creaked open, but the room was eerily still, save for the scattered dust and the dim light from his lantern. The noises stopped abruptly, leaving him with a sense of disquiet.

The most troubling aspect was the sudden drop in temperature in various rooms, with the breath of those inside turning misty in the chill. This coldness seemed to move unpredictably, following the sounds of disturbances as if the air was charged with an otherworldly presence.

Mr. Ashford and Dr. Blythe reviewed their findings in the parlor. When the sounds escalated, the pair looked at each other with restrained glee.

"This is better than we anticipated," Dr. Blythe said, adjusting his spectacles as he looked around the room. "The activity is becoming more aggressive."

Mr. Ashford agreed, stifling a laugh. "We'll need to conduct a more thorough investigation."

The noises continued throughout the night, each new sound more alarming than the last. By morning, the entire household was frazzled and sleep-deprived, with tales of the previous night's horrors spreading quickly to the staff of neighboring estates.

Chapter 15

Friday, November 22, 1811
Netherfield

The family gathered for breakfast, their faces drawn, their conversations stilted, as they exchanged glances of mutual unease. Charles Bingley, though visibly exhausted, tried to remain composed.

"This is becoming quite troubling," Charles admitted, rubbing his eyes. "What can we do to address this? Has the investigation yielded any further insights?"

"We need to continue our investigation with greater effort," Mr. Ashford said. "The escalation of activity suggests that something significant may be driving these disturbances. We will need to observe closely. Do you have any cats?"

Charles Bingley glanced at Caroline before replying. "Yes, we have a few cats, but Caroline doesn't like them." His brow furrowed. "I haven't seen any of them prowling about recently."

Caroline, clearly uncomfortable with the topic, spoke up. "I had all the cats banished from the house weeks ago."

Dr. Blythe looked puzzled. "And why was that?"

Caroline's expression hardened. "Their constant staring unsettled me. They would sit in the corners, their eyes gleaming in the dim light. It was unnerving. I couldn't tolerate it. Plus, I sneeze if they get too close."

Mr. Ashford raised an eyebrow. "Interesting. Cats can sometimes be unnerving, but their absence may have unintended effects."

Charles interjected, trying to clarify, "Caroline, while your discomfort is understandable, the cats play an important role in a household. They keep down the rat population, and rats tend to make their home in the walls and crevices of older houses like Netherfield."

Mr. Ashford nodded thoughtfully. "Indeed. Rats can cause a great deal of disturbance, both physically and audibly. Their presence might contribute to the noises you've been hearing."

Dr. Blythe nodded in agreement, his expression thoughtful. "Indeed, rat catchers are skilled in managing infestations. They use various methods...traps, poison, ferrets, and dogs. Each has its role in controlling and eradicating the pests. Mr. Bingley, you should employ the local rat catchers immediately."

Mr. Ashford added, "Ferrets are particularly effective. They can enter the rat nests and drive the rats out, making catching them easier. However, the presence of these creatures might contribute to additional noise and disturbance while they're at work."

Caroline, feeling cornered, said with a sigh, "I suppose I'll have to tolerate the return of the cats."

Charles, trying to offer reassurance, said, "We'll ensure the house cats are groomed, and their presence is limited to controlling the rats. I'll hire rat catchers today and tell them to manage their work as discreetly as possible."

Mr. Hurst turned to Louisa, a hint of frustration in his voice. "Is your sister a simpleton? She thinks she is destined to preside over a great country estate without knowing how to keep a house rat-free. That expensive school taught her nothing practical."

Maintaining her composure, Louisa replied, "Edwin, the seminary we attended in London did include household management in its curriculum. Do not blame the school for our current predicament. Blame Caroline. She is constantly costing Charles additional funds."

Mr. Hurst grumbled, "I wouldn't be surprised if the sounds and shadows we've been experiencing are all due to these beasts scurrying around at night. We'll be fortunate if the rat catcher doesn't need to open the walls."

Seeing the need to ease the tension, Dr. Blythe added, "We'll certainly consider the rat problem and ensure it is addressed thoroughly. Meanwhile, it might be helpful for us to document any further disturbances you experienced. The more information we have, the better we can understand the situation."

Charles, appearing slightly more reassured, turned to the butler. "I must consult the steward about hiring the local rat catchers. Have him meet me in the study in thirty minutes. When they arrive, please cooperate with the rat catchers and ensure they can access any areas they need to inspect. We must remove these vermin and ensure that Netherfield is comfortable for everyone."

Nichols, the butler, nodded and departed with a bow. As he walked down the hallway, his ordinarily expressionless face briefly lit with wry humor when he saw the housekeeper. He winked at her and murmured as he passed, "Mr. Bennet will be pleased."

Mrs. Nichols returned the wink with a knowing smile and continued to the kitchen, where she found three fat cats lounging around a water bowl. The cats looked up at her with contented eyes, seemingly oblivious to the commotion their presumed absence was causing in the breakfast room. Mrs. Nichols gave each one a gentle pat before attending to her other duties, secretly relieved that the household was about to get more help removing the Bingleys.

Meanwhile, Charles Bingley spoke with Mr. Ashford and Dr. Blythe in the breakfast room. He cleared his throat and addressed them, "We appreciate your patience and diligence. If there's anything else you need, please let me know."

Mr. Ashford placed his coffee cup on the saucer and said, "Thank you, Mr. Bingley. We will continue our investigation and keep you informed of any significant findings. In the meantime, we'll conduct our observations with the utmost care and respect for the property."

With that, the ghosthunters left the room and resumed their work, carefully setting up their instruments in the upper stories of the house.

When Mr. Ashford and Dr. Blythe left the breakfast room to continue their investigation, Caroline, Charles, Edwin, and Louisa remained at the table. The room was filled with the soft clinking of silverware against china, but an undercurrent of tension lingered in the air.

Caroline broke the silence with a frustrated sigh, pushing her plate away. "This place has become unbearable. I cannot stand another day of these incessant disturbances. I want to leave Netherfield."

A surprised Charles looked up from his coffee. "Caroline, abandon Netherfield? I understand the distressing situation, but we have only begun addressing the issues. Surely, we should allow the ghosthunters to complete their investigation and see if they can find rational reasons for these disturbances."

Louisa, who had been quietly sipping her tea, added, "Charles is right, Caroline. We've just enlisted professional help. It seems premature to leave when we haven't seen what can be done to eliminate gossip."

Edwin Hurst chimed in, his tone skeptical. "I'm not sure it's worth enduring this ordeal. If the ghosthunters don't succeed, we might be better off moving elsewhere. After all, the disturbances could signify that the property is not meant for us."

Her eyes narrowing with determination, Caroline added, "It is not just the disturbances. It is the discomfort of living in a house where every creak and moan is attributed to something supernatural. We are supposed to be living in comfort, not dealing with nightly horrors."

In trying to maintain a diplomatic stance, Charles said, "I understand your frustration, Caroline. However, abandoning Netherfield would be hasty. We should at least wait to hear what causes these mysterious noises."

Caroline shook her head. "I don't see the point in prolonging our suffering. We should seriously consider relocating. Living in a house plagued by such disturbances is not appealing."

With a resigned tone, Louisa said, "If the ghosthunters can't resolve these issues, we'll have to weigh our options. But for now, let's allow them to work. It wouldn't hurt to see if they can bring peace to the house."

Charles sighed. "Very well. We will wait and see what the ghosthunters discover."

The group continued their breakfast in a subdued mood, and everyone was lost in thoughts about Netherfield's future. As they finished their meal, they drifted to various areas of the house to await the outcome of the investigation.

As the day progressed, the sound of additional carriages arriving outside signaled the arrival of more visitors. The Purvis, Grant, and Philips families entered Netherfield in rapid succession, their presence adding to the growing number of curious and concerned individuals.

The first knock on the door came shortly before noon, followed by the arrival of the Purvis family. Mr. Purvis, a local squire, entered with his wife and two daughters, looking both curious and concerned.

"Good day," Mr. Purvis greeted the Bingleys. "We heard about the disturbances at Netherfield and thought it best to come by and offer our support. Ghost stories have been circulating, and we felt it necessary to share what we've heard."

Caroline, with a resigned sigh, welcomed them in. "Thank you for coming. We are currently having the situation investigated by professionals."

Mrs. Purvis, sympathetically, said, "We understand your distress. Our family has experienced supernatural occurrences. My late aunt once lived in a house that was reportedly haunted. She would often speak of unexplained noises and shadowy figures moving about. She even claimed to see a ghostly figure of a woman in a long white dress wandering the halls."

Louisa, looking intrigued yet apprehensive, nodded. "Thank you for sharing that. It seems that such stories are common."

Caroline, feeling her patience wane, attempted to maintain her composure. "Thank you for your concern, Mrs. Purvis. We are doing everything we can to address the situation."

Before more could be said, the doorknocker banged again, announcing the arrival of the Grant family. Mr. Grant, a local gentleman, entered with his wife and two sons, looking more practical but equally concerned.

"Good day to you all," Mr. Grant said, shaking hands with Charles. "We heard about the troubles at Netherfield and thought we'd visit. We've had some peculiar experiences ourselves."

Mrs. Grant said, "A few months ago, we had an incident where our barn appeared haunted. The animals became agitated, and we heard loud bangs and footsteps coming from inside. Our farmhand swore he saw a shadowy figure in the barn and refused to go near it for weeks."

One of the Grant sons added, "We also had a rat infestation in the barn, which only made things worse. The rats were causing most of the noises, but it took a while to convince everyone that it wasn't the work of ghosts."

Charles tried to maintain his composure, overwhelmed by the influx of ghost stories. "Thank you for sharing your experiences. We are addressing similar issues, and we hope the professionals will help us get to the bottom of it."

Mrs. Grant, a woman with an air of seriousness, spoke next. "I've heard that the previous owners of this estate experienced much the same. They claimed to have seen a shadowy figure on the staircase. They even moved away to escape the hauntings."

Louisa exchanged a worried glance with Charles. "Is there no end to these tales?" she asked, her frustration evident.

As the Grants took their leave, the Philips family arrived. Mr. Philips, the local solicitor, and his wife, both in their late forties and without children, joined the conversation with a more practical perspective.

"Greetings," Mr. Philips said, shaking hands with Charles. "We were informed of the recent disturbances here at Netherfield and thought we should visit."

Mrs. Philips took over, "When we lived in our previous house, we had several unsettling experiences. My husband often heard the sound of someone walking up and down the stairs at night."

"While we've heard our share of ghost stories," Mr. Philips said, "there's always been a rational explanation behind them. However, I must admit that these recent disturbances are most unusual. Before presenting a lease to you, I arranged for a complete inspection and inventory of the house and outbuildings. Based on the inspection, there was no rat infestation. As long as the cats can roam freely, you shouldn't have a problem with those disgusting rodents. If you wish, we can review those documents."

Charles, looking exhausted, tried to keep his patience. "Thank you for your concern, but as we mentioned, we hope to have clarity about these noises soon."

The conversation shifted towards the specifics of the ghost stories when the ghosthunters entered the room. Mr. Philips took the opportunity to address the pair. "Gentlemen, I trust you're finding the necessary evidence to support or disprove these reports?"

Dr. Blythe responded, "We are methodically approaching our investigation. The more information we gather, the better we can assess the situation."

Mr. Ashford added, "We appreciate the input from all the families. Each account helps us piece together the history of this house and understand the disturbances."

Mrs. Phillips added another tidbit. "You must also know of the time when a maid was found in the garden, hysterical and claiming she saw a ghostly figure by the lake. They say she left the estate in fear and never returned."

Caroline, her patience worn thin, addressed the group. "I understand everyone's concern, but we are already taking steps to investigate and address the situation. I assure you, we are doing everything possible to resolve this."

Despite her efforts to manage the situation, the arrival of more visitors and their ghost stories only added to the mounting tension at Netherfield. The day seemed destined to be filled with speculation and anxiety as everyone awaited the outcome of the ghosthunters' investigation.

Chapter 16

Saturday, November 23, 1811
Netherfield

The weather had turned colder, with a biting wind and overcast skies reflecting the somber mood within Netherfield. Mr. Ashford and Dr. Blythe completed their investigation and left behind a detailed report that confirmed the disturbances were caused by an infestation of rats rather than supernatural forces.

In the parlor, Charles Bingley read the ghosthunters' report with a sigh of relief. "It seems the noises and shadows were due to an infestation," he said, looking up from the paper. "This is a much more manageable problem than ghosts."

Caroline, still tense from the recent events, tried to look relieved. "It's good that there's a rational explanation. But I'm not looking forward to the disruption of dealing with rats."

The sound of carriage wheels and barking dogs interrupted the conversation. Outside, a small army of rat catchers, ferrets, and terriers arrived at Netherfield, ready to tackle the infestation. Two rat catchers, dressed in rugged attire with tool-laden belts, led the procession. Behind them came six sleek ferrets and four excitable terriers, all eager for their task.

The head rat catcher, a burly man named Mr. Trotter, stepped forward confidently. "Mr. Bingley, we're here to get rid of the rats once and for all. These ferrets and terriers will do most of the work, and we'll set traps and poison as needed."

Though somewhat daunted by the sight of so many critters, Charles replied, "Thank you, Mr. Trotter. Please, make yourselves at home. Let us know if you need access to any specific areas."

Mr. Trotter tipped his hat. "We'll start with the most affected areas first. The ferrets will go into the walls and small spaces, while the terriers will help with the larger openings. We should have a good idea of the extent of the infestation by the end of the day."

As the rat catchers and their animals moved through the house, an atmosphere of controlled chaos spread. The nimble and quick ferrets darted into crevices and gaps while the terriers barked energetically as they sniffed out any potential rat nests.

The staff bustled around, assisting where they could, but the commotion was not without its moments of alarm. In the late afternoon, the situation took an unexpected turn.

A loud scurrying noise emanated from the walls near Caroline's bedroom. Before anyone could react, a few rats, dislodged by the ferrets' efforts, burst out from behind the wainscoting. They dashed across the hallway, causing pandemonium among the female servants diligently working nearby.

Screams erupted as the rats darted past, their tiny feet making rapid, scratching noises. Walking through the hallway, Caroline let out a high-pitched shriek when one of the rats scampered directly across her feet.

"What is happening?" Caroline screamed, her face pale as she lifted her skirts and jumped away from the path of the rats.

One of the female servants, clutching her apron and trembling, shouted, "Rats! Rats in the hall!"

Another servant, in a panic, fled down the corridor, her scream echoing through the house. "Oh, it's awful!"

The commotion drew Charles, Louisa, and the rat catchers to the scene. Charles rushed over to Caroline. "Caroline, are you all right?"

Caroline, still shaken, took deep breaths as she cried, "No! I'm not. Having that thing run across my feet was a terrible shock."

Mr. Trotter and his team, who had been following behind with traps and tools, quickly intervened. "We'll need to get these rats under control," Mr. Trotter said, his voice steady. "I apologize for the disturbance. It seems the ferrets have driven them out faster than anticipated. We'll make sure the remaining rats are dealt with swiftly. The presence of so many rats is not typical, and we'll take steps to ensure they are all captured."

The rat catchers sprang into action, corralling the frightened rodents and setting additional traps.

Though still visibly distressed, Caroline attempted to regain her composure as the staff worked to restore some order. "Perhaps we should consider relocating to London until this is all sorted out," Caroline suggested, her voice trembling slightly. "I can't bear the thought of these rats running rampant through the walls."

Charles placed a comforting hand on her shoulder. "We'll get this sorted as quickly as possible. In the meantime, let's ensure the staff is calm and that the rat catchers are given every assistance they need."

The team continued their work into the evening, diligently capturing and placing the rats into cages. As the day drew to a close, the house became quieter. The family retired to their rooms for the night; the servants snuffed out candles, locked the doors, secured the windows, and sought their beds.

Outside, two dark figures approached the rear of the house carrying cages full of the rats captured earlier. The rats were released into a large hole leading to the study's interior wall. Knowing the proclivities of these creatures, the men were sure that exit holes would quickly appear in the room.

The household was settling for the night, and the noise and movement of the rats within the walls ceased. However, this temporary peace was disrupted when rats, driven by hunger and panic, began to pour into Bingley's study.

The study, typically a quiet and orderly room, was overrun with a writhing mass of rats. They emerged from every conceivable crevice, scurrying across the floor, climbing over furniture, and squeaking loudly as they explored their new surroundings.

Charles Bingley, who had retired earlier, was restless. He returned to his study for a final check on some paperwork and was met with utter chaos. He opened the door and saw rats scrambling over his desk, books, and papers. Their droppings covered the floor. His typically composed demeanor gave way to shock and dismay.

"What in the blazes!" Charles began, his voice rising in alarm as he surveyed the infestation. He stepped back quickly, narrowly avoiding a rat that darted across the floor. Charles slammed the door to contain the rodents. "Where the hell are those damn rat catchers?" he shouted in irritation.

The noise reached the ears of his family and servants. Caroline, who had been drifting into sleep, was jolted awake by Charles's exasperated shouts. The Hursts scrambled from their bed and donned their robes. The three converged in the hallway carrying candles before heading toward the commotion downstairs.

Charles, his face pale, summoned the servants and rat catchers urgently. "We have a situation in the study! There are rats everywhere!"

Louisa, coming to his aid, could only watch in disbelief as the staff and rat catchers scrambled to manage the situation. Tired from the day's work, the rat catchers immediately directed the terriers and ferrets into the study. No longer relying on traps, the men began impaling the rats on long poles while the terriers killed their prey. These rats would not have a second chance to invade Netherfield.

Charles's frustration reached a boiling point as the men worked, leaving a bloody mess on the floor and carpets. He paced outside the study, glancing at the chaos within; a growing sense of foreboding entered his heart. The sight of his once-pristine study now overrun by rats was too much to bear.

Caroline attempted to comfort him. "Charles, we must consider our options. This has become unbearable."

Charles turned to her. "I've had enough. This infestation has made it clear that Netherfield is no longer a suitable home for us. We need to relocate to London and request release from the rental agreement. This place may not be haunted, but it is cursed."

Though her expression was troubled, Louisa said, "Leaving seems the only reasonable solution. We cannot continue to endure these constant disturbances."

Edwin, though initially resistant, recognized the practicality of Charles's decision. "Very well. If returning to London will bring us peace and remove us from this nightmare, I will support it."

The rat catchers worked tirelessly throughout the night, gradually gaining control over the rat population. The study was steadily cleared of rats, and the tired staff worked to restore some semblance of order to the room.

Once the room was usable, Charles began making arrangements for the move. He informed the staff of their plans before returning to his bed chamber. In the morning, he wrote farewell letters to his neighbors. The decision to relocate to London was made with a sense of finality. Charles Bingley capitulated to circumstances and the desire of his family to leave the troubles that plagued their residence at Netherfield behind forever.

Chapter 17

Saturday, November 23, 1811
Pemberley

The morning was bright and clear as the cavalcade of carriages, having journeyed north for three days, finally crested a gentle hill. The air was crisp with a hint of winter's approach, and Pemberley estate stretched out below, a picturesque expanse of fields, rolling hills, and wooded glades. At the heart of the view towered Pemberley Castle, seemingly carved out of a small mountain, its grand I gleaming under the mid-morning sun. With its towering turrets and sprawling wings, the stone castle commanded an air of timeless elegance, nestled above lush gardens and the serene waters of a lake.

Their carriages stopped at an overlook, and the group disembarked, their faces reflecting awe at the first glimpse of the Darcy family's home. Elizabeth Bennet, Jane Bennet, Lady Matlock, Lady Rebecca Fitzwilliam, Colonel Richard Fitzwilliam, and Fitzwilliam Darcy gathered at the hill's crest. The dogs, Jasper and Bacon, bounded joyfully around them, their tails wagging energetically as they reveled in exploration of the nearby foliage.

Elizabeth, her eyes wide with admiration, took in the sweeping panorama of Pemberley. The estate's grandeur was even more impressive than she had imagined; its expansive grounds and majestic architecture embodied everything she had heard of it. Her gaze was drawn to the intricate details of the castle's I, how it harmonized with the surrounding landscape, and the serene beauty of the grounds that seemed to stretch endlessly.

Darcy stood beside Elizabeth, his demeanor calm and composed, though his eyes were focused on her face as she absorbed the view of Pemberley. His heart swelled with pride, seeing her face illuminated with genuine delight. The estate's grandeur reflected his heritage and was a significant part of his life.

"Is it everything you imagined?" Darcy asked softly, his voice tinged with anticipation. He felt vulnerable, wanting the home he cherished to meet her expectations.

Elizabeth turned to him, her eyes sparkling with wonder and admiration. "It is more magnificent than I imagined," she said, her voice carrying the warmth of her genuine appreciation. "Pemberley Castle is truly breathtaking. The way it stands so proudly against the mountain is beyond what I envisioned."

Darcy's smile broadened, and he took a moment to bask in her praise. His gaze lingered on Elizabeth, noting the sincerity in her voice and the way her eyes shone with excitement. "I am glad you think so," he said, his voice softening with emotion. "It holds a special place in my heart. I hope that you will find it as enchanting as I do."

Elizabeth's expression grew thoughtful as she looked out over the estate. "It's not just the physical beauty of Pemberley, though that is undeniable. It's the sense of history and how it feels alive with character. I can feel the warmth and care that have gone into maintaining the grounds and the castle."

Darcy's eyes softened, touched by her insight. "That means a great deal to me." His heart swelled with affection as he looked at Elizabeth.

Standing a short distance away, Lady Matlock and Lady Rebecca shared a warm smile as they observed Elizabeth and Darcy's interaction. The couple's mutual attraction was evident, and their expressions reflected the bond they were forming.

Lady Matlock's eyes twinkled with approval. "It's heartening to see how well Elizabeth and Darcy complement each other. Their connection seems so natural, so full of mutual respect."

Rebecca's gaze softened as she watched the couple. "Indeed. Elizabeth has brought a new light to Darcy's life, and it's wonderful to see how he gazes at her."

Lady Matlock chuckled gently. "I daresay the estate has found a new admirer. It's always a pleasure to witness someone appreciate Pemberley as much as Darcy does."

Rebecca turned her attention back to Elizabeth and Darcy, her smile widening. "And it seems that Elizabeth's admiration is genuine and heartfelt. It's not just about the grandeur of the place; it's about the love and history it represents."

Lady Matlock's eyes followed Darcy as he took Elizabeth's hand and squeezed it gently. "I think they'll make a wonderful life together here. Elizabeth's reaction to Pemberley speaks volumes about her ability to embrace and cherish what is important to Darcy."

Rebecca's voice held a note of satisfaction. "I agree. They are developing a deep understanding and respect for each other. I hope Darcy will be able to gain her love."

The two ladies shared a look of mutual understanding, knowing that Elizabeth might be a loving and supportive addition to their family.

Richard Fitzwilliam observed Darcy and Elizabeth with satisfaction, appreciating the happiness on his cousin's face.

After gazing at the impressive sight, Jane turned to Richard with a warm smile. "Colonel Fitzwilliam, I must say, Pemberley is even more splendid than I had imagined. It truly is a remarkable estate."

Richard, appreciating her genuine admiration, returned her smile. "I am glad you think so, Miss Bennet. Pemberley has always been a place of great pride for my cousin. It's heartening to learn that its charm extends beyond the family."

Jane's smile widened as she continued, "It's clear that a great deal of care and love has gone into maintaining the castle. The way it blends with the natural landscape is quite enchanting."

Richard's gaze lingered on the estate. "Indeed. My cousin Darcy has always been very dedicated to preserving the beauty of Pemberley. He values the harmony between the castle and its surroundings immensely."

Jane looked thoughtful momentarily before asking, "Has it always been such a beautiful place?"

Richard chuckled lightly. "I've known Pemberley for most of my life. As a child, I spent many holidays here, and I've seen it evolve. The grounds have always been impressive, but the Darcys continually improve it. The home farm is larger. Filling in part of the moat extended the gardens. Three additional hot houses provide fruit and exotic crops year-round. The most impressive change was the addition of indoor water closets for each suite. "

Jane's eyes sparkled with curiosity. "That must have been quite an experience, witnessing those changes firsthand."

"It was," Richard replied with a hint of nostalgia. "And it's always a pleasure to see others appreciate the estate as much as we do. I'm particularly pleased to see Elizabeth's reaction."

Jane's gaze shifted to Elizabeth, standing close to Darcy, her face alight with joy. "Yes, she seems truly enchanted by it. I am happy for her. I hope Mr. Darcy can win her heart. This place suits her very well."

Richard acquiesced and murmured, "If Darcy can repair the poor impression he made in Hertfordshire, she may learn to love him. Elizabeth and Darcy are well-matched in their appreciation for the finer things in life and their respect for what truly matters."

Jane looked back at Richard, her eyes soft. "Thank you for sharing your thoughts, Colonel."

Richard gave a courteous bow of his head. "It's my pleasure, Miss Bennet. I'm glad you can share in the beauty of Pemberley and the happiness it brings to our family."

The dogs were a whirlwind of activity, their boundless energy evident as they chased each other around the crest of the hill. Occasionally, they would pause to sniff the ground or investigate a new scent with curious noses. Their playful antics became more frantic when Jasper's sharp eyes spotted a rabbit. With an excited bark, he darted toward the creature, his movements swift and determined. Bacon followed closely behind.

Elizabeth, who had been absorbed in admiring the breathtaking view of Pemberley with Darcy, was distracted by the commotion. Her gaze followed the dogs as they raced after the rabbit, her eyes widening in alarm.

"Oh no! Look at them!" Elizabeth exclaimed, her voice tinged with concern. "They'll scare the poor thing to death!"

Darcy looked at her with amused sympathy. "I'm afraid they are rather keen hunters."

Jane, noticing the growing chaos, moved closer to Richard with an expression of worry. "We should call them back before they catch that poor creature."

Before anyone could intervene, the dogs' frantic chase led them through the group. In his excitement, Bacon collided with Elizabeth, sending her sprawling onto the grass with a startled cry.

"Elizabeth!" Darcy's voice was filled with concern as he hurried to her side. He gently helped her to her feet, his expression worried. "Are you injured?"

Flushing with embarrassment, Elizabeth glanced at Darcy with a sheepish smile. "I'm fine, just a bit dusty. The dogs certainly made their presence known."

Jane approached quickly, her concern evident. "Elizabeth, are you hurt?"

Elizabeth shook her head, a hint of amusement in her eyes. "No, just a little shaken. I'm truly fine."

Having observed Elizabeth's tumble, Lady Matlock and Rebecca approached with worried expressions. "Is everything all right?" Lady Rebecca asked, her gaze moving between Elizabeth and Darcy.

"Everything is fine," Darcy assured them. "Elizabeth had a minor tumble, but she's fine. The dogs' enthusiasm got the better of them."

Richard, observing the scene with a bemused smile, stepped forward. "It seems our dogs have a talent for creating chaos."

Elizabeth smiled at Richard, her eyes twinkling with amusement. "Indeed, they've certainly made an impression on me. This is a lively introduction to Pemberley's charms."

Panting and subdued after the rabbit escaped into a hole, the dogs returned to the group with apologetic whines and wagging tails. Their exuberance had waned, but their affectionate natures remained.

As the party regrouped and resumed their positions, Elizabeth and Darcy exchanged a glance. Darcy's eyes reflected his relief. "I'm glad you're unscathed. I hope this little mishap hasn't dampened your spirits."

Elizabeth's eyes sparkled with amusement as she brushed dirt from her gown. "Not at all. If anything, it has made my first glimpse of Pemberley unforgettable."

With a shared smile and renewed camaraderie, the group returned to their carriages for the final stretch of their journey to the castle.

Chapter 18

Saturday, November 23, 1811
Pemberley

The carriages rolled to a gentle stop in the courtyard of Pemberley Castle, their wheels crunching over the gravel behind four outriders. The horses snorted and pawed the ground, eager to be relieved of their burdens, while the trailing four outriders headed for the stables. The castle's imposing stone I, imposing turrets, and entryway stood before them. The crisp autumn air smelled of fallen leaves, pine, earth, and the faintest hint of wood smoke from the chimneys.

Staff members moved efficiently to attend to the entourage, holding the horses in place, opening carriage doors with polite nods, helping the guests disembark, and unstrapping the luggage, which was swiftly carried away to the castle's interior, leaving the visitors free to take in their surroundings.

Georgiana Darcy emerged from the castle's main entrance, her face alight with excitement. Her elegant cape flowed behind her with each hurried step as she scanned the arriving guests. Her eyes quickly found her brother, Fitzwilliam Darcy.

"William!" Georgiana called out, her voice filled with warmth and joy. She rushed to him, her arms outstretched. "It's so wonderful to see you! I've missed you so much!"

Darcy, his expression softening with affection, embraced his sister warmly, lifted her from the ground, and twirled her around. Gently placing her down, he said, "Georgiana, it's wonderful to see you as well. I'm glad you're here to greet our guests."

Georgiana's gaze turned to the newcomers, her enthusiasm undiminished. She approached Lady Matlock and Lady Rebecca Fitzwilliam, offering them a gracious curtsy. "Aunt Jessica, Cousin Rebecca, it's a pleasure to see you. I hope your journey was comfortable."

Lady Matlock smiled warmly, her eyes reflecting genuine pleasure. "Thank you, Georgiana. We're delighted to be here. The journey was quite pleasant."

Lady Rebecca added with a bright smile, "Indeed, it's a joy to see you, Georgiana. Your eager greeting has made our arrival special."

Colonel Richard Fitzwilliam joined the group with a friendly smile, his eyes twinkling with mischief. "Georgiana, it's good to see you. I trust you've been keeping things lively around here?"

Georgiana turned to Colonel Fitzwilliam, extending her hand with a chuckle. "Oh, Cousin Richard, you know how it is. There is always something to do. It's good to see you. I trust the journey was pleasant?"

Richard took her hand with a friendly grin and pulled her into a quick embrace. "It was indeed. I'm pleased to be here and see you again."

Georgiana then turned toward Jane and Elizabeth Bennet, her eyes sparkling excitedly. Darcy stepped closer, placing a reassuring hand on Georgiana's shoulder. "Georgiana, these are my friends, Miss Jane Bennet and her sister, Miss Elizabeth. Miss Bennet, Miss Elizabeth, this is my sister, Miss Georgiana Darcy."

Georgiana's eyes shone as she looked at Elizabeth and Jane. "I'm so pleased to meet you both. I hope you'll find your stay here comfortable and enjoyable. Pemberley is an extraordinary place, and we're thrilled to share it with you."

Elizabeth smiled warmly, her gaze reflecting gratitude and admiration. "Thank you, Miss Darcy. Your kindness and the beauty of Pemberley are already making this visit memorable."

Jane sincerely added, "We're looking forward to our time here. Thank you for the warm welcome."

Fitzwilliam Darcy watched the exchange with a satisfied smile, his pride in his sister evident. Georgiana glanced at Darcy and then back to the group, her eyes shining with happiness.

Georgiana's smile grew brighter as she turned and led the way into the castle. The entrance hall of Pemberley, with its high, vaulted ceilings, marble floors, mahogany tables, cushioned chairs, and luxurious tapestries, greeted them. The scent of polished wood and fresh flowers filled the air, enhancing the atmosphere of warmth and welcome.

Standing near the grand staircase, Mrs. Reynolds, the housekeeper, awaited the party with an air of composed dignity that matched the elegance of Pemberley. Her attire was immaculate, reflecting her meticulous nature, and her expression combined warmth with professional pride, embodying years of devoted service to the Darcy family. As the guests approached, Mrs. Reynolds moved forward, her eyes radiating genuine pleasure at the arrival of visitors.

Darcy stepped forward to make the introductions. "Mrs. Reynolds, may I present my dear friends and relatives? You already know Lady Matlock, Lady Rebecca Fitzwilliam, and Colonel Richard Fitzwilliam." He gestured toward the Bennet sisters with a warm smile. "These two ladies are Miss Jane Bennet and Miss Elizabeth Bennet."

Mrs. Reynolds offered a respectful courtesy to the guests, addressing them with a friendly and professional demeanor. "Welcome to Pemberley," she said, her voice carrying a sincere warmth. "It is a pleasure to have you here."

The guests responded with polite affirmations and appreciative smiles. "Thank you, Mrs. Reynolds," Jane said, her tone reflecting genuine gratitude. "Your welcome is most kind."

Mrs. Reynolds acknowledged Jane's comment and continued, "If you follow me, I will show you to your rooms. We have prepared your accommodations to ensure your utmost comfort." She led the way upstairs.

When they reached the first-floor landing, Mrs. Reynolds paused, pointing toward the right. "Lady Matlock and Lady Rebecca, you will stay in your usual rooms down this corridor. Miss Bennet and Miss Elizabeth, your suite is across the hall from them and conveniently next to Miss Georgiana's suite. A maid has been assigned to you and is standing just outside your door to assist with any needs you may have."

She then pointed to the left. "Colonel Fitzwilliam, you will stay in the opposite wing for this visit, sharing a suite with Mr. Darcy." Richard raised an inquisitive brow at the unexpected arrangement. Noting his expression, Darcy chuckled and added, "Don't worry, Richard. I promise I don't snore. We cannot have two unmarried ladies staying in the same wing with unmarried gentlemen."

Mrs. Reynolds, sensing the need to move on, interjected with a note of finality, "Refreshments will be served in the downstairs parlor in thirty minutes. Should you need anything at all during your stay, please do not hesitate to let me know."

The guests thanked Mrs. Reynolds and then proceeded to their rooms to refresh themselves after their journey. The hallways of Pemberley were filled with the soft sounds of doors opening and closing as the guests settled in. Servants moved efficiently through the corridors, helping to unpack the luggage and arrange the rooms for the guests.

Elizabeth and Jane were attended to in their adjoining rooms by their maid, who carefully unpacked their trunks and organized their belongings. The sisters engaged in light conversation as they observed the maid's efficient work.

When admiring her room's intricate details, Elizabeth remarked, "Jane, the elegance here is beyond words. I never expected anything quite so grand."

Jane, adjusting her dress in the mirror, agreed. "I feel the same. The beauty of the estate is astonishing. And Georgiana's warmth made us feel welcome immediately."

Elizabeth smiled, her gaze shifting to the window where the autumn light cast a soft glow over the gardens, the vibrant colors of the falling leaves creating a picturesque scene. "I'm eager to explore more of the grounds. The view from the hill was only a hint of the landscape."

Jane glanced at Elizabeth, her eyes sparkling with anticipation. "We should take a stroll this afternoon. Rebecca claims the gardens are enchanting, and Georgiana is such a gracious hostess."

Elizabeth nodded in agreement, her gaze wandering around the elegant room. "I'm looking forward to exploring the grounds and the gardens. The view from this window is amazing."

Jane glanced toward the window, taking in the expansive view. "We'll have plenty of time to enjoy it all." Jane moved toward the door leading to her bedroom. "However, we should wash and change into more appropriate gowns."

Elizabeth watched her sister depart and called the maid to help her disrobe before heading to the bathing room and washing away the road dust from her body.

Thirty minutes later, after refreshing themselves and donning appropriate gowns, Lady Matlock and her daughter chatted in their sitting room.

Lady Matlock remarked, "Rebecca, I'm quite happy to be here with Jane and Elizabeth. They will become good friends with Georgiana. Heaven knows the girl needs friends. Pemberley is a wonderful estate, but there are no nearby families with daughters her age. We are not at Gladstone Park often enough for you to visit frequently. The poor girl needs a sister."

"True. It is wonderful to have Jane and Elizabeth join us here at Pemberley. With any luck, Darcy will capture Elizabeth's heart and secure her hand in marriage. Then Georgiana will get a wonderful sister," replied Rebecca.

Lady Matlock smiled, looking around the room. "Yes. I look forward to watching Darcy repair her opinion of him. I suspect he may have difficulty convincing Lizzy to overlook his insulting remark at the assembly."

Rebecca's eyes twinkled with amusement. "It's clear he has great affection for Elizabeth. I look forward to watching him get to know her better." The ladies burst into laughter.

Colonel Fitzwilliam was being attended to in the opposite wing by his batman, who efficiently unpacked his belongings and arranged his room. Glancing at the neat arrangement, Richard was interrupted by Darcy, who came to check on his cousin.

Leaning casually against the doorframe that led to an adjoining sitting room, Darcy grinned. "How are you finding your accommodations, Richard? I hope everything is to your liking."

Richard looked up with a grin of his own. "Everything is perfect. Sharing a suite was unexpected, but it's not unfamiliar."

Darcy chuckled. "Indeed, it seemed the most appropriate arrangement, and it will be good to catch up."

Richard smiled and agreed, "Yes, but I'm looking forward to the refreshments Mrs. Reynolds mentioned. A bit of sustenance after our journey will be most welcome."

"You're always hungry," Darcy commented as he left the room, heading for his quarters. Now alone, Richard moved to the window and gazed over the grounds. The autumn afternoon sun cast long shadows across the rolling hills, the vibrant colors of the foliage creating a scene of tranquil beauty. "It's as splendid as ever," he murmured to himself. "It's good to be back."

In his chambers, Darcy closed the door behind him and took a moment to reflect on the day's events. He stood by the window, looking over the sight of Pemberley bathed in the afternoon's golden light.

Darcy's thoughts turned to Elizabeth. Her genuine admiration for Pemberley was particularly gratifying. He recalled how her eyes lit up at the first sight of the estate, a reaction that filled him with a profound sense of pride. It was important to him that she admired the place.

Darcy allowed himself a moment of nostalgia as he considered the changes Pemberley had undergone over the years. The castle was more than just a residence; it symbolized his family's history and achievements, a place of cherished memories and ongoing legacy. With a deep breath, he rang for his valet. He must prepare to join the others.

The aroma of freshly baked pastries and savory treats began to waft through the corridors as Darcy went downstairs, his heart light with anticipation. The scent was inviting, promising a delightful and comforting end to the day's travels. He hoped the conversation would flow easily and that laughter and shared stories would create lasting memories.

Upon reaching the parlor, Darcy was greeted by Georgiana, who was assisting with the final arrangements. The room was warm and inviting, with a crackling fire in the hearth casting a soft, flickering light across the richly decorated space.

With her hair neatly pinned and a bright smile, Georgiana looked up from arranging a tea tray and a plate of delicate pastries on a low table near the hearth. "William, everything is ready," she cheerfully said. "The guests will be arriving downstairs soon."

Darcy smiled, pleased with the preparations. "Excellent. I'm looking forward to a pleasant afternoon with everyone."

The sound of footsteps descending the stairs drew his attention. Four ladies, elegantly dressed and accompanied by a smiling Richard, entered the parlor. Lady Matlock, Rebecca, Jane, and Elizabeth entered the large room and curtseyed to Mr. Darcy, who bowed politely.

Lady Matlock, her face alight with appreciation, said, "The house is as beautiful as ever, and Georgiana is a most gracious hostess."

Lady Rebecca smiled and added, "Yes, everything seems perfect. The scents wafting from the kitchen are positively tantalizing."

Jane said, "Pemberley is wonderful. Thank you for inviting us to share your home for the holidays."

Elizabeth looked up at Darcy through her thick eyelashes, a playful smile on her lips. "Yes, thank you for inviting us. However, I am looking forward to the refreshments."

Catching the glint of mischief in her eyes, Darcy chuckled and leaned down slightly, his voice low and teasing. "Then I hope you'll find something tolerable on the various platters to tempt you."

Elizabeth's smile widened, and she gave a slight, appreciative nod. "I'm hoping there will be something delightful and tempting in every room."

The group settled onto the comfortable sofas and chairs arranged around the hearth. As servants poured tea and coffee, the conversation turned to various topics, from recent news and local gossip to reflections on their travels. The ease with which everyone interacted created a lively and engaging atmosphere, enhancing the pleasure of the afternoon. Georgiana, her curiosity piqued by the shared stories and experiences, was drawn into the discussion, her laughter mingling with the others until Darcy pulled her aside to discuss seating arrangements for dinner.

Sitting comfortably on a sofa beside Jane, Richard sipped his coffee and remarked, "It's wonderful to have you here. This afternoon promises to be most enjoyable."

A deep blush suffused Jane's neck, and she glanced sideways at Richard, her eyes soft and appreciative. "Everything here is so lovely. I'm grateful Mr. Darcy invited us." Jane lowered her voice. "Mama's plans for me and Lizzy... well, unbearable is a mild way to describe them."

Richard raised a brow, clearly intrigued by her response. "What mischief was your mother up to now?"

"Matchmaking," interjected Elizabeth from Jane's other side. She shook her finger at Richard. "You would laugh at her antics, but staying in the same room with her was getting difficult. Mama constantly berated us for refusing to follow her advice, and neither of us wanted the suitors she preferred."

"Oh, Lizzy," exclaimed Jane. "You exaggerate the situation."

Offended, Elizabeth's voice rose slightly. "Do I? Mama forced you to ride on an old nag to Netherfield to dine with Miss Bingley and Mrs. Hurst, knowing the clouds would burst open at any moment. Thankfully, you didn't get pneumonia and die when you were soaked to the skin. I suppose being forced to stay at Netherfield for days with a high fever was enjoyable?" Elizabeth's cup rattled in the saucer, almost spilling her tea.

"No, it was awful, but Mama didn't want me to get sick. She thought I would stay the night and come home in the morning." Jane tried to reason with her sister. "You know how she is..."

Concerned, Lady Matlock abruptly joined the conversation. "We do know how she is, Jane. Your mother never thinks of consequences that exceed her expectations. She probably thought staying the night would allow you to see Mr. Bingley without considering that getting wet and chilled might result in illness. If the carriage was unavailable, you should have refused the invitation to dine with the ladies; it would have been better. We have often discussed ways to circumvent Mrs. Bennet's outlandish suggestions. Why didn't you use one to stay home?"

Jane hung her head in shame, clasping her hands together. Seeing that her sister could not respond, Elizabeth said, "Lady Matlock, you've tried your best to help us cope with Mama, and I apply your suggestions daily. However, Jane cannot force herself to disobey Mama in what might be considered inconsequential matters. The diatribes that result from disobedience last for days... sometimes weeks. Being in the same house with her becomes unbearable for everyone."

Rebecca gazed at her two friends and said, "I had no idea your mother was such a problem. Why didn't you confide in us?"

"Because there's nothing you can do. Papa sends us to the Gardiners for extended visits when Mama gets overwrought. This is the first time he's sent us this far away. Please don't let our troubles affect you. We plan to have a wonderful time here." Elizabeth squeezed Jane's hand reassuringly and smiled at Lady Matlock and Rebecca.

Richard was upset to learn that Jane Bennet rode to Netherfield in the rain on a cold November day at her mother's behest to avoid an argument with the harridan. He might have lost her. Confused, He stared at Jane. "Jane, that sounds incredibly harsh. I had no idea how difficult things had become. You should not have to endure such trials for the sake of family expectations."

Jane turned toward Richard, gazed into his bewildered eyes, and murmured, "I thought escaping Longbourn was worth risking a soaking. I won't do it again."

Richard, still shaken, took a deep breath. "Well, I'm glad you're here now, and I'm even more determined to ensure you both have a pleasant and trouble-free visit. Let's focus on enjoying our time at Pemberley and leave the challenges of Longbourn behind for a while."

The conversation shifted as Georgiana spied a footman carrying a tray of freshly baked pastries. She left Darcy standing by a window to return to her guests. "I hope I'm not interrupting," she said brightly. "I ordered more treats for everyone, including lemon tarts. Perhaps a bit of sweet indulgence will brighten the mood."

Elizabeth, her eyes sparkling with gratitude, thanked Georgiana. "Lemon tarts are my favorite. Thank you, Miss Darcy." She gazed briefly at the tall, handsome Master of Pemberley, who had followed his sister to rejoin the group. *Had Darcy winked at her?*

Catching Elizabeth's glance, Darcy smiled warmly but did not comment, allowing the atmosphere to remain light and casual. He sat beside Georgiana, who was already engaging in a lively discussion about the relative merits of the various sweets. She compared the lemon tarts to the buttery shortbread and the decadent chocolate éclairs.

Richard, a great enthusiast for food, offered his opinions with good-natured humor and a sly look at Elizabeth. "I must say, Georgiana, these lemon tarts are a triumph. I must sample more to see if their flavor exceeds the strawberry tarts to ensure none are unfairly judged."

Jane laughed softly, her cheeks still pink from their earlier conversation. "You have a discerning palate, Colonel. I'm sure every pastry here is deserving of praise."

Lady Matlock chimed in with a smile. "Indeed, I have never been disappointed by Pemberley's pastry chef. It's one of the many pleasures of visiting Darcy and Georgiana."

As the conversation continued, Elizabeth was drawn into a discussion about local wildlife with Georgiana and Lady Rebecca. They spoke animatedly about the different animals that frequented the estate's grounds, and Elizabeth was soon captivated by the vivid descriptions of the various creatures.

The earlier tension melted away, replaced by a warm, relaxed atmosphere that allowed everyone to savor the repast. Laughter and pleasant chatter filled the parlor, creating a delightful backdrop to the afternoon. The guests enjoyed the sumptuous array of pastries and the congenial company.

After some time, Darcy stood and suggested, "Shall we take advantage of this lovely afternoon and explore the grounds? The gardens are still lovely, and the walking paths around the lake and streams are scenic."

The group agreed enthusiastically, and they separated to prepare for their outing. The afternoon promised to be as delightful as the parlor gathering, and everyone looked forward to the pleasures that awaited them outside.

Chapter 19

Saturday, November 23, 1811
Mischief

The crisp autumn afternoon was perfect for exploring the grounds of Pemberley Castle. Lady Matlock, Rebecca Fitzwilliam, and Georgiana Darcy meandered through the nearby gardens, their conversation drifting between family events and the latest news since summer. Their laughter and animated discussion added a touch of warmth to the cool, invigorating air.

Meanwhile, Darcy, Elizabeth, Jane, Richard, and the dogs enjoyed a leisurely walk around the lake. The sun was beginning its slow descent, casting a golden glow over the serene water and surrounding landscape. Jasper and Bacon bounded energetically near the foursome, their tails wagging with unrestrained joy.

Elizabeth was drawn to a charming stone bridge arched gracefully over a stream feeding into the lake. Framed by autumn foliage, the bridge seemed like a picturesque spot to pause and take in the view. She gently tugged Jane's coat sleeve to catch her attention. "I'm going over there," she said, her eyes bright with enthusiasm, and started walking toward the bridge.

Richard, observing Elizabeth's departure, nudged Darcy with a conspiratorial grin. "Why are you still here? Accompany Miss Elizabeth," he whispered urgently, his tone full of encouragement.

Darcy shot Richard a look of mild exasperation, the kind that only a long-time friend could interpret correctly. "You always have an opinion on my actions," he muttered, with a hint of a smile at the corners of his mouth.

Jane's soft laughter followed Darcy as he hurried to catch up with Elizabeth with a purposeful stride. He offered Elizabeth his arm as he reached her. "Please, allow me to accompany you," he said, his voice blending formality and warmth.

Elizabeth turned to him with a smile. "I'd be delighted," she replied, accepting his arm as they walked toward the bridge, leaving Jane, Richard, and two energetic dogs behind.

The two made their way across the bridge, pausing midway, leaning on the stone railing to take in the tranquil view of the stream meandering toward the lake. Darcy stood beside her, quietly appreciating the view. "It's moments like these that make Pemberley so special," he remarked softly, looking at Elizabeth's profile.

Elizabeth glanced at him, her eyes reflecting the warmth of the afternoon sun. "It truly is beautiful. I'm glad we took a moment to enjoy it."

"As am I," Darcy murmured.

Richard and Jane continued along the path. "Do you think your sister will give Darcy a chance to win her heart?" Richard asked, his tone playful yet sincere.

Jane carefully contemplated his question, a gentle smile playing on her lips. "I believe Elizabeth is open to the idea. Darcy has to prove himself to be intelligent, honorable, and kind. Whether he will win her affection depends on how well he treats people. His poor showing in Hertfordshire damaged the picture your family painted of him."

Richard nodded, intrigued by Jane's words. "It seems you have given this some thought. I must admit, Darcy has always had a certain stoicism about him that can be mistaken for pride, but seeing him at Pemberley will show Elizabeth his true personality."

Jane glanced back toward the bridge, where Darcy and Elizabeth stood deep in conversation. "Yes, there is something intimate in their interactions. Elizabeth has always been quite discerning, and I trust her judgment. If she allows herself to see Darcy's true character, she might admire him again."

Richard raised an eyebrow, his expression thoughtful. "Indeed. Darcy's efforts reflect a genuine desire to be more engaging and approachable."

Their conversation was interrupted by the playful barks of Jasper and Bacon, who spotted a meadow where a flock of sheep was grazing under the supervision of a shepherd and his collie. Their eyes were wide with excitement, and the dogs dashed toward the sheep with a sudden burst of energy.

Jane laughed softly. "It seems the dogs are having fun this afternoon. Perhaps they're trying to add a bit of chaos to the calm."

Richard chuckled. "They certainly bring a lively element to our stroll," he called out as he ran after the dogs, shouting for them to return.

The shepherd's collie sprang into action, barking furiously and attempting to herd Jasper away from the distressed sheep. The scene quickly became chaotic as Jasper's pursuit caused the flock to scatter, bleating in alarm and adding to the pandemonium. Bacon, the more obedient of the two, was swiftly captured by the shepherd when he thrust his staff in front of the poodle. Bacon recognized this symbol of authority and stopped. Richard grabbed his collar and attached his leash.

Hearing the barking and Richard's shouts, Darcy ran toward the meadow, leaving Elizabeth on the bridge. Elizabeth watched the scene with amusement.

Despite Darcy's efforts to regain control over Jasper, the dog remained oblivious to the chaos he was causing and continued to dart around the meadow, focusing solely on chasing the sheep. Suddenly, Jasper's attention shifted. His head went up, and his tail wagged harder, slapping the collie in the face.

The sound of laughter filled his ears, and he heard his name being called by a musical voice. "Oh, Jasper! Come! You are such a playful fellow!" He spotted Elizabeth standing on the bridge, her calm presence contrasting sharply with the disorder around him. With renewed vigor, Jasper sped toward her, his paws pounding against the stone, and as Jasper drew nearer, she called out with authority, "Sit!"

At the last possible moment, Jasper skidded to a halt and dropped into a sitting position, his front paws landing lightly on Elizabeth's boots. Elizabeth's initial shock turned into relief as she scratched Jasper's ears and praised him for his obedience. "Good boy, Jasper! You've caused enough trouble for one day."

Darcy arrived moments later, his face flushed with exertion. He quickly leashed Jasper, who playfully looked up at him with a tilted head and lolling tongue, his tail wagging, seemingly proud of his earlier disobedience. Having managed to herd the sheep back together, the shepherd's collie gave a tired but satisfied bark before returning to its post.

Darcy and Elizabeth walked across the bridge with Jasper, their pace leisurely as they began to practice commands. "Sit," Darcy instructed, and Jasper complied immediately. "Stay," he added, and Jasper remained still. Darcy walked away a few feet. "Come," Darcy continued, and Jasper trotted over. Darcy smiled at Elizabeth. "He's familiar with commands but has decided to obey only when it suits him."

Elizabeth returned his smile, enjoying the easy rhythm of their conversation. "He's certainly improved since the first time he knocked me down. Maybe he has selective hearing."

Darcy laughed at her jest. "True. He'll be the first dog I've owned with that quality, and I'll try to adapt to his whims." He leaned down and gently stroked the dog's head. "I thought he could become a carriage dog. His size and strength are appropriate for the job. However, he is too easily distracted. Instead of warning us of danger, he barked at every rabbit, carriage, and person he saw."

The conversation shifted to lighter topics as they walked toward a wooded path leading back to the castle. Elizabeth marveled at the man's ability to accept Jasper's foibles with laughter. The path coiled gently uphill, offering glimpses of the castle through the trees.

They strolled along the path; the gentle crunch of leaves beneath their feet provided a soothing background to their conversation. Elizabeth stole glances at Darcy, appreciating not only the beauty of the surroundings but also the relaxed and genuine manner in which Darcy interacted with Jasper.

"You know," Elizabeth began, her tone light, "it's remarkable how you handle Jasper's mischief with such patience. Most men would find it quite trying."

Darcy chuckled, his eyes twinkling with amusement. "I suppose it helps that I've grown quite fond of his antics. Plus, Jasper has a way of keeping things lively."

Elizabeth laughed softly, her eyes meeting his. "He certainly has a knack for bringing unpredictability wherever he goes. I'm glad to see you can find the humor in it."

Darcy's expression grew thoughtful as he glanced back at the bridge and the sheep meadow. "It's much like life itself, isn't it? We can't always control what happens but can choose how we respond."

Elizabeth's gaze drifted to the path ahead. "I think you're right. It's the way we handle life's challenges that shapes our experiences. Your ability to find humor and patience in Jasper's behavior speaks volumes about your character."

Darcy smiled, touched by her observation. "Thank you, Miss Elizabeth. I believe it's important to find joy in the little things, even amidst the chaos. It's something I've learned over the years. One of the most important things Jasper has taught me is never to let him off his leash if I want a peaceful walk."

Their conversation continued, weaving through topics both light-hearted and introspective. They spoke of their favorite books and recent travels. They shared anecdotes from their pasts. Each story and laugh brought them closer, and their connection grew with each step they took.

Elizabeth glanced up at Darcy, a warm smile on her lips. "This has been a delightful walk. I'm glad we could converse and enjoy the afternoon together."

Darcy's smile mirrored hers, his eyes reflecting the same contentment. "So am I. Spending time alone with you is a privilege."

They reached the castle's kitchen door, where the warmth and light from inside beckoned to Jasper. A servant opened the door to take the leash; Jasper recognized the kitchen and was happily led to his place on a rug by a closed stove, where a large bowl of water and his meal awaited.

Elizabeth and Darcy approached the main entrance of Pemberley; the sun had dipped lower in the sky, casting a softer, more golden light over the castle's façade, which seemed to invite them in, promising comfort and a cozy evening ahead.

Elizabeth commented, "It's amazing how the castle takes on a different hue as the day progresses," her voice filled with appreciation.

Darcy glanced thoughtfully at the structure. "It does have a way of changing with the light. Each time of day brings out a new facet of its beauty. I'm glad you've had the chance to see some of its variations."

They reached the main entrance, where the massive oak doors stood open. Darcy turned to Elizabeth with a gentle smile. "Shall we head to the drawing room? I believe Mrs. Reynolds has arranged a selection of warm beverages, and it would be nice to relax and enjoy some time with our friends before changing for dinner."

Elizabeth nodded, her eyes sparkling with anticipation. "That sounds wonderful."

When they stepped into the drawing room, its cozy ambiance enveloped them. Everyone else was already there, enjoying a hot beverage by the hearth. Seeing Elizabeth and Darcy, Georgiana brightened and approached them. "I'm so glad you've returned. Please, make yourselves comfortable."

Elizabeth thanked Georgiana and settled onto a plush sofa with a cup of hot tea, her gaze lingering on the fire as it crackled warmly. Darcy took his place beside her, and soon, the room filled with the murmur of conversation.

Chapter 20

Friday, November 29, 1811
Darcy

Darcy's frustration was mounting as he paced the length of his spacious chamber. The rhythm of his footsteps left impressions on the carpet, a tangible manifestation of his inner agitation. No matter how meticulously he planned, the universe appeared to conspire against him. He paused by the window, looking out at the grounds of Pemberley. The autumn foliage was a stunning sight, but it did little to calm his restlessness. He had been waiting for the perfect moment to speak with Elizabeth, to articulate his thoughts and feelings, but it seemed that such a moment was perpetually out of reach.

A week had passed in a blur of group activities, excursions, and family interactions, yet every attempt he made to secure a moment alone with Elizabeth seemed thwarted by the ceaseless company of his relatives and their guests. The closest he had come to speaking privately with Elizabeth was a fleeting encounter in the lobby the previous day when she was preparing to leave for Lambton with the other ladies. They had exchanged a few words about the day's itinerary, but the conversation had been brief and constrained by the presence of others.

His pacing grew more agitated. The family's insistence on constant companionship was both admirable and maddening. Darcy understood their desire to include everyone in the activities and conversations, but he felt that the continuous presence of others was a deliberate obstacle to his plans.

He ran a hand through his hair, trying to clear his thoughts. The evening promised another round of activities: a dinner at the castle and a gathering in the drawing room for card games. It would be another evening of idle chatter while his heart longed to debate philosophy or politics with Elizabeth.

The sound of a soft knock on the door interrupted his thoughts. Darcy opened the door, finding his sister Georgiana standing in the hall with a tentative smile.

"William, are you all right?" she asked, noting the tension in his posture.

Darcy forced a smile and joined Georgiana in the hall, his usual composure slightly strained. "I'm fine, Georgiana. Just... thinking."

Georgiana's eyes were filled with concern as she studied her brother. "You've been quite preoccupied lately. Does something trouble you? You seem more restless than usual."

Darcy hesitated, trying to find the right words to convey his frustration without causing undue worry. "I cannot find a moment alone with Miss Elizabeth. I want to get to know her better and have a more personal conversation, but it seems impossible with everyone constantly around."

Georgiana's expression softened with understanding, her brows knitting together thoughtfully. "I see. Everyone has been so engaged in the activities, and the constant company might make it difficult to find quiet moments. Perhaps you can arrange a more private encounter by adjusting your schedule."

Darcy looked at her gratefully, feeling a flicker of hope at her suggestion. "If you have any ideas, I would greatly appreciate them."

Georgiana's eyes lit up with a hint of mischief, her face brightening with inspiration. "Well, Lizzy is an early riser. She usually takes Jasper for a walk in the gardens shortly after sunrise. If you forego your usual morning ride and join them instead, you might have the opportunity to talk with her in a relaxed setting without everyone else lurking around."

Darcy's face brightened at the suggestion. "That sounds promising. Thank you, Sister."

Georgiana smiled reassuringly. "Of course, Brother. I'm glad I could help. I hope you find the chance you're looking for."

With a final, encouraging smile, Georgiana gave a little wave of her delicate hand and scampered away, her steps light and purposeful. Darcy watched her go, feeling optimistic. He took a deep breath, allowing his frustration to lift slightly. Darcy's relief was brief. He felt a hand on his shoulder. Turning, he found Richard standing behind him, a knowing grin on his face.

"Looks like you are in a better mood," Richard remarked, his tone teasing. "I can see the gears turning in that head of yours. What's the plan now? Plotting a grand romantic gesture, are we?"

Darcy raised an eyebrow, a slight smirk playing at his lips. "Richard, if you must know, I'm simply trying to find a quiet moment with Elizabeth. Georgiana suggested I join her for an early morning walk with Jasper, a good opportunity to speak with her without your constant supervision."

Richard chuckled, clapping Darcy on the back. "Ah, a morning stroll with Elizabeth. I see you've taken to romantic pursuits with the diligence of a general planning an invasion. I must say, your strategic approach is admirable."

Darcy shot Richard a sidelong glance, though his expression was light-hearted. "Very funny. If you have more words of wisdom or witty remarks, now is the time."

Richard's grin widened. "Well, if you're open to advice, be genuine; she'll appreciate that far more than any grand gestures or elaborate schemes."

Darcy appreciated the insight. "I'll keep that in mind. Finding the right balance between private conversation with Elizabeth and the whirlwind of group interactions is proving more challenging than I anticipated."

Richard's eyes softened slightly with understanding. "It's a challenge, but one worth the effort. And who knows, perhaps today will be the opportunity you've been hoping for. I warn you, don't let me catch you rehearsing your lines in front of the mirror."

Darcy laughed, shaking his head. "I promise, no rehearsals."

As Richard turned to leave, he gave Darcy one last teasing look. "Good luck, Darcy. You have missed the opportunity for a morning walk today, but there's always tomorrow. And remember, no pressure. It's only your future happiness at stake."

Darcy watched Richard walk away, his spirits buoyed by the encouragement and wondering when Richard would cease interfering. With a renewed sense of purpose, Darcy headed to his study. He must rearrange his schedule to accommodate Georgiana's suggestion.

Upon reaching his study, Darcy settled into his chair and began sifting through the stack of daily correspondence. Most letters were routine updates and business matters, but one, bearing the distinctive handwriting of an unknown gentleman, caught his eye. He opened it, his curiosity piqued. He sought the signature. The letter was from Mr. Bennet.

November 25, 1811

Longbourn, Meryton

Mr. Darcy,

I trust this letter finds you and my daughters well. I must inform you of a somewhat amusing turn of events at Netherfield Park. It appears that our recent visitors have been driven away—not by any fault of the establishment or the company, but rather by a lively rat infestation that erupted over the weekend. Indeed, the rats particularly liked the Bingleys' sumptuous quarters.

Miss Bingley, unbeknownst to her brother, banished the house cats. This banishment proved to be disastrous. The house was inundated with hundreds of rats. It is a fine testament to the adaptability of our modern society that the smallest creatures can so swiftly upend one's social aspirations.

From the accounts of my servants, the situation was quite chaotic. The Bingleys, being rather fond of their comfort, decided that an infestation of the more pestilent kind was not to their liking. This morning, the spectacle of Mr. Bingley and his sisters fleeing Netherfield was like watching an army in retreat. It is the talk of the neighborhood. Their retreat to London, leaving the rat catchers in charge of the battle to reclaim the estate for humanity, will amuse our twenty-four families in the immediate future.

I hope that the next time someone rents Netherfield, the mansion will be free of any vermin attempting to overtake it. Of course, Mr. Phillips will alter all future rental agreements to require the tenants to keep the three indoor cats the owner provides inside the manor house.

In any case, I trust you are enjoying your time at Pemberley and managing to keep your affairs free of such pestilent disturbances.

Please pass on my regards to your entire party. I look forward to hearing all about your adventures.

Yours,

Thomas Bennet

DARCY'S LIPS QUIRKED into a smile as he finished reading the letter. Mr. Bennet's humor, though often sharp, had a way of lightening the mood. Darcy could easily picture the chaos at Netherfield, the Bingleys' discomfort, and the rats claiming their territory. It was a minor, amusing distraction from the pressing concerns weighing on him.

With a chuckle still lingering on his lips, Darcy set the letter aside. He focused on the rest of his correspondence, methodically sorting through the pile. Important matters were marked for immediate action, while less urgent tasks were delegated to a second pile. The routine was comforting, a reminder of the order and control he prided himself on maintaining.

When his house steward/correspondence secretary entered, each letter was reviewed. The man sat at a small writing desk, quickly answering each missive according to Darcy's instructions. Darcy read and signed the replies while Mr. Sanders sealed the signed missives. The bulk of the accumulated correspondence was gone until the weekly packet from London arrived on Monday. He dismissed Mr. Sanders with a tight smile, knowing the man had more important duties to occupy his time.

As he reviewed his schedule, Darcy focused on finding time to speak privately with Elizabeth. He mentally adjusted his plans to accommodate an early morning walk with her, ensuring that any pressing business matters would be handled after breakfast. He allotted three hours in the afternoon for meetings and administrative tasks, confident that this arrangement would allow him to fully engage in his conversation with Elizabeth without the usual interruptions.

After finishing his work, Darcy stood and stretched, feeling the tension in his shoulders lessen. He locked his study door, his mind shifting to the afternoon's social obligations. The castle was alive with activity, and Darcy moved toward the music room.

The music room was Georgiana's favorite retreat, and as Darcy approached, he was greeted by the gentle strains of a pianoforte. The sound was a soothing melody that drifted through the hallways, drawing him closer. He stood quietly in the open doorway, careful not to interrupt the delicate performance.

Inside, Georgiana's nimble fingers danced gracefully over the keys. Her brow was slightly furrowed in concentration, and her face was serene, illuminated by the soft afternoon light filtering through the room's large windows.

Lady Matlock and Miss Jane Bennet were seated on a velvet sofa. They leaned close together, their heads bowed in whispered conversation. Jane's cheeks were flushed with amusement, her eyes sparkling as she shared a private joke with Lady Matlock. The light-heartedness of their discussion was a pleasant contrast to Georgiana's focused playing.

Across the room, near the long windows draped with flowing curtains, Miss Elizabeth engaged in lively conversation with Rebecca and Richard. Elizabeth's laughter rang out, clear and bright, as she animatedly recounted a story. Rebecca's eyes sparkled with mirth, and Richard's deep, hearty laughter added to the convivial atmosphere.

Darcy took a moment to appreciate the scene. The room was filled with a warm, inviting ambiance, and the music was a gentle backdrop for the occupant's cheerful interactions. He inhaled deeply, savoring the tranquility that seemed to permeate the space. His earlier frustration began to dissolve, replaced by a sense of calm.

Darcy entered the room and went to a comfortable chair near the piano. The chair was upholstered in a rich brocade that complemented the room's decor. He settled into it, feeling the plushness beneath him and the sense of peace that the room provided.

"Georgiana," he said softly, not wanting to startle her, "I hope you're not too engrossed to entertain a visitor."

Georgiana's fingers stilled on the keys as she looked up. Her face brightened with a warm smile, her eyes reflecting genuine pleasure. "William! I was just practicing a new piece. I'd be delighted to have your company."

Darcy's gaze softened as he met her eyes. "It sounded lovely. I'm glad I came. I enjoy listening to you play."

Georgiana's cheeks flushed with pleasure at his compliment. "Thank you. I've been working on this piece for several days. It's not perfect yet, but I'm hopeful it will be soon."

Lady Matlock and Jane looked up from their conversation, smiling at Darcy. Lady Matlock shared, "Darcy, we were just discussing the latest gossip from London. It seems you've escaped the clutches of town speculation for now."

Darcy chuckled. "I'm grateful for the respite. And it's nice to see everyone so engaged. Is there anything in particular I should know about?"

Rebecca called out, "Richard and I were reminiscing about some amusing anecdotes from our last season in town. Our London friends are always good for a story or two."

Still standing with Richard and Rebecca, Elizabeth said, "I had little gossip to share and had to rely on amusing your cousins with a story about our indoor cat, Petunia." She moved closer to Lady Matlock and sat in an armchair near her sister. Richard followed her example, and the group settled into a semicircle around the piano.

Darcy leaned back in his chair, wondering why everyone was discussing events in London. Savoring the tranquil atmosphere of the room, he turned his attention to Georgiana's music. The conversation around him was light and pleasant, and he felt a pang of contentment that had been elusive recently.

Darcy decided it was the perfect moment to share Mr. Bennet's letter. Reaching into his jacket pocket, he pulled out the folded paper. The letter had been a source of amusement and distraction for him earlier, and he was eager to share it with the others.

"While we're all enjoying this lovely afternoon," Darcy began, addressing the group, "I received a rather entertaining letter from Mr. Bennet this morning. I thought you might appreciate a bit of humor."

Georgiana paused her playing and looked up with interest. Lady Matlock and Jane turned their attention to Darcy, curiosity piqued. Elizabeth, who had been conversing with Rebecca, glanced at him with an expectant smile.

Darcy unfolded the letter carefully, his eyes scanning the lines before he read the letter. At its conclusion, a ripple of laughter broke out among the listeners. Jane's eyes widened in amusement, and Lady Matlock's lips twitched into a smile. Even Georgiana, who had resumed playing softly in the background, seemed to enjoy the story.

The room erupted in laughter. Elizabeth's eyes twinkled with mirth, and she glanced at Darcy with an appreciative grin. "My father certainly has a way with words. I can only imagine the chaos at Netherfield."

Richard chuckled, shaking his head. "It's a good thing we didn't encounter such a situation during our visit."

Darcy added, his voice steady. "'I must say, the spectacle of Mr. Bingley and his sisters fleeing Netherfield like an army in retreat was something I wish I had seen. Fortunately, the situation has been rectified with the assistance of some local vermin catchers, and the house is once again in a state of order."

Lady Matlock, still smiling, said, "Indeed. Mr. Bennet's letter has certainly lightened the mood. Thank you for sharing it with us, Darcy."

Georgiana looked at Darcy with a teasing smile. "Even from a distance, your friend's misadventures make for delightful reading."

Darcy nodded, pleased with the positive reaction. "I thought everyone might enjoy it. Sometimes, a bit of humor is just what we need to brighten our day."

As the laughter subsided, the conversation shifted back to lighter topics, with the group discussing recent events and sharing their own stories. The room was filled with the pleasant hum of conversation, punctuated by occasional laughter. Darcy felt a renewed sense of ease, the earlier tension melting away as he enjoyed the company of friends and family, the music from Georgiana's pianoforte providing gentle harmony to the afternoon's camaraderie.

Chapter 21

Friday, November 29, 1811
Elizabeth

The afternoon sunlight filtered through the music room's long windows, casting a warm glow over the group as they conversed and enjoyed Mr. Bennet's letter. Elizabeth, feeling contented, glanced around the room with a smile. The shared laughter had been a welcome distraction from her thoughts, and she was eager to savor the remainder of the day.

As the conversation gradually ebbed, Elizabeth excused herself from the group and returned to her room to prepare for the evening meal. She reflected on the past few days, considering the various conversations and her growing familiarity with Darcy and Georgiana. She enjoyed their company immensely and was curious about Darcy's intentions and frequent absences during the day.

Elizabeth's mind wandered back to the letter she had received from her father that morning just as the group prepared for their day's activities. Elizabeth withdrew the letter from her pocket and unfolded it, letting its familiar script bring her a sense of connection to home. Mr. Bennet's words were always a mix of humor and practicality, and this letter was no different. It was a brief but thoughtful note that offered a snapshot of life at Longbourn.

November 25, 1811

Longbourn, Meryton

My Dearest Lizzy,

I trust this letter finds you in good health and spirits. Life at Longbourn has settled into its usual rhythm since your departure. Your mother remains absorbed in her schemes, focusing on Kitty and Lydia. She is determined to secure their futures, though her methods remain as zealous and unrealistic as ever.

Kitty and Lydia are in good health despite their recent escapades, though Lydia's spirited nature continues to cause minor disturbances. I have managed to keep her enthusiasm in check, though it requires much patience. On the other hand, Mary continues her studies with admirable diligence; her moralizing lectures now focus on the virtues of modesty and industry.

I was pleased to hear of your safe arrival at Pemberley and am heartened by reports of your evident enjoyment of Mr. Darcy's company. It would be interesting to know if your opinion of him has softened. His recent actions and your experiences thus far may have given you new perspectives on his character.

Do convey my regards to Jane, the Darcys, and your friends. I look forward to hearing more about your adventures and your views on Mr. Darcy as time permits.

Yours affectionately,

Papa

ELIZABETH FOLDED THE letter thoughtfully, reflecting on Mr. Bennet's questions and observations. Her father's wit and concern were always evident in his correspondence, but this letter focused on Mr. Darcy. She recalled the earlier conversation with Darcy and his recounting Mr. Bennet's sardonic letter about the Bingleys' predicament with the rats. The amusement she found in Mr. Bennet's humor mingled with curiosity about her father's interest in her developing relationship with Darcy. *Why?*

Elizabeth smiled and considered how her perceptions of Darcy might change with her growing experiences. Darcy was courteous and engaging, and while her initial reservations were significant, their interactions had softened. She was eager to share her observations with her father, though she knew it would be a while before she could put her reflections into words.

The thought of writing to her family and updating them on her experiences at Pemberley brought Elizabeth a sense of comfort and connection. She knew her father's letter was both an inquiry and an encouragement toward establishing a better relationship with Darcy.

Elizabeth prepared for the evening meal and the following entertainment by selecting a simple gown in a light green shade that complemented her eyes. The evening was chilly, and she opted for a wool shawl to keep warm. Adjusting her hair and checking her appearance in the mirror, Elizabeth thought about Darcy. His determination to be pleasant was evident, and she wondered if it was a true reflection of his personality.

When Elizabeth stepped into the drawing room, she admired the intricate arrangements of flowers and elegant candelabras on the side tables, their flickering flames casting a soft, warm glow across the room. Seasonal garlands of oak leaves, interspersed with deep red berries, were draped along the mantelpiece and the edges of the windows. The room was a vision of autumnal splendor, with rich hues of gold and amber reflecting the warmth of the evening. The scent of roasted meats and freshly baked bread wafted through the air, mingling with the aroma of spiced wine and fragrant herbs.

Lady Matlock and Rebecca were chatting with Georgiana and Jane near the fireplace. At the same time, Richard and Darcy were engaged in a lively discussion about the day's events, enhanced by laughter and the clinking of glasses.

Georgiana called out, "Elizabeth, you look lovely this evening," Georgiana took Elizabeth's hand. "What do you think of the decorations?"

Elizabeth smiled, her eyes absorbing the beauty of the room. "Thank you, Georgiana. You look lovely, too. The décor is enchanting, the arrangements are beautiful, the room feels inviting, and I'm looking forward to the evening."

Darcy heard her comment and approached her, his expression warm and welcoming. "I'm glad you're pleased with the decorations, Miss Elizabeth," he said, his voice carrying a note of pride. "Georgiana and the staff have put great effort into making this evening special."

Lady Matlock joined them, holding a goblet of spiced wine. "Elizabeth, dear, have you tried the mulled wine? It's a recipe from one of our old family traditions, and I think it's quite delightful."

Elizabeth accepted the glass with a grateful smile. "I haven't had the chance yet, Lady Matlock, but I'm looking forward to trying it."

She took a sip, savoring the warm, spiced flavor. "It's delicious," she said, her eyes reflecting genuine enjoyment. "Thank you for sharing this with me."

As the conversation continued, Richard made his way over with a plate of delicacies, offering them to Elizabeth with a grin. "Here, try one of these. They're the chef's latest creation, and I think you'll find them quite delectable."

Elizabeth accepted a small pastry, taking a bite and savoring the flavor. "Oh, these are delightful. Do I detect a hint of lemon?"

Observing the interaction with a sense of contentment, Darcy joined in with a chuckle. "Richard is known for his culinary discoveries. I believe he's determined to ensure that we never go hungry."

Richard, catching Darcy's remark, grinned widely. "Well, it's not difficult with the remarkable cook you have at Pemberley. I'm merely here to make sure the standards are maintained. Besides, it's always more enjoyable to sample new creations with good company."

When the butler announced dinner, Darcy extended his arm to Lady Matlock, guiding her toward the family dining room. Richard escorted Georgiana and Rebecca while Jane and Elizabeth followed closely behind.

The dining room was elegantly set with a large round table at the center, facilitating informal and intimate seating arrangements. The room was warm and inviting, with flickering candlelight casting a soft glow over the polished mahogany table and the fine china. The scent of savory dishes wafted through the air.

Darcy sat beside Elizabeth, with Richard seated to Jane's right. Lady Matlock and Rebecca occupied the opposite side of the table, with Georgiana sitting between them, ensuring a lively exchange of conversation and ideas. The discussion was animated and engaging, covering a wide range of topics from the day's events to amusing anecdotes from the past.

Richard's stories of his travels in Portugal were particularly captivating. He recounted his experiences with infectious enthusiasm, his commentary laced with humor and insight.

"You wouldn't believe the market in Lisbon," he said with a twinkle in his eye. "I was convinced the vendors were trying to sell me every fish in the sea! The market was a riot of colors and sounds. Stalls overflowed with vibrant fruits and vegetables—apples, pears, figs, and grapes glistening in the sunlight. The air was thick with the salty scent of the sea, mingling with the aroma of freshly baked bread. Vendors shouted their prices, their voices competing with the crowd's clamor. It was as if the entire city had gathered there, each person haggling with determination. And the fish! Oh, the fish! Every imaginable kind, from the smallest sardines to the largest tuna, laid out on beds of crushed ice. It was a scene of organized chaos, and I loved every moment."

Jane smiled, her eyes sparkling with amusement and a glance at her sister. "I can only imagine. Did you manage to escape with your purse intact?"

Richard chuckled. "Barely. The charm of the market made me forget all caution. It was delightfully chaotic, and I must say, the seafood was worth every penny."

Sitting beside Elizabeth, Darcy joined the discussion with his characteristic wit. "Richard has a knack for attracting adventures in the marketplace or a quiet village. It seems he's always involved in some escapade."

Elizabeth turned to Darcy, appreciating his sharp intellect and engaging manner. "Indeed, Mr. Darcy. Your stories are just as enthralling. I've enjoyed hearing about your various endeavors and perspectives on the world."

"My adventures in foreign lands are limited to viewing various estates. My tales are boring compared to my cousin's adventures," Darcy replied.

Lady Matlock contributed anecdotes and observations to the discussion with tales of Edinburgh.

"Edinburgh is a city of contrasts," Lady Matlock began, her eyes sparkling with fond memories. "The Old Town's winding, cobbled streets are steeped in history, each corner revealing a new story. I recall walking down the Royal Mile, where the scent of fresh bread from the bakeries mingled with the crisp, cool air. The ancient buildings, with their dark stone facades, seemed to whisper secrets of the past."

Rebecca nodded enthusiastically. "And the New Town is equally fascinating, with its elegant Georgian architecture. The wide streets and grand squares are a testament to the city's growth and prosperity. I remember visiting the bustling markets, where vendors sold everything from fresh produce to fine fabrics. The people were always so welcoming."

Lady Matlock laughed. "Do you remember the tale of Greyfriars Bobby? The loyal dog who guarded his master's grave for fourteen years? Such stories add a touch of magic to the city."

Georgiana smiled, her eyes moving between the two women. "It sounds like Edinburgh is a place where history and the present coexist beautifully. I would love to visit someday and experience it for myself."

Elizabeth was thoroughly engrossed in the discourse flowing around the table as the meal progressed. The combination of stimulating conversation, delectable food, and the warmth of good company created an atmosphere of genuine pleasure.

After the meal, the guests retired to the drawing room for after-dinner entertainment. Her eyes sparkling with anticipation, Georgiana clapped her hands together, her excitement evident. "Let's play charades! It's always such fun, and it's been ages since we last played."

"Ah, charades," Darcy said with a smile. "The game that reveals both hidden talents and questionable improvisational skills."

Richard, always quick with a quip, added, "And it's an excellent way to see who truly has a knack for dramatic expression—or lacks it entirely."

Teams were quickly formed, with Jane and Elizabeth paired with Georgiana, while Darcy, Richard, and Rebecca formed the opposing team. Lady Matlock excused herself from the activity, desiring to watch the proceedings. The game commenced enthusiastically.

Darcy was first up for his team and took his role with dramatic flair. He mimed "The Tempest" with exaggerated gestures of stormy seas and wild winds. His performance was so convincing that even Lady Matlock was drawn into the spectacle.

Elizabeth watched Darcy with amused admiration. His ability to convey the essence of each charade with such skill captivated her. Her eyes followed his every movement, and she occasionally caught his gaze before blushing and looking away.

When it was Elizabeth's turn, she was tasked with "A Midsummer Night's Dream." Her portrayal of the fairy queen was met with hearty applause. She fluttered about the room, casting imaginary spells with sweeping gestures and a twinkle in her eye, her performance both enchanting and endearing.

Darcy leaned toward Elizabeth and said, "You know, you have a rather magical way with charades. I almost believed in fairies for a moment."

Elizabeth laughed, her cheeks flushed with delight. "Thank you, Mr. Darcy. You know where to find me if you ever need a fairy queen for a grand ball."

Richard became a comical pirate as the game continued, his exaggerated swagger and booming voice earning him roars of laughter from the room. Rebecca attempted to mime "The Lady of the Lake" with all the subtlety of a dramatic heroine, her expressive gestures drawing chuckles and applause.

By the time the game concluded, the group was in high spirits, their laughter echoing through the drawing room. The competition had been fierce, but the joy of the evening overrode any desire to claim victory.

With the game over, Elizabeth conversed with Darcy about literature, travel, and philosophy.

"It's fascinating," Elizabeth said, leaning slightly forward, "how literature can offer such profound insights into human nature. I've always believed that the greatest authors reveal truths about ourselves we might not even recognize."

Darcy nodded, his expression thoughtful. "Indeed. Books can serve as mirrors, reflecting both our virtues and our flaws. They challenge us to think deeply and grow."

Elizabeth tilted her head, intrigued. "Do you have a favorite book or author that has particularly influenced your views?"

Darcy's eyes softened as he considered the question. "One that comes to mind is 'The Pilgrim's Progress.' Its allegory of personal growth and redemption has always resonated with me."

Elizabeth smiled, appreciating his choice. "A timeless classic. It's amazing how certain works can remain relevant and thought-provoking through the ages."

Their conversation flowed easily and was marked by a surprising depth of understanding. They exchanged ideas and insights, and Elizabeth discovered Darcy's thoughtful and engaging character. The evening's activities forged a deeper connection between them, and the warmth of the discussion added to Elizabeth's admiration of Darcy.

The night concluded with a selection of musical performances by Georgiana and Rebecca, plus a few impromptu vocal contributions from Lady Matlock, Jane, and Elizabeth. The music filled the room with a soothing ambiance, and as the guests drifted away, Elizabeth felt a sense of satisfaction and contentment.

Chapter 22

Saturday, November 30, 1811
Disruption

The blizzard had arrived as if summoned by a magic spell, blanketing Pemberley in a pristine layer of snow overnight. The morning sun could not pierce through the thick, swirling flakes that continued to fall, transforming the estate into a winter wonderland. The world outside was muffled, the usual sounds of the countryside hushed under the thick, white quilt.

Elizabeth awoke to snow-covered grounds stretching as far as the eye could see. The view from her window was breathtaking; the trees and rooftops held a delicate frost that glistened like diamonds in the weak sunlight. She marveled at the beauty, feeling awe at nature's many facets. She had been looking forward to taking the dog out for their usual romp in the gardens. Georgiana had promised to join her, and the prospect of a brisk walk with the energetic canine had been a highlight of her mornings at Pemberley. Today, a walk with Jasper was out of the question.

In the breakfast room, Elizabeth was greeted by the scent of freshly baked bread and brewing coffee mingled with the aroma of the hearth fire, creating a comforting cocoon against the cold outside. The residents drifted into the room, filling their plates from the sideboard and taking their seats.

A disappointed Darcy joined the group and looked out the window wistfully. "We've been granted an early winter storm," he remarked. The snow is still falling heavily, and the wind is fierce. I doubt the roads will be passable today."

Richard, always one to make light of a situation, grinned and said, "Well, it appears that nature has conspired to give us a day of enforced leisure. How fortunate we are!"

Her cheeks flushed with excitement, Georgiana said, "I love the snow. It's so magical and serene. Do you think we'll be able to go sledding later?"

With a gentle smile, Jane added, "It would be wonderful to go sledding. Though the snow and the wind must first stop."

Lady Matlock looked up and said, "We must ensure everyone stays warm and comfortable. A day like this calls for cozy fires and perhaps indoor entertainment. The snow is too deep to venture outside."

Elizabeth, her spirits buoyed by the lively conversation and the prospect of a snowy day, turned to Darcy. "It seems we might have a day of unexpected relaxation. What do you plan to do with your time today?"

Darcy met her gaze with amusement and replied, "I must check on the outdoor staff. They must clear snow from the courtyard and buildings. But I must admit, I'm also looking forward to some leisure time. Perhaps we could all engage in some indoor games or storytelling." He glanced at the long windows that opened onto the patio.

The snowfall showed no signs of letting up, and the wind began to howl outside. The sight of the swirling snowflakes and the heavy drifts accumulating against the windows made it impossible to consider venturing out.

Seeing Elizabeth's disappointed expression, Darcy placed a comforting hand on her shoulder. "I'm afraid your walk with Jasper will have to wait for a better day," he said softly. "The storm has made it rather impractical for humans to go outside without a shovel, tall boots, and warm coats."

Elizabeth sighed in disappointment. "I suppose it's for the best. We wouldn't want to risk getting lost in such a storm, but I look forward to seeing Jasper and Bacon enjoy the snow through a window once the staff clears a path."

The group quickly adapted to the situation. Darcy and Richard organized a team of footmen to clear the patios, garden, courtyard, and driveway, ensuring the snow could not cause significant damage. The two men, bundled up against the cold, worked diligently with the staff to manage the snow's effects while the rest of the ladies remained inside.

Elizabeth, Jane, Georgiana, Rebecca, and Lady Matlock decided to seek out the warmest drawing room in the castle and settle in for a cozy afternoon. Georgiana suggested, "Why don't we make the most of this snowy day by engaging in restful activities? I brought my embroidery downstairs and would be delighted to work on it while we chat."

Very fond of crafts, Lady Matlock agreed. "That sounds wonderful. I've begun a new sewing project and could use some company. Discussing our various projects as we work will be a pleasure."

Eager to contribute, Jane retrieved her embroidery hoop and joined Georgiana at one of the low tables with her sewing supplies. "I've been working on a new pattern for a handkerchief. It's a bit intricate, but I enjoy the challenge."

Intrigued by the prospect of practicing her skills, Rebecca asked, "Do you mind if I join you? Sewing will be a lovely way to pass the time."

Elizabeth sat by the fire, knitting a wool cap, feeling the warmth seep into her bones. An hour later, she looked up from her task and glanced toward the crackling flames and the snow-laden windows when Darcy and Richard entered the drawing room.

Darcy said, "Since our plans to walk the grounds have been thwarted, how about a chess game or cards to pass the time? I've been itching to practice my strategy."

Richard enthusiastically responded with a grin. "A game of chess sounds splendid. I've been practicing my opening moves. Perhaps you'll find me more challenging than usual!"

Intrigued by the prospect, Elizabeth said, "A friendly competition is a great idea. I'd be happy to watch and play the winner."

With Darcy and Richard preparing the chessboard, Georgiana, Jane, Rebecca, and Lady Matlock continued embroidering and sewing. The room was filled with the gentle hum of conversation, the rustle of fabric, and the occasional laughter.

When the chess game commenced, Elizabeth and the others exchanged their thoughts on the day's events. Looking up from her sewing, Lady Matlock remarked, "It's rather charming how the storm has brought us all together in such an intimate way. We rarely have the chance to engage in these simple pleasures."

Georgiana agreed. "Indeed. It's a reminder that sometimes the best moments are those spent with loved ones."

Rebecca, her hands deftly maneuvering her embroidery needle, added, "This is the first time I've seen this many ladies engaged in needlework. It's usually only Mama and me."

Lady Matlock said, "I'm sure Jane and Elizabeth sew often with six ladies at Longbourn. At times, I regret having no other daughters."

The chess game proceeded with intense focus, punctuated by occasional playful banter. Elizabeth abandoned knitting to demonstrate a keen interest that matched the men's competitive spirit in their chess match. Occasionally, a move was met with a cheer or a groan, adding to the game's overall enjoyment.

As the afternoon wore on, the group transitioned to card games, which provided a change of pace and a chance for everyone to showcase their luck and skill. Laughter and friendly competition filled the room as they played, with Elizabeth winning a few rounds, much to her delight.

The snow continued to blanket the world outside, with no signs of letting up. The view from the windows was a mesmerizing blend of swirling white and fading light. The group enjoyed a hearty dinner, and as they dined, conversations turned to plans for the following day. They discussed the possibility of snowball fights, sledding, and other winter activities; their excitement was tangible despite the raging blizzard.

Chapter 23

Monday, December 2, 1811
Pemberley

The return of warmer weather and heavy rain brought unexpected complications to the castle's inhabitants. The deep blanket of snow began to melt rapidly, transforming into torrents of water that rushed down the mountain and through the estate. Streams swelled, their banks straining under the pressure, while silt and mud spilled over, creating an unsightly mess along the edges.

The lake, usually a serene focal point of the grounds, was now brimming with water. Its surface glistened under the weak sun but threatened to overflow onto the surrounding beach and grass as streams continued to flow into it, creating waves and large ripples. The once neat and manicured lawns surrounding the castle on three sides were becoming soggy and saturated, making it difficult for the footmen and gardeners to maintain the estate's usual standards.

Water formed puddles in the courtyard and lapped at the stone steps leading into the rear entrance. The air was filled with the earthy scent of wet soil and the faint, musty odor of dampness.

Darcy stood by the window in the drawing room, gazing out at the scene. "This is quite the predicament," he murmured, rubbing the back of his neck. "We must address the drainage issues before rain falls again or the temperature drops below freezing."

Georgiana joined him, her brow furrowed with concern. "Will the paths be usable? I worry about how everyone will navigate the estate."

Darcy grimaced, his expression serious. "I'll instruct the staff to clear the minor culverts of debris and dig trenches to guide the runoff toward the streams. Fortunately, the stables are on higher ground, and the remaining section of the moat at the castle's rear is intact. If it fills up, the staff can open the water gate to direct excess water into the underground tunnel, which will empty into the river. At times like this, I regret our grandfather's decision to fill most of the moat and convert the area into pleasure gardens. The lower park and paths will be muddy."

Just then, Richard entered, shaking his head as he observed the view. "The lake is rising faster than anticipated. If this continues, everyone will wade through puddles for a week."

"Exactly," Darcy replied, a hint of frustration creeping into his voice. "I'll call for the groundskeeper and consult him on a plan to manage the potential problems concerning our private roadways and trails. Thankfully, our groundskeeper and steward wisely instructed the staff to shovel the snow away from the castle and other structures into the moat. We have enough supplies to negate the need to travel to Lambton for a few weeks. Hopefully, a few days of good weather will dry the roads and paths."

After consulting with the groundskeeper, Darcy was ready to relax with his friends and family. He went to the doorway and spoke to the footman. "Please order a tea tray and have a maid bring it to this room." The footman left, and Darcy returned to the room and claimed an armchair near the fireplace.

The tea arrived as Jane and Elizabeth entered the drawing room. Elizabeth felt the tension and asked, "What's happening outside? It seems the weather has changed dramatically."

"Indeed," Darcy replied, turning his attention to the ladies. "The snow is melting far too quickly, causing quite a mess around the grounds. We're discussing ways to manage the water runoff before it causes permanent damage."

Jane's eyes widened with concern. "Oh dear! I hope it doesn't disrupt the gardens too much. They were so beautiful before the storm."

Darcy's expression turned serious. "Thank you for your concern. My staff will be working to prevent as much damage as possible." He glanced around the room, noticing that Lady Matlock and her daughter were missing.

"Richard, where are your mother and sister?" he asked.

Richard shrugged nonchalantly. "How would I know? I'm not their keeper." However, his surreptitious glance at Georgiana did not escape Darcy's notice. Georgiana looked down at her feet, a mischievous smile tugging at the corners of her mouth.

Darcy raised an eyebrow, suspicion growing. "Is there something I should know?"

Before anyone could respond, a commotion erupted from the hallway, consisting of muffled laughter, scampering footsteps, and the unmistakable sound of barking dogs. Elizabeth exchanged a curious glance with Jane, both suppressing smiles.

Lady Matlock and Rebecca burst into the room, each cradling a plump house cat in their arms. Lady Matlock held Sir Whiskers, a dignified long-haired gray cat with striking eyes, while Rebecca cuddled Miss Poppy, a fluffy young calico with a perpetually amused expression.

Trailing behind them were Jasper and Bacon, their tails wagging furiously. The feline guests intrigued the dogs, their noses twitching and their eyes alert.

"Mother, what on earth are you doing?" Richard asked, struggling to keep a straight face.

Lady Matlock grinned impishly. "We thought a little entertainment might lift everyone's spirits during this dreary weather."

Rebecca chimed in, her eyes sparkling with mischief. "Yes, and what better way than a visit with our beloved pets?"

Darcy sighed in amused exasperation. "I'm almost afraid to ask, but what exactly did you have in mind?"

Lady Matlock set Sir Whiskers down gently on a plush rug. "We thought the cats might hide, and the dogs will attempt to find them. It will be a splendid diversion!"

Georgiana clapped her hands softly. "Oh, that does sound amusing!"

Elizabeth chuckled. "I must admit, I'm curious to see how this develops without causing a disaster."

Richard shook his head, laughing. "This has the makings of a grand fiasco."

Lady Matlock waved a dismissive hand. "Nonsense! It will be perfectly controlled. Besides, the cats are quite used to the dogs. They even cuddle together at times."

Rebecca placed Miss Poppy beside Sir Whiskers. The two cats exchanged glances that conveyed a mutual understanding of the silliness ahead. Meanwhile, Jasper and Bacon sat obediently, their excitement at being in the drawing room barely contained.

"Now," Lady Matlock began with the authority of a seasoned ringmaster, "the rules are simple. The cats will hide somewhere in the drawing room, and after counting to twenty, the dogs will search for them."

Darcy pinched the bridge of his nose but couldn't hide his smile. "Very well. But please ensure the game remains... civilized."

The felines sauntered away with their tails held high as if to say they were not participating in a game but simply exploring the room. Sir Whiskers nestled under a wool shawl that cascaded over the arm of a chair, and Miss Poppy perched precariously atop some books, endangering a decorative vase and a small covered bowl.

Lady Matlock began the countdown, and the entire room joined in. "One... two... three..."

At "five!" Rebecca encouraged the dogs, saying, "Go find them," pointing randomly around the room.

Jasper and Bacon sprang to their feet and trotted forward, noses to the ground. Bacon sniffed diligently around the room's perimeter while Jasper became distracted by a stray ball of yarn near Georgiana's embroidery basket.

Bacon soon picked up a scent and headed toward Sir Whiskers. Sensing impending discovery, Sir Whiskers made a dignified dash across the room. The sudden movement caught Jasper's attention, and he abandoned the yarn to join the pursuit.

Seeing a cat stalked by two eager dogs made the onlookers laugh. Sir Whiskers leaped gracefully onto a low table, then onto the back of a sofa, where he sat and began grooming himself nonchalantly.

Meanwhile, Miss Poppy decided to join the fun. She meowed loudly, capturing the dogs' attention, then hopped down from the books onto Jasper's back, sending the books flying. She subsequently lept to the floor and padded toward the doorway. Jasper and Bacon followed her, tails wagging, but the calico deftly sidestepped them, causing the dogs to bump into each other. She reversed course, darted between their legs, and headed for a cushion, where she curled up with a soft "Meow."

Richard slapped his knee. "I haven't seen such coordination since the last officers' ball!"

Elizabeth wiped a tear of laughter from her eye. "Your pets are quite the performers."

Lady Matlock beamed. "I told you it would be entertaining!"

Darcy shook his head, chuckling. "I must admit, Aunt, your scheme has lifted the mood."

Georgiana giggled as Jasper, realizing he'd been outsmarted, settled for bringing the ball of yarn to Miss Poppy, dropping it at her paws in a gesture of canine goodwill. The cat regarded the offering with regal indifference before batting the yarn playfully.

Rebecca clapped her hands. "Look! They're playing ball together!"

The dogs and cats continued their gentle frolic, much to the delight of the assembled company. The earlier concerns about the estate's flooding were momentarily forgotten as everyone sipped a cup of tea and watched the impromptu pet antics.

After a while, Lady Matlock declared, "I think our performers deserve a treat." She produced a small pouch of bacon bits from her pocket, handing them to the eager animals.

Once the pets settled down, the group moved to the seating area.

Richard leaned back in his chair. "Mother, I must concede, your idea was a success."

Lady Matlock sipped her tea with a satisfied smile. "I'm glad you all enjoyed it. Sometimes, a little whimsy is just what we need."

Darcy glanced at Elizabeth, who was still smiling. "It appears my family's penchant for theatrics has its advantages."

Elizabeth met his gaze warmly. "It certainly makes for delightful company."

Georgiana set down her teacup. "Perhaps later, we could teach the dogs some new tricks. I've been working on a few commands with Jasper."

Rebecca nodded enthusiastically. "And I can show you how Miss Poppy plays fetch. She's quite talented for a cat!"

The afternoon passed pleasantly, with stories, laughter, and the shared enjoyment of simple pleasures. Darcy felt a profound sense of gratitude. Despite the challenges outside, within Pemberley, there was joy and camaraderie.

Turning to Elizabeth, he said softly, "Thank you for embracing my family's... unconventional methods of entertainment."

She smiled softly. "There's never a dull moment here, is there?"

"Indeed not," he replied, his eyes reflecting her mirth. "And for that, I am grateful."

Lady Matlock stood and stretched gracefully. "Well, that was a splendid afternoon's entertainment. I believe a fine meal and perhaps some music later would be the perfect way to conclude the day."

Everyone agreed, and as they left the drawing room, the lingering echoes of laughter served as a pleasant reminder of the joy that could be found even in the most unexpected circumstances.

Chapter 24

Tuesday, December 3, 1811
Elizabeth & Darcy

Elizabeth Bennet opened her eyes slowly, the soft morning light filtering through the curtains, and yawned, shaking off the remnants of sleep. She pushed aside the luxurious bedding, feeling the room's chill against her skin as she swung her legs over the edge of the bed. The glowing coals in the fireplace cast a warm, flickering light that danced across the walls, inviting her to rise and embrace the day.

She glanced at the large clock on the mantel and noted that dawn was due to break, promising a bright and beautiful morning. A sense of determination washed over her. She was eager to escape the castle's confines, to step into the crisp air and explore the grounds that had captivated her heart. Quickly, she dressed in a simple yet comfortable walking gown, pairing it with sturdy boots.

Thoughts of Jasper and Bacon, the playful dogs she had grown fond of during her stay at Pemberley, filled her mind. She could almost envision their eager faces, their tails wagging in anticipation. They would love an early morning romp, and she could think of no better companions for her walk. With the weather finally turning in their favor, she felt happy about taking them out for a long ramble.

Determined, Elizabeth made her way to the pantry, where she knew the treats for the dogs were kept. As she walked through the castle, the faint sound of wind whipping through the barren branches of the oak trees and the distant chirping of birds beginning their morning songs permeated the thick walls of the estate. A few early-rising servants bustled about in the kitchen, preparing breakfast.

Peeking around the kitchen door, she caught sight of the cook, who turned to her with a cheerful smile. "Good morning, Miss Bennet! Off on a walk, are we?"

"Good morning! I plan to take Jasper and Bacon for a long walk," Elizabeth replied, her enthusiasm shining through. "I was hoping you might have an apple to spare." She offered a bright smile to the older woman, hoping to charm her into yielding a treat.

"Best watch out for the mud, then! The melting snow has turned the grounds into a mess," the cook warned, her eyes sparkling with mischief. "But I dare say the dogs will love it." She handed Elizabeth a large, crisp apple, its red skin gleaming in the light.

"I appreciate the warning. I'll keep an eye out! Thank you for the apple!" Elizabeth laughed as she tucked the treat into her coat pocket, grateful for the cook's kindness.

Elizabeth went to the nearby room where Jasper and Bacon were nestled on a cozy rug near the hearth. As she entered, the two dogs perked up at the sound of her footsteps, their tails wagging vigorously as they bounded over to greet her.

"Good morning, boys! Are you ready for a walk?" she asked, chuckling as she scratched behind their ears. Both dogs responded with delighted barks, their enthusiasm infectious as they leapt around her.

With the dogs happily following, Elizabeth slipped out of the castle and onto a gravel path toward the lake. The air was crisp and refreshing, filled with the faint scent of damp earth and pine, invigorating her senses as she walked. The landscape around her transformed with each step; in the distance, she saw the once placid lake swollen from the melting snow, overflowing its banks and swallowing a large portion of the beach.

"Oh dear," Elizabeth murmured, observing the water lapping eagerly against the shore. "It seems the lake is quite full today."

Bacon sniffed at the path's edge, his nose twitching as he explored the new scents accompanying the thaw. Meanwhile, Jasper was intent on investigating every nook and cranny along the way, darting into the underbrush with playful abandon.

As she continued along the path, Elizabeth marveled at the beauty of Pemberley. The oak trees, now bare of their autumn leaves, stood tall and proud against the clear blue sky, their branches reaching upward as if embracing the sun. The early morning sunlight filtered through the branches, casting dappled shadows on the ground.

"Let's see what adventures await us today," she said to the dogs, her spirits lifted by the morning's beauty. With each step closer to the lake, a sense of excitement bubbled within her.

After deftly skipping over multiple puddles of muddy water, Elizabeth arrived at an area near the lake above the overflowing water. Here, she had a clear view of the grassy edge of the rocky beach, which held small pools of water. When they arrived, the dogs were immediately drawn to the water's edge, barking excitedly as they splashed through the shallow puddles, sending muddy droplets flying into the air.

"Careful now! We don't want to get too muddy!" Elizabeth called out, her laughter ringing out as Jasper bounded around, his playful antics prompting Bacon to chase after him. The two dogs reveled in the moment, their joy infectious until Bacon caught sight of several ducks swimming in the middle of the lake.

With a sudden burst of energy, Bacon jumped into the water and headed toward the flock at an incredible speed, his wet fur glistening in the sunlight.

"Bacon! No!" Elizabeth shouted, her voice tinged with exasperation. She rushed after him, the thought of the chaos that might ensue swirling in her mind.

Fitzwilliam Darcy awoke to the soft glow of dawn filtering through the curtains. The pale light signaled the beginning of a new day, one he hoped would bring the opportunity he sought to spend time with Elizabeth. Darcy rose from his bed and dressed swiftly, choosing attire suitable for the outdoors—a warm coat, sturdy boots, and a woolen vest to ward off the morning chill. Today, he intended to join Elizabeth on her morning walk with the dogs.

The castle was quiet at this early hour, the usual bustle of servants and guests yet to begin. Darcy made his way toward the kitchen. The scent of freshly baked bread and brewing coffee greeted him as he entered the warm kitchen, where a few staff members were working.

"Good morning, Mr. Darcy," the cook said, looking up from her preparations with a pleasant smile.

"Good morning," Darcy replied, nodding courteously. "I thought I'd take advantage of the fine weather. Could I trouble you for some bread and perhaps an apple?"

"Of course, sir," she responded promptly, handing him a wrapped slice of bread and a shiny red apple. "Miss Elizabeth was just here, doing the same. Took the dogs out for a walk, she did."

Darcy's heart skipped a beat. "Miss Elizabeth has already left?"

"Aye, just a few minutes ago. Headed toward the lake with Jasper and Bacon," the cook informed him.

"Thank you," he said. Pocketing the snacks, he turned and headed quickly toward the side entrance.

Stepping outside, he was greeted by the crisp morning air. The sun was just beginning to rise, casting a golden hue over the estate. He glanced toward the path to the lake, hoping in vain to see Elizabeth.

Setting off briskly along the gravel path, Darcy's boots crunched softly beneath him. The landscape glistened with dew, and the fresh scent of pine and damp earth filled his senses. He walked with long, determined strides, his eyes scanning the path ahead for any sign of Elizabeth.

After several minutes, he spotted Elizabeth in the distance. Her figure was unmistakable—graceful and poised, even from afar. The dogs frolicked around her, their joyful barks sounding distant. A smile tugged at the corners of his mouth as he watched her, but a bend in the path soon obscured his view.

Not wanting to lose sight of her, Darcy quickened his pace. Just as he approached the curve, a sharp, feminine cry pierced the morning air.

"Bacon! No!"

His heart leapt, and without hesitation, Darcy broke into a run. Concern propelled him forward as he imagined what might have caused that cry. The thought of his Elizabeth in distress was unbearable.

Rounding the bend, he saw Elizabeth near the lake's edge, hands on her hips in exasperation as Bacon plunged into the swollen waters, paddling furiously toward a flock of ducks. Jasper barked excitedly from the shoreline, his tail wagging uncontrollably.

"Miss Elizabeth!" Darcy called out as he approached, slightly out of breath. "Is everything all right?"

Elizabeth turned, surprise evident in her eyes, her lips softening into a warm smile. "Mr. Darcy! I didn't expect to see you here."

He stepped beside her, his gaze shifting from her flushed cheeks to the mischievous dog in the water. "I heard you call out. I thought you might need assistance."

She laughed lightly, a musical sound that eased his worry. "I fear Bacon has decided to take a swim with the ducks. He's quite the rebel this morning."

Darcy watched as Bacon swam energetically, the ducks quacking indignantly as they fluttered just out of his reach. "He seems determined," Darcy remarked with a hint of amusement.

"Too determined, perhaps," she replied, shaking her head. "I hope he doesn't catch a chill."

"Allow me," Darcy offered. He stepped closer to the water's edge and shouted, "Bacon! Come!"

Bacon paused, looked back at Darcy, and began to swim toward shore. Elizabeth raised an eyebrow, impressed. "You have a way with him."

"Practice," Darcy said modestly. "He's a good dog, just easily excited. He usually behaves better than Jasper."

When Bacon reached the shore, he shook himself vigorously, sending a spray of water and mud in their direction. Jasper pounced upon Bacon, and the dogs rolled into a mud puddle. They bounced to their feet, shaking mud, water, and debris into the air. Darcy and Elizabeth stepped back swiftly but not swiftly enough. Their boots and coats were splattered with the muck.

"Oh dear," Elizabeth said, biting her lip to suppress a giggle. "I suppose a little mud is inevitable today."

Darcy chuckled, his eyes meeting hers. "It seems so. Perhaps we should continue our walk before they find more trouble. May I join you?" He offered his arm to her.

"I would be delighted," she replied, her heart lifting at the prospect of spending time with this enigmatic man. She placed her hand on his arm, her smile radiant in the morning light.

They began walking away from the lake, the dogs happily trotting ahead. The sun climbed higher, illuminating the dew-kissed foliage around them.

Elizabeth glanced at him sideways, searching for something to say. "The blizzard was quite the unexpected spectacle."

"It was," Darcy agreed. "Though the aftermath has been disagreeable. The volume of melting snow has caused some trouble around the estate."

"Yes, I've noticed the overflow," she said, gesturing toward the lake. "And the trees lost their leaves. But the landscape is still beautiful."

"Very much so," he said, though his gaze rested on her rather than the scenery.

They walked in comfortable silence for a moment before Darcy spoke again. "I've meant to thank you for your company. It's been a pleasure having you and your sister at Pemberley."

"The pleasure has been ours," Elizabeth replied sincerely. "Your family has been most welcoming."

He hesitated before continuing. "I hope we might have more opportunities to spend time together without the rest of our party."

She looked up at him, her eyes searching his. "I would like that."

"Tell me," Darcy began, "do you often rise this early for walks?"

"Whenever I can," Elizabeth admitted. "There's something peaceful about the world at this hour."

"I agree. It's one of the few times the estate feels truly tranquil."

They continued along the path, their conversation flowing easily. They spoke of books they had read, places they wished to visit, and their pets' quirks. Darcy felt a warmth growing between them, a connection that gave him hope.

Jasper suddenly darted off the path as they neared a small grove of fir trees, barking enthusiastically at a squirrel that scurried up a trunk. His ears lifted slightly, perked forward briefly, and his tail wagged like a banner behind him. Not to be left out, Bacon bounded after him with a joyful bark, his paws kicking up little sprays of earth as he ran.

Elizabeth watched with amusement, a bright laugh escaping her lips. She shook her head, her eyes sparkling with delight. "Heavens! I didn't know Jasper could lift his ears like that!" she stared at the dog while sneaking a sideways glance at Darcy. With a playful smile, she added, "They're incorrigible when they find a critter to hunt."

"Yes," Darcy replied, his own smile softening his features. His gaze followed the dogs but then returned to Elizabeth, lingering momentarily. "They keep life interesting," he added, a hint of affection in his tone.

They paused, and Elizabeth released his arm, standing side by side watching the dogs investigate the tree's base, circling it with great interest and sniffing eagerly at the ground. Elizabeth took a deep breath, the crisp morning air filling her lungs. She closed her eyes briefly, tilting her face toward the sky as a gentle breeze caressed her cheeks and stirred the loose tendrils of hair around her bonnet.

"Thank you for joining me this morning," she said softly, opening her eyes and turning to look at him. Her expression was sincere, her eyes reflecting the soft light of the morning sun. "It's been... pleasant."

"The thanks are mine," Darcy replied, his voice gentle. He met her gaze steadily, his dark eyes warm and attentive. "I've been hoping to spend time with you."

She raised an eyebrow ever so slightly, a hint of curiosity and something else he couldn't quite read flickering in her eyes. A subtle smile played on her lips. "Have you?" she asked, her head tilting inquisitively.

"Yes," he admitted, with a touch of earnestness. His jaw tightened slightly. "There are things I've been wanting to say."

Before he could elaborate, Bacon and Jasper came bounding back toward them, muddy and panting, their tongues lolling out in canine grins. Bacon shook himself vigorously, droplets of water and bits of leaves flying from his coat.

Elizabeth laughed lightly, stepping back to avoid the shower of mud. She held up a gloved hand in mock defense. "Perhaps we should head back," she suggested, her eyes dancing with amusement. "Breakfast will be served soon."

"Perhaps we should," Darcy agreed, a reluctant smile tugging at the corners of his mouth. He offered her his arm again, his gesture courteous yet hopeful.

She accepted gracefully, her fingers resting lightly on his sleeve. As they turned back toward the castle, the dogs trotted ahead, occasionally glancing back to ensure they were following.

They walked in companionable silence, the soft crunch of their footsteps melding with the distant songs of birds. Darcy glanced at Elizabeth out of the corner of his eye. Her cheeks were flushed from the cool air, giving her a rosy glow, and a stray curl had escaped to brush against her cheek. She seemed deep in thought, her eyes fixed softly ahead.

He felt a swell of determination mixed with a touch of apprehension. He resolved to find the right moment to express his feelings fully. For now, he was content to walk beside Elizabeth, matching his steps to hers, the simple pleasure of Elizabeth's company filling him with quiet joy. The vision of a shared future lingered in his mind, warming him against the morning chill.

Chapter 25

Tuesday, December 3, 1811
Pemberley

While Darcy and Elizabeth walked toward the castle, the dogs trotted ahead, their fur muddied from their earlier escapades by the lake.

"We should have the staff give them a proper bath," Darcy suggested, eyeing the state of the dogs with amused resignation. "They've certainly enjoyed themselves this morning."

Elizabeth laughed softly. "Indeed they have. Though I think they enjoy being dirty."

"Perhaps," Darcy replied, "but I doubt the household staff will appreciate their enthusiasm for mud if they trail it all over the carpets."

They approached the kennels, where the staff typically cleaned the canines. The path was still damp, with patches of slick, muddy ground. As they neared the entrance, Jasper veered playfully toward Bacon, giving the large poodle a good-natured bump.

Caught off guard, Bacon stumbled sideways and collided with Darcy. The unexpected shove caused Darcy to lose his footing on the slippery ground.

"Whoa!" he exclaimed, trying to regain his balance.

Elizabeth, her arm linked with his, felt him sway and instinctively tried to steady him.

"Careful!" she urged, but the combined weight and momentum were too much. As Darcy fell, Elizabeth was pulled down, unable to release his arm and save herself from tumbling to the ground.

They landed on the damp grass, a tangle of coats, limbs, and laughter. The dogs, mistaking the fall for an invitation to play, began circling them excitedly, their wagging tails and muddy paws adding to the commotion.

"Are you all right?" Darcy asked, propping himself up on one elbow, his face etched with concern despite the smile tugging at his lips.

Elizabeth looked at him, her eyes sparkling with amusement. "I believe so. Though I never envisioned our morning walk ending like this."

Darcy chuckled. "Nor I." He attempted to stand, but Jasper nudged Darcy's knee with his wet nose. The unexpected push sent Darcy off balance, and he slipped back down, landing with a splat beside Elizabeth.

She laughed outright, pointing at the dogs. "It seems they have other plans for us!"

"Indeed," Darcy agreed, his tone wry. "They are quite determined to interfere with us today."

With renewed effort, Darcy managed to get to his knees. Just as he was about to rise, Jasper bounded forward, eager to play. His playful shove to Darcy's shoulder was well-intentioned but ill-timed, causing Darcy to lose his balance again. This time, he tumbled sideways, landing partially atop Elizabeth.

A moment of startled silence hung between them. Darcy's eyes met hers, his cheeks flushing with embarrassment. "Miss Elizabeth, I am so sorry," he stammered, quickly rolling away.

Elizabeth's cheeks were tinged pink, but her eyes danced with mirth. "No harm done, Mr. Darcy. Perhaps we should concede defeat and remain here until rescue arrives," she teased.

At that moment, the kennel master came into view, accompanied by two assistants armed with leashes. As they approached the floundering couple, the men's boots squelched against the ground. The assistants skillfully captured the exuberant dogs, who offered little resistance beyond playful wriggles. Bacon glanced back with a joyful bark, his tail wagging furiously and his eyes shining with mischief. Jasper panted happily, his tongue lolling out as he was led away.

The kennel master extended a sturdy hand to Elizabeth, who was attempting to rise from the ground. "Allow me, Miss," he offered kindly, his weathered face showing a hint of concern. Elizabeth accepted his help, her cheeks flushed and a stray curl tumbling over her forehead. She laughed lightly, brushing her muddied clothing with delicate fingers, her eyes sparkling despite her disheveled appearance.

"Thank you," she said, her voice warm.

Darcy was still struggling to regain his footing on the slippery ground. Darcy accepted the help of another servant with an embarrassed nod and a mumbled word of thanks. As he stood upright, he attempted to brush off the mud clinging to his coat, his fingers smearing it further in his efforts.

Georgiana, Lady Matlock, Rebecca, Richard, Jane, and Mrs. Reynolds emerged from the castle, their faces reflecting their concern and barely suppressed laughter. Several maids followed closely behind, carrying towels and blankets, their eyes widening at the unexpected condition of Darcy's garments.

"What happened?" Georgiana called out, her brows knit in worry as she hurried toward them. Her hands clutched her cloak tightly around her shoulders, the brisk air reddening her cheeks.

Richard grinned broadly, his eyes alight with mirth as he took in his cousin's bedraggled state. "Well, this is a sight I never expected to see," he teased, crossing his arms over his chest. "Darcy, taking a leisurely roll on the ground?" His chuckle was deep, causing his shoulders to shake.

Lady Matlock approached with a sly smile, one eyebrow elegantly arched. "Is this a new form of morning exercise you've discovered?" she inquired, her tone laced with playful sarcasm. She glanced between Darcy and Elizabeth, noting the muddy paw prints on their clothes.

Elizabeth smoothed her skirt, a soft chuckle escaping her lips. "Your enthusiastic pets outmaneuvered us," she explained, laughter still evident in her voice. Her eyes met Lady Matlock's with a twinkle, her embarrassment giving way to amusement.

Jane stepped forward, her face lined with concern as she reached out to touch Elizabeth's arm gently. "Lizzy, are you hurt?" she asked softly, eyes searching her sister's face for any sign of injury.

"No, Jane, I'm perfectly fine," Elizabeth reassured her sister, placing her hand over Jane's in a comforting gesture. "Just a bit... disheveled." She offered a reassuring smile.

Darcy finally regained his aplomb, standing straighter despite the mud streaked across his coat. He ran a hand through his tousled hair, a sheepish expression crossing his features. "Perhaps we should have kept the dogs leashed," he admitted, his voice wry as he glanced down at his muddied boots.

Rebecca giggled behind her gloved hand, her eyes dancing with amusement. "You both look like you've been playing in the mud," she remarked, pointing to the evidence with a delicate finger. Her laughter was light and infectious.

"With the dogs emerging victorious," chortled Richard, giving Darcy a playful clap on the back that left a new smudge on his already soiled coat. His eyes sparkled with mischief as he enjoyed the rare opportunity to jest at his cousin's expense.

Georgiana tried to suppress her amusement, her lips pressed tightly together, but a small giggle escaped despite her efforts. "Come inside, both of you," she urged gently, her eyes sympathetic. "Let's get you cleaned up before you sicken." She gestured toward the castle.

Lady Matlock took charge, her demeanor authoritative yet kind. "I'll have the servants draw warm baths and prepare fresh clothes," she declared, nodding to Mrs. Reynolds. "Use the back entrance to avoid trailing mud through the entire house," she added, a hint of sternness offset by the understanding smile on her face.

Mrs. Reynolds stepped forward, her hands clasped neatly in front of her apron. "This way, Mr. Darcy, Miss Elizabeth," she directed, her tone respectful and efficient. She motioned for the maids to follow, their arms laden with towels as they stood ready to assist.

Elizabeth exchanged a glance with Darcy, her eyes reflecting apologetic amusement. "Well, that was quite the adventure," she said softly.

Darcy met her gaze, his eyes softening as a genuine smile broke through his earlier embarrassment, giving her a glimpse of his elusive dimples. "Indeed it was," he agreed, offering her his arm with a slight, formal bow. "Shall we?"

She accepted gratefully, her fingers resting lightly on his forearm. As they began to walk toward the house, she laughed softly. "I suppose we've provided ample entertainment for everyone this morning."

"Unintentionally, of course," Darcy replied, his tone dry but his eyes betraying his amusement. He glanced over his shoulder to see the group behind them still watching, some stifling laughs, others shaking their heads with fond exasperation.

The couple retreated to the back entrance, their footsteps squelching softly on the damp ground. The maids hurried ahead to open the doors, their faces politely impassive despite the twinkle in their eyes and the faint smiles tugging at the corners of their mouths. Inside, the warmth of the house embraced the bedraggled pair; Darcy and Elizabeth exchanged a brief, amused glance as they stepped over the threshold to travel on a path of towels to the scullery room, where they removed their muddied coats and boots. It was a relief to rid themselves of the weight of their soaked garments.

Their personal servants appeared promptly, their hands deftly reaching to assist Darcy and Elizabeth in removing as much mud and grime as possible from their garments and persons. Elizabeth shivered slightly as she slipped off her gloves, her fingers trembling subtly. A stray lock of hair clung damply to her cheek, and she brushed it aside with a quick, graceful motion. Darcy noticed her slight discomfort and offered a sympathetic nod before turning his attention to his disheveled state, attempting to smooth down his tousled hair with little success.

"Miss Lizzy," her maid spoke kindly, her eyes reflecting genuine concern. "A warm bath will do you good. Let's get you upstairs." She gestured gently, her hand lightly touching Elizabeth's elbow.

"Thank you, Sally," Elizabeth replied gratefully, offering a warm smile. Her eyes met the maid's for a moment, appreciation evident in their depths.

As Elizabeth began to follow Sally, she turned back to Darcy, her gaze meeting his. A soft smile played on her lips. "Despite the unexpected tumble, it was an agreeable walk," she said, a hint of mirth dancing in her eyes.

He inclined his head with a small smile, his features softening. "Agreeable indeed. Perhaps we should allow Richard and Jane to walk the dogs next time," he replied, a teasing glint appearing in his eyes.

"Or simply accept that with Jasper and Bacon, unpredictability is guaranteed," she said playfully, her eyebrows arching slightly as she suppressed a laugh.

"Quite so," he agreed, his gaze holding hers for a moment longer. There was an unspoken understanding between them, a subtle shift in the air. The corners of his mouth curved into a broad smile before Elizabeth turned to depart.

Richard sidled up to Darcy as Elizabeth disappeared up the servants' staircase, a mischievous grin spreading across his face. "Well, cousin, you've certainly made the day interesting," he remarked, one eyebrow raised in mock admiration. He folded his arms casually, leaning slightly toward Darcy.

Darcy sighed good-naturedly, a faint flush coloring his cheeks. "Not the impression I intended to make," he admitted, a sardonic smile tugging at his lips. He ran a hand through his damp hair, causing it to stand up even more.

"Nonsense," Richard clapped him on the shoulder with a hearty pat. "A bit of levity suits you. Besides, it seems Miss Elizabeth was more amused than offended." His eyes sparkled with knowing amusement.

"I can only hope," Darcy replied, though a hint of a smile softened his stoic expression.

"Come along," Richard urged, nodding toward the stairs. "Let's get you cleaned up before you frighten the entire staff." He snickered, his laughter rich and infectious, as he nudged Darcy forward.

In her room, Elizabeth sank into the warm bath prepared for her, the soothing water embracing her and easing any lingering chill. She let out a contented sigh, her muscles relaxing as she leaned back against the tub. Her fingers traced idle patterns on the water's surface, her mind drifting to the unexpected turn of events—the feel of Darcy's hand clasping hers as they stumbled, the shared laughter that echoed between them, the way his eyes had softened, revealing a tenderness she hadn't seen before.

Her cheeks warmed at the memory. There was a subtle shift in her feelings toward the man. She couldn't quite name it yet. Her gaze unfocused as she stared at the water, feelings of what might be love stirring gently in her heart.

Darcy stood by his window after bathing and changing into fresh clothes, the crisp fabric contrasting his earlier disarray. He gazed over the grounds where sunlight highlighted the spot where they had tumbled. Despite the initial embarrassment, he felt the muddy incident had brought them closer. Elizabeth's easy laughter and graciousness had eased his discomfort, allowing him to see a new facet of her charm.

Perhaps, he mused, a private smile tugging at the corner of his mouth, unpredictability had its merits. He recalled the sparkle in Elizabeth's eyes and how her lips curved when she teased him. He hoped the morning's events had opened the door to deeper understanding—ideally with less mud and no audience.

Chapter 26

Tuesday, December 10, 1811
Pemberley

Elizabeth stared at the blank sheet of paper lying on the writing desk. A quill pen and an open ink bottle rested beside it. Sighing deeply, she lifted the pen and dipped it into the ink.

She hesitated momentarily, watching as a single droplet of ink threatened to fall from the quill's tip. She gave the tip a gentle tap against the mouth of the bottle. The droplet fell into the abyss. The pristine surface of the paper challenged her, its emptiness a mirror of the uncertainty swirling in her mind. She held the pen lightly above the page, but no words came.

Elizabeth leaned back in her chair, her gaze drifting to the window. The interaction between her and Darcy over the past week played over in her mind, starting with the unexpected tumble, the warmth of his arms as he tried to keep from falling, the various walks in the gardens, discussions in the library, visits to the Peaks, and his intense lingering glances that spoke volumes yet left so much unsaid. Her heart fluttered at the memories, but a wave of confusion came with it.

"Why is this so difficult?" she murmured to herself. "It's just a letter."

She had promised her father she would write weekly, updating him on her stay at Pemberley. But how could she possibly convey all that had transpired? How could she explain the gradual shifting of her feelings toward Mr. Darcy without revealing too much?

Setting the pen down, she stood and began to pace the room. The soft rustle of her skirts was the only sound as she moved, her thoughts a tangled web of emotions.

"Perhaps I should start with something simple," she thought. "Just the ordinary happenings." Returning to the desk, she took a deep breath and began to write.

Pemberley Castle, Derbyshire

December 10, 1811

Dear Father,

I hope this letter finds you in good health and spirits. Our stay at Pemberley has been most eventful, and I am eager to share some of our experiences. I will refrain from describing the estate again.

Over the past week, Jane and I have spent many pleasant hours walking the paths and admiring the lovely scenery with Jasper and Bacon. Those canines are magnets for trouble. If they are not chasing after a helpless critter, they are knocking people into puddles. Yes, they sent me flying into a puddle... a muddy puddle. I am fine, but I had to purchase a new coat. Lady Matlock insisted on paying the bill since Bacon was partly to blame.

A soft smile tugged at her lips as she continued.

Georgiana is a delightful young lady, shy but exceedingly kind. We have enjoyed playing duets together on the pianoforte, and her skill is remarkable. She has asked to be on a first-name basis, and we agreed. Only Mr. Darcy stays on a formal basis. Sometimes, I think he is jealous when the Fitzwilliams call me Lizzy.

Elizabeth hesitated before mentioning more about Mr. Darcy. Her feelings toward him had undergone such a transformation that she scarcely knew how to express them.

She stopped again, re-reading her words. They felt inadequate, failing to capture the complexity of her emotions. With a sigh, she set the pen down once more. "This is hopeless," she muttered.

A knock at the door interrupted her thoughts. Elizabeth looked up from the page before her, the quill poised uncertainly in her hand.

"Come in," she called, her voice tinged with mild surprise.

The door opened to reveal Jane, her serene smile offering immediate comfort. Her eyes shone affectionately as she stepped into the room, her hands slowly closing the door.

"Elizabeth, I thought I might find you here," Jane said softly, tilting her head slightly. "You've missed tea." She raised an eyebrow, a hint of playful reproach in her expression.

"Have I?" Elizabeth glanced at the small clock on the mantel, her eyebrows arching in mild astonishment. "I hadn't realized the time," she admitted, a slight flush creeping into her cheeks.

Jane stepped further into the room, her gaze drifting to the writing desk cluttered with scattered papers and an open ink bottle. "Are you writing to Papa?" she inquired.

"Attempting to," Elizabeth replied, a rueful smile tugging at the corners of her mouth. She set the quill down with a soft sigh, her shoulders slumping slightly. "Though I'm not making much progress."

Jane approached the desk, her footsteps light upon the carpet. She placed a comforting hand on Elizabeth's shoulder, her eyes compassionate and warm. "Perhaps I can help?" she offered, tilting her head as she searched her sister's face.

Elizabeth looked up at her sister, gratitude shining in her eyes. She gestured to the chair opposite her with a graceful sweep of her hand. "I would welcome it," she said sincerely, her smile brightening.

As Jane settled into the chair, smoothing her skirts neatly as she sat, she leaned forward slightly, her eyes reflecting warmth and understanding. Her hands folded gracefully in her lap, and a smile played at the corners of her lips, her expression encouraging.

Elizabeth sighed softly, fidgeting with the quill as she turned it between her fingers. "I find myself at a loss for words," she confessed, her gaze dropping to the page before her. "So much has happened, yet I cannot express my impressions adequately." Her brows knit together, and a hint of frustration flickered across her face.

Jane regarded her sister thoughtfully, tilting her head ever so slightly. "I see. I wrote about our excursions, the blizzard, and the heavy rains. I described the cats and dogs roaming the castle and our general evening activities. So you don't have to mention any of those things." Jane twirled a curl around her finger, pondering her words. Are you going to write about Mr. Darcy? Papa wants to hear your thoughts about the gentleman." Her eyes searched Elizabeth's face, noting the subtle changes in her expression.

Elizabeth felt a blush rise to her cheeks, a delicate pink tint spreading across her skin. She avoided Jane's gaze momentarily. Gazing directly into Jane's eyes, she said, "Partly," she admitted, her voice barely above a whisper. "My entire perspective regarding that man has shifted, and I'm unsure how to convey that to Papa." She glanced up, her eyes full of uncertainty.

Jane reached out to place a reassuring hand over Elizabeth's. "Why not start with the simple truth?" she suggested, her thumb brushing lightly against her sister's knuckles. "Tell him about your experiences. You don't need to reveal your change of heart at once." Her eyes held a tender sincerity, offering comfort without judgment.

Elizabeth's tension eased as she absorbed Jane's words. "Perhaps you're right," she murmured. Determination settled over her features as she straightened her shoulders. She picked up the pen again, the familiar weight grounding her. She dipped the quill into the ink, her fingers steady as she began to write.

One particularly amusing incident occurred while walking with Mr. Darcy, Richard, Jane, and the dogs, Jasper and Bacon. We found ourselves in quite a predicament with a flock of sheep, an angry collie, and their shepherd. Full of energy, the dogs managed to move the sheep in several directions.

She glanced at Jane, who smiled encouragingly. Feeling more confident, Elizabeth continued.

It was a moment of genuine laughter and levity, something I had not anticipated sharing with Mr. Darcy. His good humor and kindness in that situation revealed a new aspect of his character.

The more time I am in his company, the more I realize how mistaken I was in my earlier judgment of his character. He is an intelligent man of integrity and depth, devoted to his family, and considerate of those around him.

I understand that first impressions can be misleading, and I am grateful for the opportunity to see beyond them. Pemberley has not only been a place of physical beauty but also of personal growth. The library is two stories high, and thousands of books line the shelves. I spend hours in there reading.

Everyone engages in games, music, and delightful afternoons of charades that leave us all laughing. Lady Matlock and Georgiana have decided we are to put on one of Shakespeare's plays. They are searching the trunks in the attic for costumes.

Please give my love to everyone. I look forward to sharing more stories with you soon.

Your affectionate daughter,

Elizabeth

Setting the pen down, Elizabeth felt a sense of relief. "Thank you, Jane," she said warmly. "Your presence has helped more than you know."

Jane reached across the desk to squeeze her hand. "I'm glad to help, Lizzy."

Elizabeth folded the letter carefully, sealing it with a bit of wax. "I'll send this off with the next packet to London. I must write to Mama and our sisters, too."

"True. I plan to finish my letters after dinner. The courier is scheduled to ride to London tomorrow. Shall we go join the others?" Jane inquired. "I'm sure they will be glad of our company."

"Yes, of course." Elizabeth stood, smoothing the folds of her dress. As they approached the door, Elizabeth glanced at her sister with a knowing smile. "You seem happier, more at ease."

Jane considered this. "I suppose I am. Being away from home and associating with caring friends has lifted my spirits."

They walked down the grand staircase together, the soft murmur of conversation guiding them toward the parlor. The aroma of freshly brewed tea and the sweet scent of pastries filled the air.

Entering the room, they found Georgiana at the pianoforte, her fingers gliding over the keys in a delicate melody. Mr. Darcy stood nearby, his attention entirely on his sister's performance. As Elizabeth and Jane entered, he looked up, a subtle warmth lighting his eyes.

"Miss Bennet," he said, inclining his head. "Miss Elizabeth."

"Mr. Darcy," they replied in unison.

Georgiana finished her piece, turning to greet them with a shy smile. "I'm so glad you're here. Would you care to join me for a duet, Lizzy?"

"I would be delighted," Elizabeth replied, moving toward the instrument.

Sitting beside Georgiana, she felt Mr. Darcy's gaze upon her. A quiet confidence settled within her. The uncertainties that had plagued her earlier in their acquaintance receded, replaced by a gentle anticipation.

The music filled the room as they played, weaving a tapestry of emotional harmony. Elizabeth glanced at Georgiana, whose expression radiated pure joy. Sharing this moment felt significant, a connection with the younger Miss Darcy and perhaps with her brother.

When the piece concluded, the room filled with enthusiastic applause from those gathered. Elizabeth and Georgiana exchanged delighted smiles as they rose from the pianoforte bench. Elizabeth smoothed her skirts and tucked a stray curl behind her ear, her cheeks flushed with the pleasure of performing with a musical prodigy. Georgiana clasped her hands together, her eyes shining with happiness.

Mr. Darcy approached them with a measured stride, his posture relaxed. His eyes reflected genuine admiration as he looked first at his sister and then at Elizabeth. He inclined his head slightly, a soft smile gracing his features.

"That was beautifully done," he remarked, his voice warm and sincere. "You perform exceedingly well together."

"Thank you," Elizabeth replied, meeting his gaze with a bright smile. She felt a pleasant warmth rise within her under his attentive look. "Your sister's playing is wonderful." She gestured gracefully toward Georgiana.

Georgiana blushed lightly, a delicate pink spreading across her cheeks. She lowered her gaze modestly, fiddling gently with the ribbon of her gown. "But you have the voice of an angel, Elizabeth," she said softly.

Elizabeth laughed, reaching out to squeeze Georgiana's hand affectionately. "You flatter me, Georgiana," she replied, her eyes filled with genuine fondness. "It is your skill that inspires me."

Mr. Darcy observed the exchange, his gaze moving between his sister and Elizabeth. He noticed the ease as they interacted—the shared glances that spoke of a growing friendship. *Would Georgiana welcome Elizabeth as a sister?*

"You complement each other beautifully," he added, his voice carrying a note of appreciation. "I hope we may hear more duets during your stay."

Elizabeth glanced at him, her eyes dancing with a hint of mischief. "If that is your wish, Mr. Darcy, how could we refuse?" she replied, inclining her head teasingly.

"Yes, I would like that very much," Georgiana agreed, her fingers entwining lightly with Elizabeth's, her earlier shyness giving way to excitement.

"Then it is settled," Elizabeth said with a cheerful nod. She released Georgiana's hand and turned slightly toward the rest of the company.

"Shall we join the others?" Darcy suggested.

"Of course," Elizabeth agreed. As they walked together, she noticed the subtle way Mr. Darcy's gaze lingered on her, a new softness in his eyes.

They made their way across the room, the gentle murmur of conversation enveloping them. Elizabeth felt a contented glow settle over her—the music, the company, and the unspoken connections weaving together to create a moment she would cherish.

Lady Matlock stepped forward with a smile. "We are fortunate to have such accomplished musicians in our midst. It adds so much to our gatherings."

As the conversation flowed around her, Elizabeth felt a sense of belonging. She loved this place and these people. Her gaze locked with the tall, handsome master of Pemberley, and she felt the stirrings of hope in her heart. *Did Mr. Darcy return her feelings?*

Later, as the afternoon melted into evening, Elizabeth strolled leisurely through the gardens, the golden hues of sunset painting the sky with strokes of amber and rose. The soft rustle of her gown accompanied her footsteps on the winding path. She trailed her fingers lightly over the red berries of a holly bush, her thoughts drifting to the handsome Mr. Darcy.

She heard footsteps crunching softly on the gravel behind her and turned gracefully to see Mr. Darcy approaching. His tall figure was silhouetted against the warm glow of the setting sun, his hands tucked into his coat pockets.

"Good evening, Miss Elizabeth," he said softly. His gaze held a gentle warmth that reached his eyes.

"Good evening, Mr. Darcy," she replied, adjusting the wool shawl draped over her shoulders, the breeze stirring a few loose tendrils of hair around her face.

They walked together along the garden path, their steps naturally falling into rhythm. A comfortable silence settled between them. Elizabeth glanced sideways at Darcy, noting the contemplative expression on his face as he gazed ahead.

After a moment, he cleared his throat and turned slightly toward her. "I wanted to thank you for your kindness toward Georgiana," he murmured, his voice sincere. "She speaks highly of you."

Elizabeth looked up at him, her eyes meeting his gaze. A bright smile illuminated her features. "She is a delightful young woman," she replied sincerely. "It has been a pleasure getting to know her."

Darcy hesitated, his gaze drifting momentarily to the ground before returning to her face. A hint of uncertainty flickered in his eyes. "I hope being here is agreeable for you," he continued, his tone gentle. His fingers flexed slightly in his pockets, betraying a subtle nervousness.

"Very much so," she assured him, her voice warm and steady. She gazed over the landscape at the trees casting long shadows in the fading light. "Pemberley is a place of great beauty," she added, her eyes returning to his with a soft glow. "But the people make it truly special." A delicate blush colored her cheeks as she spoke, and she glanced away.

He seemed to consider her words carefully, a thoughtful glint in his eyes. A slow, appreciative smile curved his lips. "I am glad to hear you say that," he replied.

They paused near another holly bush, its glossy green leaves and bright red berries adding a vibrant touch to the garden. Elizabeth reached out to gently touch a sprig, her fingertips brushing against the smooth surface of the leaves. "The holly is lovely this time of year," she remarked softly, her eyes fixed on the plant.

"Indeed," Darcy agreed, his gaze resting not on the holly but on her. The golden light of sunset illuminated her profile, highlighting the graceful line of her jaw and the soft curve of her lips. He took a subtle step closer.

Elizabeth turned her head to look at him, sensing his movement. Their eyes met, and for a moment, the world seemed to fade away, leaving just the two of them enveloped in the gentle glow of the evening. There was an unspoken question in his gaze, matched by a quiet curiosity in hers.

"Miss Elizabeth," he began, his voice barely above a whisper. He hesitated, searching for the right words. "Your presence here has been... most welcomed."

She felt her heart quicken, a flutter of anticipation stirring within her. "I am pleased to hear that," she replied softly. "I have found my time at Pemberley to be... quite enlightening."

A faint smile touched his lips. "In what way?" he asked, tilting his head slightly.

She took a slow breath, considering her response. "I have come to appreciate many things," she said thoughtfully. "Your kindness, your sister, the beauty of the estate..." She paused, her gaze steady. "And perhaps, to see you in a new light."

His expression softened, a flicker of hope sparking in his eyes. The tension in his shoulders eased slightly as a gentle smile touched his lips. "I am glad to be counted among the things you appreciate," he murmured, his voice low and sincere.

"Mr. Darcy," Elizabeth began, her voice tinged with curiosity. She tilted her head ever so slightly, a few loose curls escaping from beneath her bonnet to brush against her cheek. Wrapped snugly in a wool shawl over her winter gown, her gloved hands gripped her shawl tightly. "May I ask you something?"

"Of course," he replied, inclining his head. His attentive gaze remained steady. He stood tall in his greatcoat, buttoned against the chill, a scarf wrapped neatly around his neck.

"Do you believe people can change their perceptions when given new insights?" she asked, her eyes searching his face.

He met her gaze. "I believe that understanding grows with experience," he said thoughtfully. "What we think we know can be transformed when we allow ourselves to see more clearly." His breath lingered in the cold air. The temperature was dropping.

She studied the bare branches of the trees around them, etched starkly against the pale winter sky. "I have found that to be true," she agreed softly. A gentle smile curved her lips as she returned his gaze, her eyes reflecting a newfound understanding.

A cold breeze stirred. Elizabeth pulled her wool shawl a bit tighter around her shoulders, the chill of the December evening seeping in. Mr. Darcy took a deep breath, the cool air filling his lungs as he gathered his thoughts. "Miss Elizabeth," he said quietly, his voice almost a whisper. "There is much I wish to say, but I fear it is too soon."

She looked up at him, her eyes soft and inviting. Her heartbeat quickened slightly. "You need not fear," she replied gently. "I welcome honesty." She took a small step closer, her boots crunching softly on the path.

He took a slow breath, his intense gaze holding hers. "These past weeks have been… illuminating," he confessed. "Getting to know you is a privilege. Seeing you here every day is a gift." He hesitated for a fraction of a second before reaching out to take her gloved hand. His touch was gentle as he lifted her fingers to his lips, his eyes never leaving hers as he pressed a tender kiss upon them.

Her heart quickened, a warmth spreading through her despite the chill in the air. She felt a soft blush rise to her cheeks, her breath catching slightly at the unexpected intimacy of the gesture. Before she could respond, Jane's voice called out from the terrace, bright and cheerful, interrupting the moment.

"Elizabeth! Mr. Darcy! Supper is ready!"

They both turned abruptly to see Jane and Georgiana waving from a distance, their figures framed by the warm glow of the house lights spilling onto the terrace. Elizabeth withdrew her hand gently, her cheeks warming further. Several emotions flickered across her face—surprise, embarrassment, and a lingering joy.

"Perhaps we should return," Elizabeth suggested, her voice steady despite the fluttering she felt inside. She shyly glanced up at him through her lashes.

"Yes," he reluctantly agreed. Though he composed himself quickly, his gaze lingered on Elizabeth a moment longer, his eyes conveying what words had yet to express. He offered his arm to her with a courteous nod.

She accepted gratefully, resting her hand lightly on his arm. The warmth of his presence beside her was both comforting and exhilarating. As they walked back toward the house, side by side, the crunch of frost beneath their feet mingled with the distant sounds of laughter and the soft glow of candlelight beckoning them inside.

She stole a subtle glance at him, noting the contemplative expression on his face, the way his jaw tightened slightly as if deep in thought. His proximity made her acutely aware of every shared breath, every subtle movement. The chill of the December evening was tempered by the warmth between them.

"Thank you for the walk," she said softly, breaking the silence.

"The pleasure is mine," he replied, turning his head to meet her gaze. A gentle smile softened his features. "I hope we may have the opportunity to do so again."

"I would like that," she admitted, her eyes reflecting the soft glow of lit lanterns as they drew nearer. There was an openness between them now, a silent acknowledgment of something blossoming in their hearts.

As they approached the terrace steps, Georgiana and Jane awaited them with welcoming smiles. The warm light from the open doors spilled outward, fighting against the night's oncoming darkness.

"Did you enjoy your stroll?" Jane asked, her eyes twinkling as she observed her sister's flushed cheeks.

"Very much," Elizabeth replied, her gaze meeting Jane's with subtle defiance. Elizabeth resented the interruption of her time with Mr. Darcy.

Georgiana stepped forward. "We were beginning to wonder if you liked being cold," she said playfully.

"Perhaps we lost track of time," Darcy responded, a hint of a smile tugging at his lips.

They entered the house together, the inviting warmth enveloping them as they shed their outer garments. The lively hum of conversation and the rich aromas of supper filled the air. As they made their way to the dining room, Elizabeth reflected on the moments shared in the garden... the unspoken feelings and tender looks. A sense of anticipation warmed her spirit despite the winter chill.

Throughout the meal, amidst the clinking of silverware and the flow of convivial chatter, Darcy's and Elizabeth's eyes met across the table more than once. Each shared look intensified the hope their earlier conversation stirred in their hearts.

Later that evening, as Elizabeth prepared for bed, she stood by her window gazing into the starlit night. The memory of Darcy's kiss upon her hand replayed in her mind, igniting a smile. The stirring emotion within her was no longer unnamed; it was love.

Darcy retired to his study, his thoughts consumed by the evening's events. He leaned against the mantel, eyes fixed on the flickering flames of the hearth. The feel of her hand in his, the softness of her gaze—all lingered vividly in his memory. Hope filled his heart, along with a determination to express himself more fully when the next opportunity arose.

In the quiet of their separate rooms, both contemplated the path ahead, each unaware that the other was equally absorbed by thoughts of what might be.

Chapter 27

Tuesday, December 17, 1811
Pemberley

Sir Whiskers, the large, gray, long-haired Norwegian Forest cat who ruled his feline comrades with an iron paw, crouched behind the ornate sofa in the parlor. His tufted ears were perked, and his bushy tail swished silently, betraying his intense focus. His bright eyes tracked the furtive movements of a tiny intruder—a daring mouse—scampering across the polished stone floor toward a small hole in the opposite wall.

Unaware of the upcoming drama, Jane Bennet sat gracefully on a chaise lounge near that wall, engrossed in a novel. The quiet ticking of the grandfather clock was the only sound accompanying her peaceful solitude until a soft squeak broke the silence.

Sir Whiskers, muscles coiled like a spring, pounced. The mouse, sensing danger, darted erratically, its tiny feet pattering frantically against the floor.

Jane looked up from her book, her brow furrowing slightly at the unexpected noise. The mouse veered sharply before she could comprehend the source and scurried directly toward her. With a startled gasp, Jane leapt to her feet, her novel tumbling to the floor. "Oh heavens!" she shrieked, her eyes widening as the small creature darted across her slippers.

Sir Whiskers chased the critter, his large, fluffy form moving with surprising agility. He bounded across the room, his thick fur flowing gracefully behind him. Pursuing the mouse, he knocked against a side table, sending a delicate porcelain vase wobbling precariously. The vase teetered momentarily before plummeting to the floor with a crash, shards scattering everywhere.

The din echoed through the hallway, catching the attention of Colonel Richard Fitzwilliam, who was passing by on his way to the library. His military instincts kicked in at the sound of breaking porcelain and a lady's distressed cries. He hurried toward the parlor, his boots thudding against the polished floor.

Jane quickly stepped onto a small footstool, gathering her skirts and hoping to distance herself from the unwelcome rodent and the cat.

"Please, shoo!" she loudly implored the mouse, though her voice trembled slightly. Sir Whiskers continued his pursuit, undeterred by the obstacles in his path, while preventing the mouse from reaching the safety of the hole.

Drawn by the clamor and the scent of excitement, Bacon ran past Richard and bounded into the room, knocking over a chair in the process. He barked loudly, his tail wagging with unchecked enthusiasm.

"Bacon! No!" Jane cried out, but her plea went unheeded. The poodle dashed toward Sir Whiskers, eager to join the chase. In his exuberance, Bacon collided with the footstool upon which Jane stood. The stool wobbled dangerously. Jane's eyes widened as she felt herself losing balance. She let out a small scream as the stool tipped over, sending her tumbling.

At that precise moment, Richard burst into the room. Assessing the situation in an instant, he moved swiftly toward Jane. "Miss Bennet!" he called out, arms outstretched.

He caught her before she hit the ground, but the momentum carried them both backward. They fell onto the chaise lounge, landing in a rather unceremonious heap. Jane found herself partially draped over Richard, her cheeks flushing a deep shade of pink.

"Are you all right?" Richard asked calmly.

"I... I believe so," Jane stammered, her heart racing. "Thank you, Colonel."

Before they could disentangle themselves, Lady Matlock stood on the threshold of the open door, her eyes widening at the sight before her. Behind her, several servants peered in, drawn by the cacophony of barks, hisses, and crashes.

"Good heavens!" Lady Matlock exclaimed, her gaze shifting from the overturned furniture to her son and Jane in their compromising position. Sir Whiskers sat atop a nearby table, his long fur fluffed up, eyes wide with excitement, his prey dangling from his mouth. Bacon stood in the middle of the room, panting happily as if he'd orchestrated the entire event.

Richard quickly helped Jane to her feet, both attempting to regain their composure. "Mother, this isn't what it looks like," he began, straightening his cravat with a nervous tug.

Lady Matlock arched an elegant eyebrow. "It appears to be a most... eventful afternoon," she remarked, a hint of amusement twinkling in her eyes despite her stern tone.

Jane smoothed her skirts, her cheeks still flushed. "I assure you, Lady Matlock, it was all an accident. The mouse—"

"The vase—" Richard added simultaneously.

They exchanged a brief glance before Jane continued. "Sir Whiskers was chasing a mouse, and I... I was startled and climbed onto a footstool. Bacon ran in, knocked it over, and I lost my footing. In the confusion, Richard caught me."

Lady Matlock's expression softened. "I see," she said gently. Turning to the servants clustered at the door, she addressed them with composed authority. "Please attend to the broken vase and carefully clean any remnants. We wouldn't want anyone to be injured. Also, bring in the mousers; I suspect more than one mouse uses that hole." She pointed to the small hole at the bottom of the wall behind the chaise.

The servants nodded and set about restoring order to the untidy room. One of them coaxed Bacon away with a treat while another approached Sir Whiskers, who was grooming himself nonchalantly after gulping down his prize, acting as if the chaos had nothing to do with him.

Richard offered his arm to Jane. "Perhaps we should step outside for some fresh air," he suggested. "It might do us both good after such a... lively encounter."

"That sounds like an excellent idea," Jane agreed softly, her eyes meeting his with gratitude.

As they approached the door, Lady Matlock gave her son a subtle nod, a knowing smile playing at the corners of her mouth. "Do enjoy your walk," she said pleasantly. "And do be careful of any more... unexpected surprises."

Outside the parlor, the castle was significantly calmer. Jane's tension began to ebb as they strolled down the corridor toward the doors. They donned their coats, hats, and gloves and went outside, where the late afternoon sun bathed the courtyard in a pale light.

"I must apologize," Jane said, her voice barely above a whisper. "I never meant to cause such a scene."

Richard glanced at her, his expression warm. "There's no need to apologize, Miss Bennet. If anything, I should thank Bacon and Sir Whiskers for allowing me to serve in some small way while they rid the room of that rodent."

Jane laughed softly. "Your help was most appreciated. I was falling toward the floor. You saved me from injury."

They entered the garden, the cool December air refreshing against their flushed faces. The gardens of Pemberley stretched before them, the neatly trimmed hedges dusted with the remnants of a light frost.

"It's so peaceful here," Jane remarked, her eyes reflecting the soft hues of twilight.

"Indeed," Richard agreed, though his eyes were fixed on her. "It's moments like these that make one appreciate the simple joys in life."

She looked at him thoughtfully. "I agree."

He offered his arm, and she accepted gracefully. They walked in companionable silence for a few moments, the crunch of gravel beneath their feet the only sound.

"May I ask, Miss Bennet," Richard began tentatively, "have you been enjoying your stay at Pemberley?"

"Yes," she replied. "Everyone has been exceedingly kind, and the estate is truly magnificent."

"I'm glad to hear it," he said earnestly. "It's been... enlivening to be here with you and your sister."

She smiled softly. "You are too kind."

They continued along the garden path, the conversation flowing easily between them. Richard shared anecdotes from his military service, carefully choosing lighthearted and amusing tales. Jane listened attentively, her laughter genuine and frequent.

Back inside the castle, Lady Matlock observed their retreating figures from a window, a satisfied expression on her face. Turning away, she encountered Elizabeth and Georgiana approaching.

"Is everything all right, Aunt?" Georgianna inquired, noticing the slight disarray and servants still present in the parlor.

"Quite all right, my dear," Lady Matlock assured her. "Just a bit of excitement involving Sir Whiskers and a most elusive mouse."

Georgiana giggled. "That cat does love his adventures."

"Indeed he does," Lady Matlock agreed. "But I believe all is well now."

Elizabeth glanced toward the terrace doors. "Was that Colonel Fitzwilliam and Jane I saw heading into the garden?"

"Yes," Lady Matlock confirmed, a hint of mischief in her eyes. "It seems they sought some fresh air after the... excitement."

Georgiana exchanged a knowing look with Elizabeth. "Perhaps we should leave them to it," she suggested.

"Perhaps we should," Elizabeth agreed, a smile tugging at her lips.

Meanwhile, Richard and Jane found themselves near a charming gazebo overlooking a small pond. The water mirrored the vibrant sky, and a few ducks glided effortlessly across the surface.

"It's beautiful here," Jane remarked, her gaze sweeping over the tranquil scene. "Thank goodness Bacon is not here."

Richard laughed. "That dog would jump in and attempt to retrieve a duck!" He turned to face Jane. "It is beautiful here," Richard agreed, though his eyes remained on her. "But the company makes it all the more so."

She looked at him, a faint blush coloring her cheeks. "You are most gracious."

He took a gentle breath, gathering his courage. "Miss Bennet, I hope you won't think me forward, but I have greatly enjoyed our time together."

She met his gaze, her expression open and kind. "As have I, Colonel."

"I would very much like the opportunity to know you better," he continued. "If it would be agreeable to you, would you agree to a courtship?"

A delicate smile spread across her face. "I would be delighted."

His smile widened, relief evident in his eyes. "You have made me very happy."

"And you have made me happy," Jane replied softly.

They stood together, the gentle sounds of evening enveloping them. Once uncertain, the future now held a promise that filled them with quiet joy as their hearts began to walk a single path toward a deep love.

216

Chapter 28

Tuesday, December 17, 1811
Letters

Pemberley, Derbyshire

December 17, 1811

Dear Aunt Maddy and Uncle Edward,

I hope this letter finds you in good health and spirits. It feels like ages since we last saw each other, and I have much to share with you about our stay at Pemberley.

I must tell you that Jane is positively radiant, and the reason for her happiness is something I believe will also bring joy to your heart. Over the past weeks, Jane has formed a closer acquaintance with Colonel Richard Fitzwilliam. Their friendship has blossomed most delightfully, and I am pleased to inform you that Colonel Fitzwilliam has expressed his desire to court Jane.

As you know, Colonel Fitzwilliam is a gentleman of excellent character—kind, honorable, and possessing a lively wit that beautifully complements Jane's gentle nature. His manners are impeccable, and he holds a respectable position in society, not to mention the high esteem in which his family and peers hold him. I have had the pleasure of observing them together, and it is evident that they share a deep affection and mutual respect.

The Darcys wholeheartedly support the match; their kindness toward us has been beyond measure. Lady Matlock and Lady Rebecca treat Jane with warmth and affection. Jane has endeared herself to his entire family beyond the affection and friendship we have been privileged to share with them in the past.

I know Mama will be eager to hear this news, but please leave sharing the news to Papa's discretion. Jane's letter to Papa is enclosed in this packet. Please be assured that Jane is exceedingly happy.

As for myself, I continue to enjoy Pemberley's hospitality. Mr. Darcy has been most attentive, and I find our conversations increasingly engaging. But I shall write more about that subject another time.

I look forward to sharing all the details with you in person. Until then, please give my love to the family.

Your affectionate niece,

Elizabeth

Pemberley, Derbyshire

December 17, 1811

My Dearest Father,

I hope this letter finds you well. It has been some weeks since we left Longbourn, and I miss you, Mama, and my sisters dearly. However, I write today with the most joyful news.

During our stay at Pemberley, I have enjoyed becoming better acquainted with Colonel Richard Fitzwilliam. Over the past weeks, our friendship has blossomed into a deep and abiding love. Colonel Fitzwilliam has kindly expressed his wish to court me, and I have joyfully accepted. We share many values and interests that will serve as a strong foundation for our future happiness.

Mr. Darcy and his family have been most supportive of our attachment. Lady Matlock and Lady Rebecca treat me with the warmth of a daughter and sister.

I understand the importance of family approval; your opinion means the world to me. I earnestly hope that you will look favorably upon Colonel Fitzwilliam's intentions. He intends to write and formally ask for your consent.

Please convey my love to Mama and my sisters. I am eager to share more details with you in person. Until then, rest easy knowing I am exceedingly happy and hopeful for the future.

Your loving daughter,

Jane

Pemberley, Derbyshire

December 17, 1811

Dear Mr. Bennet,

I trust this letter finds you in good health and spirits. Over the past weeks, I have had the honor and pleasure of becoming better acquainted with your daughter, Miss Jane Bennet. Her grace, kindness, and amiable disposition have left a profound impression on me. I hold her in the highest esteem and have developed a sincere affection for her.

It is with the utmost respect that I write to request your permission and blessing to court your daughter and eventually marry her. I am fully aware of the importance of seeking a father's consent and would not presume to proceed without your blessing. Only distance and the fluctuating weather keep me from riding to Longbourn and speaking with you in person.

Allow me to assure you of my honorable intentions. My family supports my desire to pursue a relationship with Miss Bennet, and I am confident that a union between our families would be met with their wholehearted approval. If your daughter eventually agrees to marry me, I will resign my commission and manage my estate personally.

Thank you for considering my request. I look forward to receiving your favorable reply.

Yours respectfully,

Colonel Richard Fitzwilliam

Pemberley, Derbyshire

December 20, 1811

My Dear Father,

I hope you read this letter before Mother's or Rebecca's. I write to you with news that brings me great joy.

At Pemberley, I enjoyed becoming better acquainted with Miss Jane Bennet. Over the years, her gentle demeanor and amiable disposition have greatly endeared her to me as a friend.

Over the past weeks, our acquaintance has blossomed into a deep affection. However, I felt undeserving of Miss Bennet's exceptional grace, kindness, and virtue. I thought she deserved to marry a gentleman unscarred by the horrors of war. Well, your dog and Georgiana's cat have inadvertently improved my life by engaging in an indoor hunt for a mouse that wreaked havoc in the parlor. I'm sure Mother or Rebecca will write with all the details.

I am delighted to inform you that Jane has accepted my courtship. She is of age, but I have written to Bennet to approve and bless our courtship out of my deep respect for him.

I am fully aware of the importance of seeking your blessing in this matter, regardless of the many occasions you suggested this course of action. Mother, Rebecca, and Georgiana danced around the room when Jane and I told them the news. Miss Elizabeth was overflowing with happiness, and Darcy solemnly shook my hand.

Father, this may sound odd, but I believe Darcy loves Elizabeth and is afraid to tell her. If he manages to propose, and Elizabeth accepts, we must have a special license at hand. Get two special licenses, one for Jane and me and the other for Darcy and Elizabeth. Bring Bennet and the licenses here when you come for Christmas.

Please convey my warm regards to my brother. I eagerly await your thoughts and hope to see you soon.

Your loving son,

Richard

Matlock House, London

December 19, 1811

Bennet,

With immense pleasure, I write to you regarding the recent developments between our families. Richard has informed me of his deep affection for Jane and his intention to marry her after a brief courtship, pending your approval. Furthermore, Richard believes my nephew, Darcy, desires to wed Elizabeth. My wife assures me that with help from Rebecca and Georgiana, your daughters will be engaged before Christmas and married before the first of January.

In light of these joyful developments, I must acquire two special licenses to facilitate the marriages without delay. You must come to London today so we can procure these licenses tomorrow morning. Your presence will make obtaining the license for Darcy and Elizabeth quickly obtainable, as opposed to presenting a letter of permission since she is only twenty.

Your daughters' happiness is of utmost importance to us all, and I am eager to ensure that all proceeds according to their wishes.

My unmarked carriage awaits you outside your front door. I know you well, go pack a change of clothes and climb into it, my friend. Your favorite brandy and cigars await!

I look forward to dining with you tonight and discussing our children.

With warmest regards,

Matlock

Chapter 29

Monday, December 23, 1811
The Pemberley Library

The late afternoon sun cast its weak light through the tall windows of the Pemberley library, illuminating row upon row of leather-bound volumes lining the mahogany shelves. The scent of aged paper and polished wood filled the air, enticing any book lover to camp in the room for hours.

Elizabeth sat comfortably ensconced in an oversized wingback chair near the floor-to-ceiling windows in a reading nook created by the perfect placement of a freestanding bookcase. The nook contained three oversized wing-backed chairs, several side tables, and a sofa. The chair's high back and enveloping wings provided a cozy retreat, shielding her from the view of anyone walking past the open door or perusing shelves in most of the room. She could lose herself in the pages of her book and read undisturbed. Elizabeth was congratulating herself on her perspicacity in closing those doors.

She turned a page, her fingers lightly brushing the paper, when the library doors burst open with a resounding crash. The abrupt noise shattered the silence, causing her to startle slightly. Peering cautiously around the edge of the chair, she saw Mr. Darcy stride into the room, his expression stormy and his movements brusque. He swung the heavy doors shut behind him with a force that echoed through the chamber.

Unaware of her presence, Darcy ran a hand through his disheveled hair. The customarily composed gentleman was now visibly agitated. He paced along the room's length; his footsteps were muffled by the rich Persian rug stretching across the floor. His jaw was set, and his eyes held a fierce intensity that Elizabeth had seldom witnessed.

She shrank back, unsure whether to reveal herself or remain hidden. A part of her felt compelled to offer comfort, but the unguarded emotion on Darcy's face gave her pause. She had never seen him so undone.

Darcy stopped near a table piled with books, his hands gripping the back of a chair as he stared unseeingly at the volumes before him. A heavy sigh escaped his lips, and he muttered under his breath, the words too soft for Elizabeth to discern.

Curiosity piqued, she watched him silently, her own heart beginning to beat a little faster. What could have caused such a reaction in a man who rarely displayed his feelings?

After a moment, Darcy moved to the fireplace, leaning one arm against the mantel as he gazed into the dancing flames. The firelight highlighted the tension etched across his brow.

He spoke again, this time louder, his voice filled with frustration. "How could everything become so complicated?" he uttered, his tone heavy with resignation.

Elizabeth's breath caught. Although she knew it was improper to eavesdrop, she could not look away. His vulnerability was a fascinating contrast to his usual stoicism.

Darcy turned abruptly and began pacing once more. "I must find a way," he declared to the empty room. "I cannot let this opportunity slip away. Not again."

Her mind raced. Was Darcy speaking of business matters? Family obligations? Or perhaps... something more personal?

As he passed near her hiding place, Elizabeth felt a pang of guilt. Deciding it was better to make her presence known than to continue covertly observing him, she cleared her throat.

"Mr. Darcy?" she said hesitantly, rising from her chair.

He stopped abruptly, his eyes widening in surprise. "Miss Elizabeth!" he exclaimed. "I did not realize anyone was here."

"I apologize," she replied, her cheeks flushing slightly. "I was reading and did not wish to startle you."

He paused to compose himself, his expression shifting toward his reserved demeanor. "The fault is mine," he said, inclining his head. "I fear I have disturbed your peace."

"Not at all," Elizabeth assured him. "Is everything all right?"

Darcy hesitated, his gaze searching hers. It seemed he might confide in her, but then he looked away. "Merely unsettled thoughts," he replied. "Nothing to trouble you with."

She stepped closer, her concern genuine. "Sometimes speaking of one's worries can provide clarity," she offered gently.

He looked back at her, the intensity in his eyes softening. "You are kind, Miss Elizabeth."

A brief silence settled between them, the crackling fire filling the void. Finally, Darcy drew a deep breath. "I have received word from my uncle, Lord Matlock," he began. "There are... matters that require delicate handling."

Elizabeth nodded encouragingly. "I hope there is nothing too distressing."

Darcy managed a small, sardonic smile. "That depends on one's perspective, I suppose."

She tilted her head slightly. "Would it help to share it?"

He considered her for a long moment. "Very well," he conceded. "My uncle has taken it upon himself to... offer an opinion on certain personal affairs. While his opinion is aligned with my desires, I feel my family's determined interference is unhelpful at this juncture."

Elizabeth's eyes widened slightly. "I see. Well, I don't… but families tend to interfere."

"True," Darcy continued, his tone betraying a hint of irritation. His gaze bore into her eyes, searching for some indication of regard.

Her heart skipped a beat. "What does Lord Matlock want?"

"He wants me to marry without delay."

The weight of his words settled upon her. "What?" she asked carefully.

Darcy's gaze met hers, a flicker of vulnerability breaking through."Such matters should be handled with care, not haste. A man wishes to gain the regard of a worthy woman without family and friends clamoring for results."

She felt a swell of empathy. "I can understand your reservations."

He took a step closer. "There are feelings involved that deserve to be expressed properly."

Elizabeth's pulse quickened. "Sometimes, those closest to us act with the best intentions, even if their methods are misguided."

He nodded slowly. "Indeed."

Gathering her courage, she ventured, "If there is someone whose feelings you are uncertain of, perhaps speaking with them directly would ease your mind."

Darcy studied her intently. "You are right," he said softly. "I have been remiss in not speaking plainly."

She held his gaze, her own emotions swirling within her. "Honesty can be daunting, but it is often the best course."

He stepped even closer, the space between them narrowing. "Elizabeth," he began, his voice barely above a whisper. "There is much I wish to say—much I need to tell you."

Her breath caught at the sound of her given name on his lips. "I'm listening," she replied, her heart pounding.

He hesitated, searching for the right words. "Since I met you, my feelings have been... conflicted. You challenged me in ways I did not expect. Your wit, your spirit—they have captivated me."

She felt warmth rise to her cheeks. "Mr. Darcy..."

He continued, determination evident in his expression. "I know I have not always expressed myself well. I have struggled between my feelings and my sense of duty. But I can no longer deny what is in my heart."

Elizabeth's eyes shimmered with hope and apprehension. "And what is in your heart?"

He took her hand gently. "I love you. Deeply, ardently, irrevocably. I wish to spend my life with you. Will you marry me?"

Emotion welled within her. "Oh, yes, I will marry you," she whispered. "You cannot know how those words of love affect me."

"Then tell me," he implored softly, pulling her into his arms.

She smiled, her eyes meeting his with unguarded affection. "My feelings have undergone a considerable transformation. Where once I harbored misunderstandings, I now see the true measure of your character. Your kindness, your integrity—they have touched me profoundly."

"Does that mean...?" he began, hope lighting his features.

"Yes," she affirmed. "I love you as well."

Relief and joy flooded his expression. "You have made me the happiest of men."

She laughed softly. "And you have brought me great happiness in return."

He raised her hand to his lips, gently kissing her fingers. "I promise to endeavor every day to be worthy of your love."

"And I promise the same," she replied warmly.

Just then, the library doors opened quietly, and Georgiana stepped inside. Seeing the two of them together, she hesitated. "Oh! I didn't mean to interrupt."

Darcy turned to his sister with a reassuring smile. "It's quite all right, Georgiana."

Elizabeth smiled at her. "Please, join us."

Georgiana moved closer, her eyes bright with curiosity. "I was looking for a book, but I can return later."

"Nonsense," Darcy said. "We were just... discussing some important matters."

Georgiana's gaze shifted between them, a knowing smile forming. "I see."

Darcy exchanged a glance with Elizabeth before addressing his sister. "Georgiana, there's something we wish to share with you," he said, a rare lightness in his tone.

Georgiana clasped her hands together eagerly. "Yes?"

With Elizabeth's hand clasped firmly in his, Darcy said, "Elizabeth has graciously accepted my proposal. You will have a sister."

A delighted gasp escaped Georgiana's lips. "Oh, that is wonderful news!" She hurried forward, embracing Elizabeth warmly. "I am so happy!"

Elizabeth returned the embrace. "Thank you, Georgiana. Your happiness means the world to me."

Darcy watched the exchange with contentment. "We wanted you to be among the first to know."

Georgiana turned to her brother, her eyes glistening with happiness. "You both deserve every happiness."

"Shall we share the news with the rest of the family?" Georgiana suggested excitedly.

"Perhaps we should," Elizabeth agreed, glancing at Darcy.

He nodded. "Yes, it's time to face the horde."

Together, they left the library, stepping into the corridor where the sounds of the household carried. As they went to the parlor, Darcy leaned close to Elizabeth and whispered, "Thank you for being patient with me. I was hoping for a perfect moment to ask, but I was thwarted by weather and pets."

Elizabeth looked up at him, her eyes shining. "It was worth the wait."

He smiled, the weight of past uncertainties lifting. "For me as well."

Entering the parlor, they found the family gathered—Lady Matlock, Colonel Fitzwilliam, Jane, and Rebecca were engaged in light conversation. At their entrance, all eyes turned toward them.

"Ah, there you are," Lady Matlock greeted them. "We were just discussing the preparations for the holiday festivities."

Darcy cleared his throat, drawing attention. "We have an announcement to make."

Richard raised an eyebrow, a teasing glint in his eye. "Well, don't keep us in suspense, Cousin."

Darcy, his eyes on the woman beside him, declared, "Miss Elizabeth has agreed to be my wife."

"This is splendid news!" Lady Matlock exclaimed, rising to embrace them both.

Jane rushed to Elizabeth's side, hugging her tightly. "Oh, Lizzy! I am so happy for you!"

Richard clapped Darcy on the back. "Congratulations! It seems we shall both be celebrating."

Darcy smiled at his cousin. "Indeed."

As the family gathered around, offering congratulations and well-wishes, Elizabeth and Darcy felt profound joy and contentment. The journey had been unexpected, filled with twists and turns, but it had led to this moment where love and understanding prevailed.

Later that evening, as the first stars appeared in the winter sky, Darcy and Elizabeth found a quiet moment on the terrace overlooking the gardens.

"It's beautiful," she remarked, gazing at the shimmering landscape.

"Not as beautiful as the view beside me," he replied softly.

She laughed gently. "You flatter me."

"I speak only the truth," he insisted.

They stood together in comfortable silence, the crisp air invigorating yet tempered by their shared warmth.

"Are you happy?" he asked after a while.

"Immensely," she affirmed. "And you?"

"More than words can express."

She leaned her head against his shoulder. "Then we are both fortunate."

"Yes," he agreed, wrapping his arm around her. "We are."

As they turned to rejoin their families inside, Elizabeth knew that she was home.

Epilogue

Tuesday, December 25, 1821
Pemberley

The crisp winter morning dawned clear and bright over Pemberley. The estate shimmered under a delicate blanket of freshly fallen snow. Inside the castle, garlands of evergreen and holly decorated the banisters and mantels while the scent of pine mingled with the aroma of freshly baked pastries and spiced cider.

Elizabeth Darcy stood by the drawing room window, gazing at the glittering landscape. Her hand rested gently on her rounded abdomen—she was expecting their fifth child in the coming months. Her four children filled her heart with immeasurable joy: William, aged nine, with his father's thoughtful eyes; Alexander, seven, so curious and adventurous; Clara, six, a mirror of Elizabeth's spirited nature; and little James, four, whose laughter was the music of the household.

"Are you ready, my dear?" Fitzwilliam Darcy approached her, his eyes warm with affection. He was as handsome as ever, and time had only added depth to his character. He placed a tender kiss on her forehead.

"Yes," she replied with a smile. "The children are eager to set off."

Soon, the entire family gathered in the grand foyer. Jane Fitzwilliam, Elizabeth's elder sister, arrived with her husband, Richard Fitzwilliam. Their four children—Matthew, nine; Emily, seven; Grace, five; and Thomas, three—were dressed in their Sunday best, eyes bright with excitement. Jane's gentle beauty was complemented by the happiness that radiated from her.

"Good morning, Lizzy!" Jane greeted, embracing her sister. "The children could hardly sleep last night."

"I believe ours were the same," Elizabeth laughed. "Christmas morning holds a magic all its own."

Mr. and Mrs. Bennet beamed as they watched their daughters and grandchildren. Mr. Bennet's sardonic smile softened as he caught his wife's eye. "Well, my dear, it seems we have quite the brood," he remarked.

Mrs. Bennet dabbed at her eyes with a handkerchief. "Oh, Mr. Bennet, who would have thought we would see this day? So many grandchildren! And all so accomplished!"

Lady Rebecca, now Viscountess Harrington, joined the family in the foyer with her husband and their three children—Philip, Olivia, and Charlotte. Her eyes sparkled with wit and contentment. "Merry Christmas!" she called out, her children joining their cousins with delighted greetings.

Mrs. Georgiana Hale, formerly Miss Darcy, entered arm-in-arm with her husband, Mr. Edward Hale, a distinguished gentleman from a neighboring estate. Their two children—Samuel and Elizabeth—were eager to join the festivities. Georgiana's shyness had blossomed into a quiet confidence over the years, and her happiness was evident.

The remaining Bennet sisters joined the family gathering. Mary, married to Mr. Nathaniel Gray, a thoughtful barrister, arrived with their two children, John and Alice. Kitty, now Mrs. Frederick Stanton, brought her three lively youngsters—Henry, Margaret, and Lucy. Even Lydia, whose impetuous youth had mellowed into a spirited charm, graced the gathering with her husband, Colonel Daniel Forster, and their son, Daniel Jr.

The Gardiners and their four children were welcomed with open arms. Mr. Gardiner's steady demeanor and Mrs. Gardiner's warmth added to the familial harmony. Their children—Sarah, Michael, Clara, and Benjamin—were delighted to reunite with their cousins.

As the church bells began to toll, the large family made their way to the chapel, which was located across the courtyard to the west of Pemberley Castle. The morning service was heartfelt, filled with carols and reflections on the year's blessings. The children's voices rang pure and clear, bringing smiles to all the assembled families.

After the service, they returned to the castle, where the excitement of gift-giving awaited. The great hall was transformed into a festive wonderland. A towering mountain of presents stood near the far wall, behind several screens decorated with ribbons and handmade garlands crafted by the staff.

"Now, remember," Elizabeth cautioned with a playful wink, "no peeking until everyone has their gifts!"

The children assembled eagerly, eyes wide with anticipation. Gifts were exchanged amid laughter and exclamations of delight. Handmade treasures, thoughtful tokens, and surprises from afar made each unwrapping a moment to cherish.

As the children played with their new toys, the adults gathered by the hearth, cups of mulled wine in hand. The warmth of the fire reflected the warmth in their hearts.

"I must say, Darcy," Richard Fitzwilliam began, a twinkle in his eye, "your hospitality surpasses itself each year."

"Indeed," Mr. Bennet agreed. "Though I suspect my second daughter's influence brings such joy to Pemberley."

Darcy smiled modestly. "It is the presence of family that truly makes this house a home."

Mrs. Bennet sighed contentedly. "All my girls married well and so many beautiful grandchildren. What more could a mother want?"

"Perhaps another grandchild?" Mr. Bennet teased, glancing at Elizabeth's abdomen. "We have yet to see the full extent of Elizabeth's love for her husband."

Elizabeth laughed, her eyes dancing. "Oh, Papa, I believe our newest addition to the family will arrive in March."

The conversation flowed easily, filled with reminiscences and shared dreams for the future. Georgiana played a soft melody on the pianoforte, her music weaving through the happy chatter.

Later, a Christmas feast was served in the dining hall. The long table was laden with roast goose, glazed ham, steaming vegetables, and an array of delectable sweets. Candles flickered, casting their light into the farthest corners of the room.

Darcy stood to offer a toast. "To the family and the blessings we share. May we continue to grow in love and happiness."

"Hear, hear!" echoed around the table as glasses were raised.

As evening descended, the festivities continued with games and storytelling. The warm glow of candles illuminated the room. The children's laughter echoed softly as they settled on plush rugs and cushions, their eyes alight with anticipation. They gathered at the feet of their grandparents, their hands clasped together or fiddling excitedly with the edges of their attire, enthralled by tales of Christmases past.

"Tell us about when Mama and Aunt Jane were young!" little Clara Darcy begged, her eyes wide and cheeks flushed with excitement. She leaned forward, her curls bouncing as she looked up at her grandmother with an eager smile.

Mrs. Bennet chuckled, her eyes crinkling at the corners as she looked fondly at her granddaughter. "Oh, there are many stories to tell!" she exclaimed, her hands fluttering in delight. She glanced mischievously at Elizabeth and Jane, a twinkle in her eye.

"Perhaps not all at once," Elizabeth interjected with a laugh, raising a playful eyebrow. She exchanged a knowing glance with Jane, who hid a soft laugh behind her hand. Elizabeth's eyes sparkled with amusement as she gently shook her head.

Outside, snow began to fall, the delicate flakes drifting lazily from the sky and blanketing Pemberley in a pristine layer of white. The large windows framed the scene, and the reflections from the candles and oil lamps within the castle cast a soft light onto the thin layer of freshly fallen snow. The adults continued to share stories, their voices weaving together in a harmonious blend that filled the room with nostalgia. The children's eyes grew heavy, their earlier exuberance giving way to sleepy contentment as they nestled closer to their siblings or rested their heads on their parent's laps.

Tired from the day's excitement, their parents gently gathered the younger children. Promises of more adventures on the morrow were whispered as the youngest children were carried upstairs, their arms wrapped around their parents' necks or rubbing sleepily at their eyes. Soft kisses were placed on foreheads and whispered lullabies accompanied them to their beds.

Once their children slept, Elizabeth and Darcy stood together at the nursery window. The moon's soft glow bathed the room in a gentle light, illuminating the peaceful faces of their sleeping children. Elizabeth rested a hand on the windowsill, her gaze drifting from the serene scene outside to the terrace below, where snowflakes drifted softly to the ground. Her breath formed a faint mist on the glass as she sighed contentedly.

Elizabeth turned to gaze at the angelic faces of her sleeping children, her expression tender and filled with love. Their soft, even breaths and rosy cheeks filled her heart with a profound joy. She felt Darcy's warm presence at her side, his shoulder brushing lightly against hers as he joined her in admiring their children.

"They are beautiful, aren't they?" he whispered, his voice filled with awe. He slipped an arm around Elizabeth's waist, drawing her closer.

"Yes," she agreed softly, resting her head against his shoulder. "Our greatest accomplishments." Her eyes glistened with unshed tears of happiness, and a gentle smile played on her lips.

"Ten years ago, who would have imagined we would be here?" Elizabeth mused, her gaze returning to the softly falling snow outside. She traced idle patterns on the windowpane with her fingertip, lost in reflection.

Darcy looked at her, his gaze tender and filled with affection. "I did, from the moment you agreed to be my wife," he said softly, a hint of a smile curving his lips. His eyes held hers steadily, conveying the depth of his feelings without needing words.

She smiled up at him, her cheeks dimpling. "Are you always so confident, Mr. Darcy?" she teased gently, arching an eyebrow. Her eyes danced with playful challenge.

"Only when it comes to you, Mrs. Darcy," he replied, a warm smile spreading across his face. He brushed a stray strand of hair away from her forehead, his fingertips lingering softly against her skin.

She turned her head, her soft curls brushing gently against his cheek, a contented sigh escaping her lips. "Our family has grown so much," she murmured, her voice barely above a whisper. "I am grateful every day for the life we have built." Her hand found his, their fingers intertwining effortlessly.

"As am I," he replied, squeezing her hand gently. He leaned down to kiss her lightly, his lips brushing against her skin like a soft caress. The gesture was tender, filled with unspoken promises.

Elizabeth gazed out the window momentarily before turning back to him, a hint of longing in her eyes. "I wish Lord and Lady Matlock were here with us to celebrate our tenth anniversary on the twenty-seventh," she said, her voice tinged with sadness. "But it is only fair that they visit Lady Catherine and Anne this year with Viscount Hedley's family."

Darcy nodded thoughtfully, his expression sympathetic. "In Anne's last letter, she mentioned that Aunt Catherine's health is declining," he said, concern evident in his eyes. "A long carriage ride is beyond her capability. It is good that Lord Matlock took some of the family to Kent for Christmastide."

Elizabeth sighed softly, her shoulders rising and falling. "I know," she admitted, her gaze dropping to the floor. "But I wish more of your family was here." She gazed down at their intertwined hands, her thumb brushing over his wedding ring.

He chuckled softly, giving her a gentle squeeze. "Where would we put them all?" he teased, his tone light. His eyes sparkled with amusement as he looked down at her.

"There's room for another fifty guests, darling man," she retorted with a playful huff, a smile tugging at the corners of her mouth. She hesitated for a moment, her expression growing more serious. Looking down, she asked softly, "Do you ever think about the Bingleys?"

Darcy's expression grew thoughtful, his gaze drifting toward the flickering candle. "Not for several years," he admitted, his voice tinged with regret. "According to Richard, Charles took Caroline to Italy in 1814 after she... disgraced herself in London. I haven't heard anything else," he muttered, his brows knitting together.

Elizabeth reached up to gently touch his cheek, her eyes filled with empathy. "I often wonder what became of them," she said quietly. "Charles was your dear friend."

He covered her hand with his own, turning his face to press a kiss into her palm. "He was," Darcy agreed, his eyes meeting hers. "Perhaps one day we shall hear news of him."

She offered a small, hopeful smile. "Until then, we can keep them in our thoughts," she said, resting her head against his chest.

He wrapped both arms around her, holding her close as he rested his chin atop her head. "You always know how to find the good in every situation," he murmured appreciatively.

Elizabeth looked up at him, her eyes shining. "It's easy when I have so much to be thankful for," she replied, lightly caressing his jawline.

He leaned down to capture her lips in a tender kiss. "And I am thankful for you," he whispered against her lips.

She smiled softly, her gaze full of affection. "As I am for you," she echoed.

He looked down at her, his expression softening, a wicked gleam in his eye. "You're beautiful," he said, his eyes meeting hers.

They shared a quiet moment before Elizabeth stifled a yawn, covering her mouth delicately with her hand. "Shall we forsake our family and retire for the evening?" she suggested, her eyes warm.

"Of course," he agreed, offering his arm. "After you, my love."

They went to their chamber, and Elizabeth immediately moved to the fireplace, where the flames cast dancing shadows on the walls. Darcy followed, his gaze never leaving her.

As they settled by the hearth, Darcy took Elizabeth's hand. "Thank you for making this castle a true home. Pemberley was beautiful, but you have made it a place of warmth and joy," he said earnestly, his eyes reflecting the depth of his feelings.

She looked up at him, her expression tender. "Our love and our family make it so," she replied, her voice filled with affection.

He gazed into her eyes, his dark with emotion. "I look forward to every day with you, Elizabeth," he murmured, lifting her hand and pressing a gentle kiss upon it.

"And I with you," she said softly, her smile radiant. Her free hand reached to rest against Darcy's cheek, her fingers tracing the familiar contours. "You have given me the greatest happiness."

He leaned in, their foreheads touching as they shared a moment of quiet intimacy. "As you have given me," he whispered.

They sat together; the soft crackling of the fire and the distant sound of the wind outside were the only noises accompanying their thoughts. Elizabeth rested her head on his shoulder, her eyes closing in contentment. Darcy wrapped an arm around her, holding her close.

Outside, the snow continued to fall, each flake adding to the pristine blanket that covered the grounds—a gentle promise of the new day to come.

The End

Author's Notes

In 1811 England, Great Danes were the epitome of hunting dogs, particularly for hunting boar and deer. Their strength, size, and courage made them excellent for holding down large game until the hunter could arrive. Additionally, the nobility often kept them as guard dogs and companions. Their prevalent colors were already well-established by the early 19th century. The most common colors for Great Danes included:

- Fawn: A golden-brown color, often with a black mask.
- Brindle: Fawn and black striped pattern.
- Black: Solid black or with white markings on the chest and feet.
- Harlequin: White with irregular black patches.

The Standard Poodle originated in Germany and was popular in France before spreading to other parts of Europe, including England. They were primarily used as water retrievers and hunting dogs. Their intelligence, trainability, and distinctive curly coats made them popular among the nobility and wealthy landowners.

In 1811, Standard Poodles were primarily used for hunting waterfowl, such as ducks and geese. Their excellent swimming abilities and intelligence made them ideal for retrieving waterfowl. Additionally, they were sometimes used for hunting upland game birds like pheasants and partridges. Hunters highly prized these versatile dogs for their remarkable ability to work in various terrains and conditions.

Standard Poodles were known for their various colors, many of which are still recognized today. These colors would have made Poodles a visually diverse and appealing breed during the Regency era. Here are some of the prevalent colors:

- Black: The most common color, known for its rich, dark hue.
- White: Popular among the nobility, white Poodles were often seen as elegant and refined.
- Brown: A rich chocolate color, sometimes fading to a lighter shade.
- Silver: Born black, these Poodles' coats would fade to a striking silver as they aged.
- Blue: A deep shade of bluish silver, often developing a brown tint as they mature.

Please imagine the dogs mentioned by name in this story as having the color and markings you favor. My choice for Darcy's Great Dane, Jasper, is harlequin, while Bacon, the Matlock's Standard Poodle, is black.

Publications

B orn to Serve

Mature Audiences Only. Not Canon. This story may contain triggers for sensitive individuals.

Immerse yourself in a unique blend of dark paranormal fantasy and the timeless world of Pride and Prejudice. In this dragon-themed saga, Zander and Kira, soulmates who birthed a galaxy, have made Earth their primary masterpiece. Their extraordinary bond and powers are central to the story.

Darcy and Elizabeth are hosts to these immortal dragon spirits. They navigate a realm where the dragon king and queen reign over an entire galaxy. This fantastical world, while reminiscent of Regency England, is brimming with magical and social differences.

In this tale of love and pride, Darcy is deeply in love with Elizabeth and fully aware of his dragon host status. Elizabeth, however, remains ignorant of her own, her dragon's voice mysteriously silent. Darcy's passionate proposal offends Elizabeth's pride, revealing his meddling in Jane Bennet's romance with Charles Bingley, leading to a stunning revelation.

Will Elizabeth overcome her pride and accept Darcy's proposal? Will dark magic complicate their future? Will the schemes of hostile relatives overshadow their happiness?

Filled with suspense, unexpected twists, and mature themes, this dark fantasy reimagines familiar characters in a new light, diverging from Austen's originals. It promises readers an unpredictable adventure as Darcy and Elizabeth pursue their happily ever after.

Jane: A Born to Serve Bonus Chapter

Mature Audiences Only. Not Canon. This story may contain triggers for sensitive individuals.

This is an extra chapter for readers wanting to know why Jane fiercely protected her sisters.

Mistaken Heart

Mature Audiences Only. Not Canon. This story may contain triggers for sensitive individuals.

In this blend of JAFF and dark paranormal fiction, young Miss Elizabeth Bennet is uprooted to London to live with the Gardiner family after her older brother, James, sells Longbourn. Following a year of mourning, Elizabeth visits her cousins, Mr. William Collins and Mrs. Charlotte Collins.

During her stay at Hunsford parsonage, Mr. Fitzwilliam Darcy and Colonel Richard Fitzwilliam arrive at Rosings Park, the residence of their aunt, Lady Catherine de Bourgh. Both gentlemen are quickly captivated by Elizabeth's charm, finding her sweet, witty, and delightfully innocent. Despite his reserved demeanor, Darcy's heart is immediately engaged. His resolve to make her his wife ignites a fierce rivalry with the more affable Colonel Fitzwilliam, a conflict threatening to tear their friendship asunder.

Elizabeth becomes infatuated with the charismatic Colonel Fitzwilliam, dismissing Darcy's quiet reserve as dislike. However, during a stroll on a crisp September day, a startling revelation shatters her romantic illusions and exposes the dark reality of dragons.

Dark Before Light

Mature Audiences Only. Not Canon. This story may contain triggers for sensitive individuals.

Embark on a journey to 1811 England with a captivating story that weaves love, intrigue, and the season's spirit. As London prepares for Yuletide celebrations, Charles Bingley relinquishes the lease for Netherfield Park. Fitzwilliam Darcy, impatient to see Elizabeth Bennet, seizes the opportunity to become the new leaseholder.

On Christmas Eve, Darcy, accompanied by his cousin, Colonel Richard Fitzwilliam, rides toward Netherfield with a single objective: to win the heart of the spirited Miss Elizabeth Bennet. As Darcy rides ahead, Colonel Fitzwilliam briefly halts in Meryton.

However, the path to love takes an unexpected turn after Elizabeth, Kitty, and Lydia Bennet venture into the woods to gather greenery for holiday decorations. Her thoughtless sisters abandon Elizabeth. Alone and vulnerable, Elizabeth encounters Lieutenant George Wickham, whose behavior deviates sharply from that of a gentleman.

In a tale where darkness threatens to obscure the light, Darcy must confront the unforeseen dangers lurking along a path in the wintry woods. Will Darcy's love prevail in the face of adversity? Will Elizabeth open her heart?

Explore the magic of the holiday season as Elizabeth and Darcy reach for a future full of happiness and joy. Netherfield Park is a place where Christmas miracles are destined to happen. Delve into this story, where the magic of the holiday season proves that the brightest light can emerge from the darkest moments.

Practice Makes Perfect

Mature Audiences Only. Not Canon. This story may contain triggers for sensitive individuals.

In this story, Fitzwilliam Darcy is a twenty-six-year-old gentleman accustomed to control and command who views the world through a lens of entitlement. He sees Miss Elizabeth Bennet as his ideal match and removes any obstacle blocking his marriage plans.

Elizabeth, a sheltered eighteen-year-old with limited social exposure, finds Darcy a perplexing enigma. His stern demeanor, rigid posture, and sparse conversation confuse her. Yet, despite his serious nature, she admires his striking features and intelligence, and she thinks about him more often than she should.

Will Richard's playful flirtations with two ladies at the vicarage become a problem? Will Darcy's jealousy ignite into fury? Can Darcy win Elizabeth's heart? Will Richard be a help or a hindrance?

Dancing With Pistols (Short Story)

In this short JAFF story, Elizabeth Bennet meets Fitzwilliam Darcy at the Meryton assembly. Darcy is immediately struck by Elizabeth's beauty, intelligence, and wit, while Elizabeth finds herself unexpectedly drawn to a charming Darcy. That night, both experience vivid dreams centered around conflicts with a common theme.

Will they overcome the manipulations and disapproval of Mrs. Bennet and Bingley's sisters? Will Jane Bennet and Charles Bingley find happiness together? Discover the answers in this engaging 30-minute quick read.

The Right Choice (Short Story)

In this poignant and reflective tale, Elizabeth Bennet Darcy recounts her journey from a challenging childhood to a secret, enduring love with Fitzwilliam Darcy. As they navigate societal expectations and personal trials, their bond strengthens, culminating in a clandestine marriage and a life filled with shared joys and sorrows. Now in her twilight years, Elizabeth faces the heart-wrenching loss of Darcy, her soulmate.

Her narrative captures the essence of their eternal love, culminating in a dream where they shed the ravages of time and walk together into a golden eternity, forever united. This story explores resilience, love, and the transcendent power of enduring bonds.

About The Author

L. Wagner lives in Texas and is happily married to a wonderful man who indulges their cat with daily treats. She enjoys writing as a hobby and enjoys reading Pride and Prejudice variations, mysteries, paranormal fantasy, and science fiction.

A Pride and Prejudice fan since the 1960s, she finally decided to contribute a few stories to the JAFF community. Hopefully, the twists and turns of her imagination will interest you.

Thank you!

Reviews help authors more than you might think.
If you enjoyed this story, please leave a positive review.

Follow me on X [Twitter]: @LindaW7446

Don't miss out!

Visit the website below and you can sign up to receive emails whenever Linda Wagner publishes a new book. There's no charge and no obligation.

https://books2read.com/r/B-A-MHLOB-RVCHF

BOOKS 2 READ

Connecting independent readers to independent writers.

Also by Linda Wagner

Darcy & Elizabeth: Finding Love
Practice Makes Perfect
Dark Before Light
Determined Interference

Dragons, Deceit, and Desire
Born to Serve
Mistaken Heart

Short Stories
Dancing With Pistols
The Right Choice

Standalone
Jane: A Born to Serve Bonus Chapter

www.ingramcontent.com/pod-product-compliance
Lightning Source LLC
Chambersburg PA
CBHW021425150726
47989CB00001B/125